COURT OF CRYSTAL

By HR Moore HL 41/22 £5

D1394500

Jew

Phlebotomy

1040

20

23ʳᵈ Dec

Titles by HR Moore:

The Relic Trilogy:

Queen of Empire

Temple of Sand

Court of Crystal

In the Gleaming Light

Nation of the Sun (coming June 20th 2021)

http://www.hrmoore.com

For the new one, who made me get a move on.

FAMILY TREES

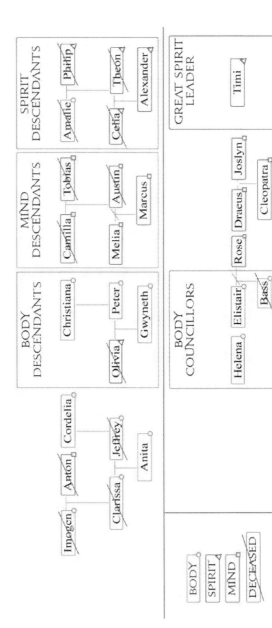

BODY DESCENDANTS

Imogen — Anton — Cordelia — Christiana

Clarissa — Jeffrey — Olivia — Peter

Anita — Gwyneth

MIND DESCENDANTS

Camilla — Tobias

Melia — Austin

Marcus

SPIRIT DESCENDANTS

Amalie — Philip

Celia — Theon

Alexander

GREAT SPIRIT LEADER

Timi

BODY COUNCILLORS

Helena — Elistair

Bass

Rose — Dracus — Joslyn

Cleopatra

BODY
SPIRIT
MIND
DECEASED

THIS FAMILY TREE CAN ALSO BE FOUND AT WWW.HRMOORE.COM/COURTTREE

CHAPTER 1

Matthew and his army halted. The fatigue from their long march fell away as they watched billowing smoke reach, like a toxic hand, into the sky.

A deep gloom settled across the landscape. Kingdom, ancient and impervious, had been forced to its knees, bowing to disaster, crying for help.

The moment passed, and the army rallied. They careered forward as one, no order needed to send them to their work.

They reached the sad, battered capital, and the devastation washed across them like the shock wave that had caused it. Matthew stood, momentarily bewildered, this not at all what he—or any of the others—had expected. The city was theirs for the taking. No organised army to defend it, no one at all to stand in their way.

He snapped to action, issuing orders to the other self-selected leaders of the revolution. He headed straight to the temples, or—more accurately—to the ruins where the temples had stood.

The sight that greeted him was worse than anything he'd imagined; dead strewn carelessly around, limbs protruding from under chunks of debris. The temples were gone, either crashed to the ground, or disappeared into one of several great chasms that had opened beneath them.

A dusty mist hung in the air. That which had billowed into the sky now fell to settle on all below; faces, clothes, bodies. The world was tinged with grey.

Amid the chaos, a few were beginning the task of bringing order. They instructed the uninjured to sort the wounded into groups. They were constructing a perimeter, herding those without physical injury—but dazed and shaking with shock—back a safe distance. Others went about the morbid business of inspecting bodies, discovering if they belonged to the living or the dead.

Matthew studied those who had assumed control—the people to whom others were naturally looking for instruction. There were four or five of them working as a group, moving through the wreckage, issuing orders as they went. Matthew recognised them, surprised to find they were all senior councillors, not a Descendant in sight. He let them continue. His men would arrest them in good time, but there was no point in halting their work.

Matthew turned his attention to searching for the real danger to his cause; those with the authority to declare themselves in charge once the dust settled: the Descendants themselves.

He moved through the carnage, no one raising their eyes to look at him, no one even seeming to notice his army, who had poured across the wreckage. The devastation was too huge.

He approached the entrance to the Spirit Temple, which lay discarded on the ground. His eyes scoured mound after mound of wreckage for any clue, when a flash of red caught his eye. He moved closer, climbing over an enormous fallen pillar, to find a man in a battered red cloak hovering over the lifeless figure of a woman. He was shaking her, frantically trying to coax her back to life, saying, 'Anita. Come on, Anita. Wake up.'

The man in the cloak heard Matthew approach, and turned to appeal for help. 'Please,' he said, 'please help me move her to safety. I can't wake her.'

'Of course,' said Matthew, beckoning to two of his men to help. He'd recognised Marcus immediately, and delight at his good fortune bloomed inside.

* * * * *

A sharp sting across her cheek jolted Anita awake. She was lying on her back in a dark room, on a cold, hard floor. A splitting pain shot through her head as she sat up, trying to orientate herself, trying to force her foggy mind to remember.

Visions flashed in front of her eyes, of the Relic, the temples, Alexander, the world crashing down around her… Marcus pulling her out. Out of nowhere, a hand flashed into view—a hostile hand—attempting to strike her face once more. Anita dodged right, the hand missing its mark, but the movement sent another electric pain tearing through her mind.

'This is all your fault,' hissed a voice Anita recognised, but couldn't place.

She said nothing, waiting for the pain in her head to subside.

'That's just like you,' it came again. 'Stay silent. Play the innocent. Pretend your hands are clean.'

Anita looked up at the same moment her head delivered who it was. 'Gwyn,' she said, 'Gods… where are we?'

Anita looked around. They appeared to be in a study, with a floor of polished marble, and a colossal desk dominating the room. Two uncomfortable-looking upholstered chairs sat on one side of the desk, a black leather chair on the other.

The walls were a deep green, sucking in what little light two ornate lamps provided, one on the desk, the second standing on the floor, next to a solid-looking oak door.

The room contained little else: a wooden filing cabinet, a drinks stand, a window obscured by heavy drapes. Ugly, crude modern art adorned the walls, their subjects staring down with malice, goading those who looked up from below.

Gwyn laughed a cruel laugh. 'Knowing you, you probably set this up. Were you working with the rebels from the start? Did you agree some nice little deal to get all the Descendants killed through that stupid stunt? Were you using Marcus and Alexander? Revelling in watching them run around after you like lost puppies...'

'... Gwyn,' said Anita, contemplating how much her head would hurt if she attempted to stand, 'I have no idea what you're talking about. The rebels are in Kingdom?'

Gwyn sneered at her, clenching her jaw before walking to the opposite wall. She brooded a moment before answering. 'I suppose that makes sense... you're not clever. You were probably just a pawn.'

Anita let her get it off her chest, staying silent, too preoccupied by the throbbing in her head to rise to Gwyn's bait.

Gwyn let out a huff of resignation. 'The rebels arrived in Kingdom shortly after the temples collapsed. There was nobody to resist them, no one realized what was happening until too late.

'The rebels sought out and arrested anyone holding a position of power; academics, councillors, and, of course, the Descendants. You, Marcus, and I were being moved here—to a Mind councillor's home—

when the remnants of Marcus' army ambushed the rebel guards. Marcus' soldiers spirited him away, I presume to safety. They didn't even try to rescue us. The rebels put us in this room shortly after we got here, and nobody has been back to check on us since.'

'The door's locked?'

'No,' said Gwyn, scornfully. 'They went to the trouble of capturing us and putting us in what amounts to a cell, but thought it unnecessary to turn the lock on their way out...'

'Guards?' asked Anita, refusing to be drawn into a fight.

'I don't know. I haven't heard anyone coming or going, or anyone talking outside. But the walls and door are thick.'

'How long have we been here?'

'Hours. It was light when we got here, and it's been dark for ages.'

'And they didn't say when someone would be back to talk to us? Or to give us food and water?'

Gwyn laughed heartlessly. 'Look, Princess, I know you didn't see the devastation out there—it all got a bit much, and you fainted—but I very much doubt feeding and watering us is high on anyone's priority list right now.'

Judging by the lump on her head and the pain when she moved, Anita hadn't simply fainted, but again, she let it go. 'Why did they bring me?' she asked. 'As far as they know, I'm neither a councillor nor a Descendant, so why am I here? Especially as I was unconscious?'

'Marcus was hovering over you like a worried puppy,' said Gwyn. 'Obviously still a lovesick idiot.'

Anita rolled her eyes, showing irritation for the first time. 'What about Alexander?' she asked. 'Is he here too?' She held her breath as she waited for the answer,

Gwyn's energy telling her it wouldn't be what she wanted to hear.

'They couldn't find him.'

'Couldn't find him?' said Anita, trying to get a handle on the sudden rush of panic coursing through her insides.

Gwyn shook her head. 'No.'

Memories flashed in front of Anita's eyes. 'Marcus told me Alexander was helping to get people out through the Mind Temple.'

'How could he possibly have known that?'

'He said it to make me leave…' She was such an idiot… 'Alexander was thrown back into the Mind Temple; I saw it. Did they search there?'

'The Mind Temple's nothing but a hole in the ground,' said Gwyn. Anita was surprised to hear something almost like kindness in her tone. 'He's most likely at the bottom of that hole, covered in temple remains.'

Anita bowed her head. She refused to believe it. 'He must have found a way out.'

A dull thunk cut across the room and their heads snapped around in unison to face the noise. The door swung inwards, revealing two men. 'Marcus?' said Anita.'You're free to go, Anita,' said a man Anita didn't recognize. 'You can leave with Marcus.'

'Who are you to hold anyone hostage?' said Anita, the words out before she'd had a chance to thoroughly consider her predicament.

'My name is Matthew,' said a middle-aged man with solid eyes and a grounded demeanour. Something in his energy didn't quite add up. 'I'm the leader of the revolution. We have taken over Kingdom—what's left of it, after the damage you people inflicted. We'll be establishing a new way of doing things. Now, are you going, or would you prefer to stay here with your cell mate?'

'Gwyn's coming too,' said Anita, resolute. 'We're not leaving without her.'

Matthew laughed, and Marcus shot her a wary look before saying, 'Anita, all the way here, and at every opportunity since, Gwyn has been trying to sell the idea—to anyone who will listen—that everything is entirely your fault.'

'What?' Anita said on an exhale, her shoulders slumping, turning to look at Gwyn.

Gwyn averted her gaze. 'Go,' she said, sliding down the wall to sit on the cold, marble floor. 'Just go.'

Anita considered her options, briefly entertaining the idea of insisting Gwyn be allowed to come with them, or staying to devise some method of escape. But she had a far better chance of locating Alexander from the outside. She left, Marcus placing his hand firmly on her back, guiding her in the direction of the exit. She ignored the warmth of his touch.

They reached a spacious entrance hall, decadently decorated yet uncomfortably sparse. Anita wondered whom had, until earlier in the day, occupied this residence. Were they still alive?

'... I'll come back tomorrow,' said Marcus, ushering Anita through the door. 'Until then, my men will continue to work with yours.'

'Tomorrow the fun begins,' said Matthew. His eyes were steely, but his energy contained only good intentions.

'Goodnight, Matthew.'

* * * * *

Anita sat in a garden of beautiful red trees, running water, and rounded bridges. It was like nothing she'd

11

ever seen, enclosed by the rest of Marcus' Mind residence. It was warm, despite the bitter night air that had gnawed at her bones on the walk back through Kingdom.

Footsteps shook her out of her reverie. Footsteps that belonged to Marcus, and another man Anita didn't recognise. 'What's going on?' asked Anita, trying to read their intentions from their energy.

'Good to see I'm not the only one out of the loop,' said a thin man with auburn hair and frustrated features.

Marcus held the man's gaze, then Anita's, lingering just a moment too long. 'Anita, this is Sol. I know he doesn't look like much, but don't let that fool you. Sol is the most effective member of my personal guard, and I'm assigning him to look after you.'

'What?' said Sol and Anita together.

'Are you mad?' snapped Sol. 'First you risked your life to go back for her, and now you expect me to risk mine to keep her safe?'

Anita shot Sol a dirty look. 'I don't need looking after.'

Marcus said nothing for several seconds, appraising the pair. 'Anita, if you're staying here with us, I would feel better if you had a guard to keep you safe. Sol, as long as you work for me, you'll do what you're told.'

'Why?' said Anita.

'Because Matthew wasn't the only one who heard Gwyn blame all of this on you. Plenty of councillors and academics heard too, not to mention anyone else we passed. Gwyn wasn't discrete in her accusations.'

Anita exhaled, closing her eyes. All she wanted to do was find Alexander, and Cleo, and Cordelia, and by now, the entire world would think she was behind the disaster.

'You're also the true Body Descendant,' said Marcus. 'We have to assume you're needed to return the Relic to the Gods.'

Anita raised her eyebrows and shot a sideways look at Sol.

'Don't worry, you can trust him.'

'She's the Body Descendant?' said Sol. 'What about Gwyn?'

'Our parents switched us when we were babies,' said Anita, impatiently. 'It's a long story.'

'And you'll have ample opportunity to explain in the days ahead,' said Marcus, 'but for now, Sol, please leave us. Anita and I have a lot to discuss.'

Marcus sat on the bench beside Anita. Silence fell between them, the thud of Sol's retreating footsteps the only sound.

Marcus' calm, confident new demeanour didn't escape her; nobody was in any doubt about who was in charge. Such a shift in the short time since his father's death...

The footsteps faded, and they relished the quiet for a few moments before Anita brought them back. 'How is it you're best friends with Matthew of the rebellion?' Marcus had insisted they not discuss anything on the walk back to his residence—lest someone overhear—but now she wanted answers.

'Or is it Matthew of the revolution?' he replied.

'You, of all people, a sympathiser?'

'I'm a pragmatist. All that matters now is rebuilding. People think we sent the Relic back, and we have a rare chance to do something good, to build a decent world.'

'You've become quite the philosopher...'

'Anita, please,' he said, facing her.

'Sorry,' she mumbled. 'Too long in a cell with Gwyn; must have rubbed off on me. What happened after I blacked out?'

Marcus took a deep breath, looking out over the garden. His energy, although subdued, bubbled with a new intensity. 'The temples collapsed. Everything, absolutely everything, came crashing down, and a cloud of dust engulfed us. It was like a blizzard. I could barely see my own hands, let alone what was going on around us. I covered our faces and waited for the dust to settle; there wasn't much else I could do.

'I don't know how long we were there before it began to clear, but the next thing I knew, I was looking up at Matthew. To start off with, it seemed like they were just trying to help. They moved us to an area with other survivors, provided water, and were treating injuries.

'Then I realized the people being added to our area weren't random; they all held senior offices, as either councillors or academics. We were planning our escape when Matthew's men realized we'd worked it out, called for backup, and moved everyone to the residence you woke up in.'

'How did you get away?'

'Sol,' he said, simply.

Anita gave him a 'go on' look when he didn't continue.

'One of the injured councillors collapsed on route and Sol used the confusion as an opportunity to grab me. He knocked out the man guarding me, and, along with the rest of my personal guard, got me back here.'

'How come your personal guard was still intact?'

Marcus looked her in the eye. 'Anita, I'm not conspiring with Matthew. I'd ordered my guard to stay with my army, just outside of Kingdom. It wouldn't have looked right for me to turn up to send back the

Relic with a full complement of guards; what would people have thought?'

'So, your entire army's intact?' she asked, feeling her first glimmer of hope since coming round to a slap across the face from Gwyn. Marcus nodded. 'And that's how you got Matthew to release me? The threat of force?'

'Typical Body,' laughed Marcus. 'No. I told him you're the only one we have left who's qualified to analyse the energy readings from the observatory. I also told him Gwyn was lying when she said everything was your fault. I made him see it would be better for everyone if you came back with me... it's called diplomacy...'

'And he went for it, just like that?'

Marcus nodded.

'He didn't try to keep you there too?'

'No. But he knows about my army. I can't imagine he wants fighting in the streets.'

'The unspoken threat of force,' said Anita, pointedly.

Marcus laughed. 'Yes, I suppose so.'

Anita shoved him, regretting it as his energy leapt. She stood up and walked to one of the bridges, purposefully putting space between them, leaning against the cool stone.

'What happens next?' she said, her tone serious. 'I have to stay here? Making occasional guarded trips to the observatory, to monitor the energy?'

'You make it sound like I intend you to be my prisoner!'

'Aren't I?'

'Of course not. You're free to leave any time you please—and to come back again—but you shouldn't underestimate the danger you're in. If people believe the temple collapse was your fault, you won't be safe. Not anywhere.'

'You could issue a statement, telling them what really happened.'

'And what did really happen, Anita? Why were you in the temples, when you told Gwyn you'd stay away?'

Anita took a deep breath. 'You think I had something to do with it?'

'I think you know something about what happened that you haven't told me yet. But that's not to say I think it's all your fault.'

She looked him squarely in the eyes, not really seeing him, buying time as her brain processed her options. Every way she looked at it, her best option was to tell Marcus everything she knew. There was no suggestion that Marcus was her enemy, and if she wanted to find Alexander and the others, she needed allies.

'Something had been bothering me about the way we were sending back the Relic. It was a constant niggle at the back of my mind, made worse by a note I found from Bass, saying there was something he'd been unsure about too.'

Marcus raised his eyebrows but didn't interject.

'But Elistair and I worked through everything a hundred times. We went through the calculations, completed test runs, and read every scholarly article we could find. We found nothing to suggest it wouldn't work, so we went ahead. The final tests went fine, as you know, apart from one small thing that kept replaying in my mind.'

'What?' asked Marcus, eagerly.

'The gust of energy that knocked Gwyn over after the first test.'

A smile twitched at the corner of Marcus' mouth. 'Go on.'

'That was the problem,' she said. 'I couldn't see past how funny it was when Gwyn fell flat on her arse... Anyway, when it was time to send the Relic back, I was on the beach, trying to meditate. I figured I should try to use the time for something more productive than worrying, but that image kept replaying over and over. And then it came to me: the energy backlash.'

'The what?' said Marcus. 'You mean the gusts after we sling-shotted the boulders? That was a backlash?'

Anita nodded. 'Equal and opposite forces,' she said, simply.

'Meaning?'

'When you propel something one way, there's always another equal and opposite force that pushes back. Now, of course, not all the energy used to send something skyward is felt as a backlash, as some of it is used to move the object through the air, however, the larger the object, the larger the force required to move it, and the larger the backlash.'

'But I thought the energy used to send the Relic and the boulders skyward was the same?'

'Yes, it was the same, as although the boulders were bigger than the Relic, they were the same weight. But that doesn't really matter. The thing we hadn't accounted for was the volatility of the energy within the object itself. With something like a boulder, the volatility is extremely low; rocks don't have exciting properties. However, with something like the Relic...'

'... we don't really understand what it is, let alone what it's made of, or how it would react to a force.'

'Exactly.'

'And that's what destroyed the temples? The backlash from sling-shotting the Relic?'

'I think so... I don't see what else it could have been. I tried to get back in time to stop it, but the guards on the door of the Body Temple wouldn't let me in, and by the time I got round to the Spirit Temple, it was too late.'

Marcus' look blackened. 'Gwyn.'

Anita gave a shrug. 'What's done is done. The question is what we do now.'

Marcus sat in silence for a few long moments, Anita's words hanging in the air. A tranquillity settled over the garden that was entirely inappropriate, given the horrors outside the front door.

'We have to find a way to carry on,' he said. 'We'll work with the rebels to establish a new kind of rule; one that ensures fairness. We'll help everyone affected by this, and monitor the energy, which will hopefully bounce back. Once the world is stable again, we'll find the Relic, and send it back for real.'

'What about the others? Alexander, Cleo, Cordelia, Helena, Elistair...? What about our friends?'

'If they're alive, they'll turn up. We'll search the hospitals, and once we clear the rubble...'

'... we might find their dead bodies?' she said, bitterly. 'Or maybe they're already out there, piled up with the rest of the dead?'

'Anita,' said Marcus, gently. 'If they're alive, we'll find them. But you have to prepare yourself for the possibility they're not.'

'You think I don't know that?' she said, her voice harsh. 'We need to get back out there and look.' She knew her suggestion was madness, given everyone thought she had single-handedly caused the temples to come crashing down…

Marcus moved towards her, Anita tensing as the gap between them narrowed. She was wary, like a wild animal, not sure whether to run.

He reached her and drew her into his arms. She hesitated for a moment, but the familiar hardness of his chest pressed against her face. She inhaled his scent, and her arms wrapped around him of their own accord, finding comfort in the strength of his embrace.

Their energy mingled, and Anita relaxed into him, the weight of what had taken place seeming to dissipate between them, becoming a little lighter than before. He reached up and stroked her hair. 'We'll find the others,' he said softly. 'Alexander will be alive. He's resourceful. If anyone could have survived, it's him.'

Anita pulled away. His proximity was comforting, but their energy was edging towards something... else.

'Marcus...' she said, trying to keep her voice neutral.

'... I know,' he said, firmly.

She turned away, trying to refocus, not missing the jump in his energy when he saw the flush that had spread across her cheeks.

CHAPTER 2

They sat around a big oval table, the rebels on one side, the remaining Descendants and councillors on the other. Marcus had made it a condition of the meeting that the councillors held hostage could attend, along with Gwyn, of course.

They had agreed to meet at a neutral location, in a house in the centre of Kingdom, owned by a prominent Spirit academic. Or at least, it had been, before the academic had disappeared into the chasm under the temples. His housekeeper had survived and agreed they could use the place. She had even provided refreshments, laid out on the glass table before them.

The house was entirely modern, designed to impress. The boardroom in which they sat appeared to be suspended in mid-air, glass walls on all sides, as well as above and below. The room looked out onto carefully manicured gardens, the table hovering over an oval-shaped pond in the garden below.

The glass box was one of several similar boxes, linked by suspended glass walkways. The main living quarters wrapped around the garden in a way that reminded Anita of Marcus' internal water garden, but on a significantly larger scale. She marveled at the sheer enormity of this complex, right in the heart of

Kingdom, when Matthew's intense voice permeated her thoughts.

'Firstly, I think we should have an update from both sides on the rescue efforts to date. We've had a week to work our way through the carnage, and I feel as though we're finally making some headway. Would you agree?' he asked Marcus.

'I would,' said Marcus. He turned to Sol and nodded.

Sol detailed the work Marcus' army had been doing, from clearing the temple site to sorting through the dead. They had set up stations where those who had lost friends and relatives could carry out the morbid task of identifying bodies. They had reopened the rationing stations, ensuring supplies from the Wild Lands—meagre as they were—still made it through to the city.

They had cleared the remnants of the Body Temple, and were now working on the Temple of the Spirit. They hadn't found a survivor from within the wreckage for two days, with the Mind Temple proving particularly challenging, given the gaping cavern in the floor. Although Anita already knew all this, she couldn't help the unbidden bolt of loss that shot through her at his words.

She'd argued with Marcus that they should send soldiers into the hole to search for survivors. She'd offered to go herself, but Marcus had talked her out of it. He'd told her it was too dangerous, that he couldn't put his people in unnecessary danger, and that she was too important to those who still survived for her to go in herself.

She had reluctantly agreed, however, had insisted she see the site in person. Marcus had told her not to go, but seeing as she wasn't his prisoner, she had. Sol and two of his men had accompanied her to keep her safe. They'd blended in well, Anita wearing the black uniform of Marcus' private guard, and nobody had so much as looked at them as they'd crossed the wreckage.

The scene had been worse than Anita imagined. It had taken them half an hour just to climb through the temple remains, to reach the yawning hole where the altar had once stood. The hole was enormous. All that had once existed beneath that section of the temple was now a distant memory. She'd crouched at the edge and focused her energy, searching for any tiny trace of life, any minuscule flicker of force to indicate someone was alive in the depths.

Sol had looked on nervously, watching her every movement, poised to leap forward, should she slip. But he'd kept quiet, knowing the reaction she would give him if he told her to move away.

She'd stayed there for a full hour, willing something to come up out of the depths. By the time she stood to leave, she knew there was no hope of finding anyone down there alive.

Sol finished his report and Matthew nodded to the man seated to his right, indicating that he should follow. He was fair-haired with green eyes and fine features, and Anita raised an eyebrow as she felt Gwyn's energy leap.

The man, Joshua, informed them of the work Matthew's rebel army had been doing. It centred around tending the injured and arranging burials for the dead. They'd taken over a field on the outskirts of Kingdom and turned it into a graveyard, digging human-sized holes in neat rows, ready to receive those who hadn't made it out alive.

As Joshua's report came to a close, all eyes shifted to Matthew and Marcus, flitting between the two, waiting to see who would speak first. Marcus said nothing, looking at Matthew expectantly, deferring to his agenda. Matthew's features remained impassive, but he inclined his head before speaking. 'What about the energy?' he asked. 'Has it bounced back?'

Anita felt the press of expectation settle on her. She looked around and collected her thoughts before beginning.

'As you know, I am yet to return to Empire, to the observatory, so what I am about to say will need to be validated. However, from the rudimentary instruments I have at my disposal, it would seem the energy has not bounced back.

'I would stress that the readings vary wildly. The energy appears to have upswings followed by downswings. The readings point to a very slight upward trend overall, but nothing drastic. It's impossible to say if the volatility is linked to the return of the Relic, or the collapse of the temples. We'll only know for sure once our wounds start to heal.'

'*The return of the Relic*?' smirked Gwyn. 'You're still keeping up that charade?'

Anita resisted the temptation to look at Marcus, concentrating on his energy to discern his reaction. It leapt, laced with nervous apprehension, but before either of them could respond, Gwyn continued.

'You see,' she said, practically batting her eyelashes across the table, 'what makes this whole sickening mess even more tragic, is that the apparent return of the Relic was all just a big ruse. She,' she said, gesturing menacingly towards Anita, 'came up with the idea. She said we could trick the energy into lifting by making it appear we'd returned the Relic to the Gods.'

'What?' said Matthew, turning his gaze to Marcus and Anita. 'It was all a hoax?'

'No,' said Anita, defensively. 'At the beginning of the energy crisis, Bass and I were, of course, paying close attention to the energy. When Christiana died, we expected a shock. Many believed the Body line would end with her death. As you all know, we did experience a shock, the likes of which we had never seen before, and more than that, the duration of which we had never, in our wildest predictions, expected.

'However, the most interesting observation was the point when the energy started to react. It wasn't her actual death that caused the energy decline, but the announcement of it. It's not events themselves that influence the energy, but peoples' reactions to them. People control the energy, through our hopes, fears, beliefs, and perceptions.'

'So you tried to manipulate the energy by faking the return of the Relic?' asked Matthew.

'Yes, in essence, but I won't take credit for the idea. We had to do something to try and stabilise the energy, otherwise, we were headed for a crisis far worse than the one we're in now. We had no idea how to return the Relic to the Gods, so this was the next best thing, given what we observed after Christiana's death. And let's not pretend we had any other options. It was the *only* idea any of us had to lift the energy. It was Bass' vision,' she said, looking pointedly at Gwyn. 'He was working on it when he was killed.'

Gwyn shrunk under the scrutiny of Anita's accusing grey eyes. 'Maybe Bass would have realized what was wrong with the calculations sooner than I did. If he had lived...'

'... you purposely planned to deceive the entire population?' said Joshua, sharply. 'How could you ever consider that to be ethical?'

Anita raised her eyebrows. '*Ethical?*' she snapped. 'Did you not hear what I just said?'

'I...' he tried to respond, but she cut across him.

'We were facing the starvation of the entire population. Food supplies were diminishing, crops had failed, fish stocks were declining… it was only a matter of time before something happened to the drinking water, and we had no way to reverse it.

'Austin didn't help, of course, using the uncertainty for his own selfish purposes, refusing to take action, telling all who would listen that we were scaremongering.

'Alexander and Bass battled to get rationing agreed by the council, but it wasn't enough without an energy response. We came up with every idea we could to lift the energy, but there was nothing; nothing that would make even the slightest dent. The only thing big enough to matter was returning the Relic. And do you know how much time and effort the Descendants put into returning the Relic?' she asked, looking directly at Joshua.

He averted his gaze.

'None,' she said, looking around the room. 'Not a single minute of their precious time did they dedicate to fulfilling the prophecy. They spent a great deal of time lining their own pockets. They hosted parties where they sipped whisky and ginger champagne, but when it came down to it, they did not a thing to solve the one problem that mattered.

'But to avert the impending implosion of our world, that was the only thing that would make a difference. Seeing as we didn't know how to send it back, we made it seem as though we had. We were going to send it back for real once we'd dealt with the problem of stabilising the energy. It seemed logical to solve one crisis at a time.' Anita stopped talking, a little embarrassed at the duration of her speech.

Joshua said nothing, still refusing to look at Anita, so Matthew took over. 'Where's the Relic now?' he asked. 'And what do you plan to do with it?'

'We sent it to the Salt Sea,' said Anita, 'although we haven't heard from the Institution members who were supposed to retrieve it. We don't know if that's because of the chaos here, or because there's a problem.'

'So the Relic could be anywhere?' said Matthew, sounding concerned for the first time.

'You know as much as I do,' she said, refusing to be cowed.

'It could have fallen into anybody's hands,' said Matthew, 'meaning it could make a reappearance? Which would cause the energy to plummet again?'

'That is a possibility,' said Anita, 'not that we really know what's happening with the energy.'

'What do you all think we should do to contain this mess?' Matthew asked of the room, casting his eyes up and down the table.

'We need time,' said Anita. 'We need to find out what happened to the Relic, and the rest of the Institution members, and what's happening with the energy. Once we know the truth of the current situation, we can make a plan to deal with it.'

'And how do you propose we learn all of that?' asked Joshua, seeming to have regained his confidence.

'I need to go back to Empire, to the observatory, and study the readings there. We need to find Helena and the other Institution members, to see if they know anything… if they're still alive. And we should send people to the Salt Sea, to see what took place there. Aside from that, we should continue to restore order in our capital.'

'Which brings us to what you plan to do next?' said Marcus, directing the tide of attention back towards the man on the other side of the table.

'We will do what we've always intended,' said Matthew, 'which is to establish a democracy. We'll continue to clear up the mess, and once that's under control, we'll hold fair and free elections. We'll ensure candidates from all backgrounds can stand. When we have an elected leadership, my army will become their army, to be directed as they see fit. It goes without saying that the army will also ensure those with the means do not stage a coup.'

'There are none other than I who have the means to stage a coup,' said Marcus, dryly, 'aside from Amber, but nobody knows where she's gone.'

'Amber?' said Matthew. 'She's gone?'

'Yes,' said Marcus, shrugging his shoulders. 'She didn't like it when I changed the way my father ran things. She took those in my army loyal to her and melted away, presumably to somewhere in the Wild, but nobody seems to know where. It's strange for such a big group to go entirely unnoticed, but none of our sources have been able to locate them to date.'

'Maybe they travelled by sea,' said Matthew.

'Maybe,' said Marcus, 'not that it matters. She's gone, and unless she's able to recruit a large number of people, her army won't be a match for ours combined.'

'Ours combined?' said Matthew, raising his eyebrows in surprise.

Marcus nodded. 'I have no desire to stand in the way of what you're trying to achieve. There was a time when I might have, but not any longer.' Marcus threw a sideways glance at Anita. She sat very still as she listened to his words.

'We need to work together now,' said Marcus. 'I won't stand for election, but I'm sure there is much I can do to add credibility to your cause. Gwyn and I are well placed to help smooth the transition to a different kind of rule.'

Gwyn nodded her agreement.

Anita was speechless, both because of Marcus' proposal, and Gwyn's easy assent.

'Then we shall meet again in a few days to discuss how to proceed. I'll send word to let you know when and where,' said Matthew. Anita read the relief flooding his energy.

'We'll try to locate the Relic, and will pull together a full report on the status of the energy before we meet again,' said Marcus, turning to look at Anita, who inclined her head.

The meeting adjourned and Matthew left with his people, making a point of leaving Gwyn and his prisoner councillors behind. None of the prisoners remarked on Matthew setting them free. Instead, they silently slipped away, presumably to look for their loved ones. Marcus and Anita left swiftly, winding their way back to Marcus' residence, Sol a discrete distance behind.

'I'm going to the observatory, am I?' asked Anita, her tone accusatory, but her features playful.

'Have you gone deaf?' said Marcus. 'As I said, I'm sending you to the observatory.'

'You're *sending* me to the observatory?'

'You really must be having trouble with your hearing…'

Anita shoved Marcus sideways, harder than she strictly needed to, feeling Sol's energy react as he tried to work out if she posed a genuine threat to his boss.

'Aren't you protecting *me* these days?' said Anita, spinning to look Sol in the eye. 'Is that not the case, Marcus?'

Marcus smiled. 'I'm pretty sure I still take priority.' He shoved her to the edge of the street, so she had to step in a puddle.

Sol rolled his eyes and retreated to a safe distance.

Anita removed her feet from the puddle and whirled around, preparing to retaliate. Before she could, she felt the dull thud of an impact, followed by a sharp pain in her leg, which buckled underneath her. Her brain tried to process what was going on, when another pain shot across her skin, this time on her arm, a brick hitting the floor beside her.

She reacted instinctively, turning towards her attacker as she pushed herself to her feet. Marcus grabbed her hand, urging her into a run towards his residence. Sol's rapidly approaching footsteps eliminated her impulse to resist. She followed Marcus' lead, everything a blur until they were inside the safety of his home.

'What was that?' she breathed, as Sol ushered them into a study in the middle of the house.

'The result of Gwyn's campaign against you, would be my guess,' said Sol, forcing Anita down onto a chaise longue, so he could check her over.

His hands were cool against her skin and somehow calming.

'You have cuts, and there will be bruising, but other than that, you're fine,' he said. 'Wait here; I'll get the first aid kit.'

'Yes Sir,' said Anita, more light-heartedly than she felt.

Sol returned from a cupboard by the door with dressings for her leg and arm. Marcus scrutinised Sol's every move from where he perched across the room. Anita noted his raging energy as she battled to come to terms with the attack.

'Who do you think it was?' Anita asked, looking between Sol and Marcus for answers.

'I don't know,' said Sol, carefully bandaging up her leg.

'Neither do I,' said Marcus, getting up to pace in frustration. 'It may have been random; an opportunistic individual.'

'There are enough people who have lost a loved one,' said Anita. 'You can't blame them for wanting someone to punish.'

'You think it's that simple?' asked Sol.

'You don't?' she replied.

'I saw the looks Gwyn gave you, and she told the rebels about the Relic, trying to pin the whole thing on you again. I wouldn't put organising an attack past her,' he said, moving on to bandage the wound on her arm.

'You think she would go that far? She's bitter and twisted, but...' Anita stopped mid-sentence as she met Marcus' ashamed eyes. Her mind flashed back to the most recent Chase, showing her images of Marcus and Gwyn attacking her.

'She's done it before,' he said quietly. 'We did it before.' His voice was almost a whisper as he held her gaze with nervous eyes.

Anita's eyes turned steely as the events of the previous few weeks flooded back. 'Stop fussing over that,' she snapped at Sol, getting to her feet and heading for the door. 'I'm leaving for the observatory in the morning.'

'I'll come too; it's not safe...'

'... I'll be perfectly fine,' she said, cutting Marcus off. 'Goodnight.'

She retreated to the stillness of her room, feeling more alone than she ever had, praying to the Gods to return her friends, praying above all for Alexander, and for Cleo.

CHAPTER 3

A few days later, Anita arrived at the observatory in Empire, and felt the same strange pull she always did, like the building was sucking at her energy. She took comfort from the familiar sensation, enjoying the coolness of the brass against her skin as she climbed the stairs.

The everyday noises of the observatory greeted her when she emerged at the top; at least nothing here had changed.

She circled the room, running her hand over the dials and levers that she and Bass had toiled at together. She carefully put the instruments to work, pulling a report on the data collected since her last visit.

Cogs whirred, and lights flashed. Anita watched them for a while as they hurried to do her bidding. The contented silence soon turned to resentment; resentment at the need to sit alone.

She stood abruptly, striding to the ladder that led to the roof, bursting out at the top, to find, to her complete shock, her best friend lying asleep on the biggest receiver. Anita checked for a moment, not sure she trusted her eyes, blinking several times before cautiously calling out, 'Cleo? Is that you?'

The figure sprang to her feet, snatching up the knife lying at her side, wielding it aggressively. Cleo took a moment to recognise Anita. When she did, her mouth fell open and her arm fell back to her side. 'Anita?' she said, stepping forwards. 'Where have you been?'

'I could ask you the same question,' said Anita, indignant at Cleo's suspicious tone.

Cleo smiled. 'Sorry. You can't be too careful these days,' she said, moving to where Anita stood, pulling her into an embrace. 'I'm so glad you're okay.'

'You too,' said Anita, hugging Cleo tight. 'Have you seen Alexander? Is he here too?'

Cleo took a step back. 'No. He's missing?'

'Nobody's seen him. Marcus thinks he's at the bottom of the hole under the Mind Temple.'

Anita sighed and walked to the edge of the building, where she sat, legs dangling over the side. Cleo joined her.

'I'm sorry,' said Cleo.

'He's not dead.'

Cleo's energy was unsure, but she didn't contradict Anita. 'What happened to you?' she said instead.

'I was on the beach, trying to meditate, trying to open the brass cylinder in my head, when I realized what Bass had been worried about.'

'What Bass was talking about in his note?' said Cleo.

'Yes. It was the backlash he couldn't account for.'

'The backlash?'

'The same energy that caused Gwyn to fall over in the tests, but much, much stronger.'

'That's what caused the temples to collapse? Not the wrath of the Gods, or some conspiracy by the people who moved the Relic there?'

Anita laughed. 'Afraid not.'

'Damn. That would have been much better.'

'Really?' said Anita, sceptically.

'Well, no, but it would have been more interesting.'

'You realize this is a breakthrough discovery? We know more about the Relic and its power; that's pretty interesting.'

'If you say so,' said Cleo. 'You still haven't answered my question though. Where have you been?'

'As I'm sure you've noticed, I realized too late to stop the experiment, but I ran back to the temples to try. I was halfway to the front of the Spirit Temple when everything started to collapse. I tried to get to the front, to find Alexander, but Marcus pulled me back and got me out before the whole thing caved in. After that, the rebels held me hostage.' She paused and turned to look at Cleo. 'You know the rebels have taken Kingdom?'

'Of course,' said Cleo.

Anita rolled her eyes. 'Sorry, Miss Gossip, just checking. Anyway, then Marcus negotiated my freedom. They also captured Gwyn, but he left her behind.'

Cleo laughed. 'I'm sure he did,' she said, nudging Anita.

'Oh, stop.'

Cleo laughed.

'Anyway, I stayed at Marcus' for a while. We met with the rebels and agreed I would report back on the state of the energy at the next meeting.'

'So here you are.'

'So here I am,' she agreed, turning serious. 'Have you heard from the others? Cordelia? Elistair? Your dad?'

Cleo's features darkened, and she shook her head. 'Dad's safe. He got me out of Kingdom and back here, but the others…"Have any of their bodies been found?'

Cleo shook her head. 'Not for any of them, and not for Helena or Timi either.'

'The others from the Institution?'

'Rose and Melia are back at the farm, although Melia's in a wheelchair; she lost the use of both her legs. Peter's dead. Rose saw a pillar fall on him.'

'Poor Gwyn,' said Anita.

'I know,' said Cleo. They looked out over Empire in silence. 'So what happens next? What else did you discuss with the rebels?'

Anita took a deep breath. 'Marcus is going to work with them. He's going to denounce his claim to rule and help set up democratic elections.'

'Will he stand?'

'Apparently not.'

'What about Gwyn?'

'She didn't say. But she has no army to support her like Marcus, so either way, she's less of a threat.'

'You know she's been telling everyone it's all your fault?'

Anita rolled her eyes. 'Yes, I know. I was attacked yesterday; I'm assuming as a direct result.'

'Attacked? By whom?'

'Don't know. We didn't stick around to find out, but I can't think of any other reason for a stranger to throw rocks at me.'

'You never know, could just be one of Alexander's fan girls... or Marcus' for that matter.'

Anita punched her best friend playfully on the arm.

'Do you think Gwyn was directly behind it?' said Cleo.

Anita shrugged. 'Maybe. She also told the rebels we didn't actually send the Relic back.'

'What?'

'I think she was trying to find another way to turn everyone against me. I mean, it's good they know, but I'd love to know what she's up to.'

'Me too,' said Cleo.

'There's one more thing,' said Anita, turning so she could see Cleo's reaction.

'Yeah, what?'

'When I ran into the Spirit Temple, the guy you were dancing with at the ball, the one who keeps running away?'

'Yes,' said Cleo, her energy coming alive.

'He was standing at the back, leaning against a pillar, and he said something weird.'

'What?' asked Cleo, impatiently.

'He said, *you know.*'

'Huh?'

'I responded the same way, but he just repeated those same words.'

'You know what?'

'I'm not certain, but I think maybe he knew the temples were going to collapse.'

'That's crazy,' said Cleo, defensively, 'how could he possibly have known that?'

Anita looked at Cleo. 'Tell me, who is this mysterious man of yours, with energy like none other, who keeps disappearing into thin air? What's his name? What does he do for a living? What skills does he possess? Who does he work for?'

'You know I have no idea,' huffed Cleo, 'but it's a bit farfetched to assume he knew the temples were going to fall down.'

'Why?'

'Because... because he lives in the Wild.'

'You mean the Wild where the Relic was discovered?'

'Generations ago.'

'Maybe that's the point of the Magnei,' said Anita, 'that they know things about the Relic. You said yourself, he's likely one of them.'

'Fine,' said Cleo. 'I suppose we have to entertain the possibility that he knew, although it's extremely unlikely. What are you going to do about it?'

'We're going to find him and ask him, of course.'

* * * * *

Anita spent the next two days retrieving and analysing the data from the observatory. Cleo brought food, and Anita slept a few uncomfortable hours curled up on the floor, refusing to face Cordelia's empty house. By dusk on the second day, she was finally happy she understood the readings. She was getting up to leave, bringing her muscles back to life after sitting for so long, when a voice from behind made her jump.

'Are you coming to the Institution meeting? We need to get going if we're going to make it on time.'

She spun around, thinking both of how she could defend herself, and wondering how she had neither heard nor felt the person's approach. She was relieved to see Marcus, even if his features did transform into a smug smile when he saw the panicked look on her face.

'Sorry, didn't mean to give you a fright,' he said, triumphantly.

'From your delight, I would say that's exactly what you intended,' she said, throwing a screwed-up ball of paper at him.

'And I bet you're dying to know how I did it.'

They both knew she was, but she wouldn't give him the satisfaction. 'Yes, I am coming. I take it we're travelling together?'

'I thought you could use a chaperone. We wouldn't want a repeat of the incident in Kingdom, with no one there to protect your poor defenceless derriere.'

Anita raised her eyebrows. 'My what?'

Marcus shrugged. 'So I've selflessly come to your service, with my renowned warrior skills.'

Anita shook her head and shoved him out of the way so she could descend the stairs. 'I have no words,' she said.

Marcus chuckled as he followed her out of the building, but his energy betrayed his relief.

He took the uncharacteristic step of driving them to the meeting himself, having, for some reason, dispensed with his driver. Anita could feel Sol's familiar energy trailing them, so they weren't entirely alone. 'A little mundane for you, isn't it?' said Anita.

'What?' said Marcus.

'You know exactly what,' she said, continuing when he showed no signs of answering. 'I've travelled with you in coaches, cars, and on horseback, and you always have the showiest, most ostentatious steed available. But, except for the horse, I have never once seen you drive yourself.'

'Cutbacks,' he said, smiling mischievously.

Anita laughed. 'Your father owned half the world.'

'Hmm, you're right, he did.'

'So...?' she said, looking sideways at him while using her arms to show he should go on.

Marcus huffed. 'Can't a man be a little mysterious?'

'Not with me.'

This time, Marcus raised his eyebrows. 'I dropped the chauffeur to impress girls,' he said. 'They seem to dig down-to-earth guys.'

'Fine, don't tell me, but I'll find out eventually.'

'I don't doubt it,' he said, his energy unexpectedly plummeting.

'Marcus, what's...' she said, but he cut her off.

'... I came to pick you up,' he said, quickly, 'because I wanted you to know that whatever happens at the meeting, I know it wasn't your fault.'

Her energy jumped at his words. 'They don't think...?'

'... I don't know. Who knows what Gwyn's convinced the rest of the world of by now…'

'Where are we going?' she asked. She'd assumed the meeting would be at the farm, where the Institution usually conducted business, but they weren't travelling in that direction.

'We're holding the meeting at the castle. I've got a squadron of my army stationed there, so we'll be safe.'

'Don't you think that's a little much? From what I can tell, life is continuing in Empire much the same as it did before. It's like nobody's noticed what happened in Kingdom, or maybe they just don't care.'

'Isn't that how it always happens? There's a disaster, and everyone runs around like headless chickens for a few days, donating clothes, money, food. Once they've told everyone they know how charitable they've been, they go back to their ordinary lives, and forget all about it.'

'Depressing, isn't it?' said Anita.

'Human nature, I suppose. The only time people make a real stand is if they personally feel the pain.'

'You'd think they might worry about food rations.'

'They probably don't realize there's anything to worry about.'

* * * * *

Marcus and Anita walked into the study that had, until so recently, belonged to Austin, Marcus' deceased father. Cleo and Rose were already there, along with Cleo's father, Draeus, and Marcus' mother, Melia.

Cleo raised an involuntary eyebrow when she saw Marcus and Anita enter together. Anita threw her a dirty look; now was not the time.

Anita and Marcus greeted their fellow survivors, then sat on the worn leather sofas by the fireplace, a fire roaring in the hearth. Marcus relayed to the others what had taken place in Kingdom, telling them everything, including Matthew's plan to create a democracy.

'And what are your intentions in all this?' asked Melia, her suspicion clear.

'As I told Matthew, I have no desire to rule. I intend to help him set up a system that's fair to all. What I do once that's done, I cannot say.'

'You expect us to believe you'll willingly give up all your power?' Melia continued, pushing her son further than the others would have.

'I didn't say I planned to give up all my power,' laughed Marcus. 'I will still have property, money, no doubt connections, but I have no desire to become embroiled in the politics of leading the world. I'm not naturally good at it, and I find it tedious.'

The door opened, and their heads swung in unison towards the noise. All eyes fixed on Gwyn's haughty form as it sauntered into the room. 'We all know you're not cut out for politics. Nor you,' she said, picking out Anita with her eyes. 'Far too rash. I, on the other hand, was born for this.'

Anita fought to stifle a smirk. Rose, thankfully, answered on behalf of them all.

'Gwyn,' she said, 'it's good to see you. I'm so very glad you're safe. I'm sure we all are.'

'I'm sure,' said Gwyn.

'Marcus was just bringing us up to speed on developments in Kingdom,' said Rose. 'I don't think you've missed anything you don't already know.'

'Good,' said Gwyn, sitting next to Rose. 'I'm just dying to hear what Anita's found out about the energy.'

All eyes swung to Anita, who forced a smile. 'We were just getting to that,' she said, not giving Gwyn the satisfaction of showing her irritation. 'As I'm sure you all know by now, I've been going through the energy readings from the last few weeks.

'Before we carried out the plan to return the Relic, the energy was in steady, although shallow, decline. The pace of deterioration had slowed considerably. We think because of the rationing, and the announcement of the plan to return the Relic. Up until the Relic's return, the readings continued in a relatively consistent manner. Then, on the day itself, the readings show a marked increase, followed by a monumental decline, which, given how low the levels were anyway, is not good.'

'The dip would surely be expected,' said Rose, 'given what took place.'

'Of course,' said Anita. 'But what I think is more interesting, is the rise that was recorded before the event. This shows people genuinely believed sending the Relic back would make a difference.'

'Just not the difference they expected,' said Gwyn.

'No,' said Melia, 'nobody saw that coming.'

'Not until it was too late,' said Anita, meeting Melia's cold eyes.

'And what's been going on since?' asked Cleo, moving them on before things got nasty.

Anita pulled her eyes away from Melia and addressed the others. 'Since then, the energy has been extremely volatile. It bounced back a little a few hours after the temple collapse, and it's been going up and down for seemingly no reason ever since. Occasionally it rises and then almost seems to get stuck, bouncing along consistently at a higher level for a few hours, before crashing again. Any semblance of the stability we had before has gone, and it's impossible to say what the broader effects will be.'

'Great,' said Gwyn.

Anita ignored her and continued. 'The strangest thing is that there's something different about the energy's intensity, or potency maybe. It's like there's less energy overall, like some of it has... disappeared.'

'There was a theory the Relic acted like a magnet for energy,' said Rose. 'Maybe that was true, but now there's nothing to pull the energy to us?'

'There's evidence to support that theory, however, that wouldn't explain an overall drop in potency, as the Relic would suck the energy to its new location. We have receptors that trace energy from all over the world, not just from Empire and Kingdom.'

'Does that mean we could use the receivers to locate the Relic?' asked Cleo.

'You don't know where the Relic is?' said Gwyn.

'No,' said Rose, irritated. 'We sent scouts to the Salt Sea, and when they got there, they found the Institution members sent to retrieve the Relic dead, and not a sign of the Relic itself.'

'So someone stole it?' said Anita. This was new information to her too.

'It appears so,' said Rose, quietly.

'Who else knew where we were sending it?' asked Anita. 'The list was short, wasn't it?'

'Yes,' said Rose, 'aside from all of us,' she gestured around the room, 'Helena, Elistair, Alexander, Timi, Peter, and Anderson were the only ones who knew.'

'Unless someone tracked the test boulders,' said Marcus, looking to Anita for her thoughts.

'It's possible,' said Anita. 'If someone had known what we were doing, they could have used an energy meter, like those used to lock onto animals during a Chase.'

'But they would've had to know about the tests in advance, to be prepared with a meter,' said Cleo. 'Someone would've had to let something slip. Or, more likely, one of the people on that list stole the Relic themselves.'

'Or several of them working together,' said Gwyn. 'I mean, only Dad's body has been found, so it could have been all of them, for all we know.'

'But, for what reason?' said Anita. 'Why would Helena or Elistair or Alexander want to steal the Relic?'

'They could have found out something we don't know,' said Gwyn.

'Helena never trusted Timi,' said Cleo, 'and there's always been something shifty about Anderson.'

'It could have been any of them, or none of them,' said Draeus. 'It's just as possible someone overheard a conversation between two of us, or that an opportunistic trader saw where the Relic landed and took it for themselves.'

'We should investigate all possibilities,' said Rose.

'I can keep my ear to the ground on the trader front,' said Draeus. 'I'm due back at the Cloud Mountain to deliver more supplies in a week, so I can sniff around a bit when I'm there. If Timi's still alive, that's where he would have gone.'

'I'll come with you,' said Rose. 'I want to see him myself, if he's alive. Institution business,' she added, when Draeus looked like he might protest.

'Fine,' he grumbled.

'I'll stay here and pull the Institution back into shape,' said Melia. 'I'm hardly mobile, and the remaining members need instruction. They don't know where to look, now Helena's gone.'

'You won't disband the Institution?' said Marcus.

'Not on your life,' said Melia.

'But what about the rebels? Will you tell them of your intention to carry on?'

'Yes, probably. We won't try to stand in their way. We think democracy is a good thing, but energy stability is still our goal. And anyway, our senior leadership is intact. Decisions like that are made well above our heads.'

'Will you take over as handler for all of Helena's recruits?' asked Cleo.

'No. I don't have time to look after that many people, and even if I did, the leadership wouldn't like it. They don't like anyone to know too much about what's going on. They'll send someone new to look after the four of you, I'm sure,' she said, nodding in the direction of Marcus, Anita, Gwyn, and Cleo.

'They can try,' said Anita, 'but I don't consider myself to be a member of the Institution, so I won't be following orders.'

'Me neither,' said Marcus and Gwyn together.

Cleo stayed uncharacteristically quiet.

'Handlers are not necessarily about orders,' said Melia. 'They're essential for the dissemination of valuable information.'

'I'll wait and see who it is,' said Cleo, 'then pass judgement.'

'Seems reasonable,' agreed Anita. 'I'll obviously continue to monitor the energy, and will keep you and the rebels in the loop on any findings.'

'And I'll continue to work with the rebels on setting up the election,' said Marcus.

'As will I,' said Gwyn.

'We'll need to make an announcement, of course, denouncing the old system and throwing our support behind the new one,' said Marcus. 'Leaving out any mention of the Relic.'

'You don't think there should be some reference to it?' said Anita. 'Isn't that the premise the whole election will be based on? That the prophecy has been fulfilled, the world is free from the Gods, and therefore the Descendants no longer have a mandate to rule?'

'You think we should say it was successful, despite the obvious?' said Marcus.

'I wouldn't phrase it quite like that, but yes. If we want the energy to respond, people have to really believe things are about to get better. If you leave out any mention of the Relic, they're going to get suspicious.'

'But if we lie to them again, and they find out, wouldn't that make things worse?' asked Rose.

'Maybe,' said Anita. 'But if they find that out, we'll have more pressing concerns anyway, like avoiding being lynched.'

'So long as nobody suspects the rebels know the truth, it wouldn't be the end of the new system, even if it came out,' said Cleo.

'People would worry that it would anger the Gods to support a new regime, if the Relic was still in the world,' said Marcus.

'In which case,' said Cleo, 'the only option is to keep the whole thing under wraps.'

'And hope whoever stole it doesn't have grand plans to announce its continued existence,' said Gwyn.

CHAPTER 4

'So, you agree?' said Marcus, ignoring everyone except for Matthew in the glass room in Kingdom they were still using for meetings. 'Gwyn, you and I should make a joint statement, telling the world the return of the Relic was a success. We'll also announce the structure of the new system and election dates.'

Matthew looked Marcus in the eye. 'Given the state of the energy, I don't think we have much choice,' he said, quietly. 'We need to cut rations again, and I won't be responsible for the anarchy that telling the world the truth would bring. However, for the same reason, if it were to get out that the Relic is still in the world, we will deny all knowledge.'

'I agree that would be for the best,' said Marcus. 'We'll schedule the announcement for two days from now. Will you be ready to explain the structure by then?'

'We're ready now,' said Matthew. 'We will no longer divide politics along temple lines, where the tendency is for each temple to strive to prove their superiority over the others. Instead, there will be two halls, both elected, but with different reasons for existence.

'The primary hall will comprise several political parties, although, of course, what type and how many remains to be seen. The primary hall will house the world's President, and key individuals with different responsibilities, from finance, to education, to health. It will also house representatives from every region. They will debate issues and set policies, with the overall goal of energy stability and enhancement.'

'Sounds like the structure we already have,' said Gwyn, defensively.

Matthew nodded. 'Yes, but unlike the Descendants and councillors, those representing the people will be elected.'

Marcus shot Gwyn a disapproving look. 'What will the second hall do?' he asked, keen to hear Matthew's full plan.

'The second hall will be full of academics and specialists,' said Matthew, 'who will both inform debate in the primary hall and instigate it by bringing new findings to the fore.'

'Like the academics we have today,' said Gwyn.

'Again, they will be elected,' said Matthew. 'The primary hall will hold an election every four years, and the second hall will do so every seven; longevity and consistency being of importance here.

'Furthermore, there will be no specific leader to the second hall. Instead, each member will serve a term of several months in the role of Clerk, when their research schedule allows. This role will be administrative: setting up votes, determining future topics of debate over and above what the primary hall requires, and ensuring debates keep to schedule.'

'Sounds like you've got it all planned out,' said Gwyn.

Matthew looked at her with cutting eyes, making her shrink in her seat. 'We've been contemplating revolution for years,' he said, slowly. 'What else do you think we've been doing in that time?' He paused, the air turning heavy.

'I... uh...' She floundered under the scrutiny of his gaze, then gestured for him to continue.

'What about the temples?' asked Anita.

'What about them?' said Matthew. 'Now the world is free from the Gods, what relevance do the temples have?'

Anita looked aghast. 'Development of skills, tradition, worship of the Gods—to whom we have not, in fact, returned the Relic. Comfort, community; the list is endless.'

Matthew's face was a detached mask as he replied. 'They'll continue much as before, so long as the people support them. We won't disband them or tear them to the ground, nor will we prevent the usual ceremonies. However, they won't play a central role in the way we govern. The temples have been a tool of subjugation for too long; we shouldn't romanticise them.'

'And you would be foolish to underestimate the power they still hold,' said Anita, her features set. 'Whether you like it or not, energy is about emotion. People have grown up with the temples as a central part of life. Schooling, celebrations, festivals, every prominent time in our calendar is linked to those temples. People have strong emotional connections to them. It would be dangerous to undermine, or worse, make trivial, every important moment in almost every person's life. I can't imagine what that would do to the energy.'

'They'll still be around. People will adapt,' said Matthew. 'That's the way it has to be.'

'Really?' said Anita. 'According to whom? Because, to my knowledge, nobody has yet been elected, so nobody has the right to make a proclamation like that.'

Matthew held her gaze a moment, the room collectively holding its breath, waiting to see how Matthew would respond to such an open challenge. To their astonishment, he backed down.

'You're right,' he said, palms facing the ceiling as he spoke, 'I don't have that mandate, and you're also correct that I should not assume the people will support my view. However, I will campaign for a move away from a society so closely linked to the temples.

'I'm sure they'll have a place in our lives for decades to come—maybe even centuries—but ultimately, the people should be in command of our destiny. People, with their own minds, weighing up options in the light of facts.'

'It's a shame,' replied Anita, 'that you are determined to bring about change across the full spectrum of society, except where it's needed most. Why can't the temples evolve to exist in harmony with your vision? Not least, because if you don't get the temples on side, you'll forever live with the threat of being overturned by some extreme faction that your policies will have inadvertently helped create.'

* * * * *

'He's such an idiot,' said Anita, polishing off her third glass of Cleo's latest alcoholic concoction—something to do with cucumber, vodka and elderflower that went down much too easily.

'Well, despite that, he's taken control of the entire rebel army, and he's probably less of an idiot than the Descendants,' said Cleo, then remembered Marcus was with them. 'Sorry, no offence.'

Marcus laughed and shook his head. 'Aside from his views on the temples, I don't think his plan is bad.

He wants energy stability, as we do, and their proposed structure makes a lot of sense.'

'Oh, stop being so sensible,' said Anita. 'It's not at all like you, and it really doesn't suit you.'

Cleo rolled her eyes. 'Another round?' she said, not waiting for their answer before making her way to the train's bar, for the fourth time in quick succession.

They were travelling back to Empire. Anita wanted to get back to the observatory, to prepare for the announcement, and Cleo wanted to look for something in the archives.

Marcus had been vague about his reasons for accompanying them. It was especially strange, given that he would have to return to Kingdom the following day, to prepare for the announcement.

'Step aside,' said Cleo, elaborately, as she reached the bar, elbowing the poor bartender out of the way. 'Let me show you how it's done.'

Anita laughed, pulling her gaze away from Cleo to take in the rest of the ornate carriage. Beautiful wooden carvings framed intricate artwork that gave the dark space a cosy feel. Wall lamps cast a low light over small circular tables, around which sat lavishly upholstered mahogany chairs.

The sun had recently set on the horizon, and an attendant had closed the crushed velvet curtains, making the carriage feel even smaller. The rocking of the train encouraged them to relax for the first time in days. In here, Anita could almost believe the world was still normal.

Marcus looked playfully at Anita. 'I think being sensible suits me quite well, thank you very much.'

Anita's eyes sparkled, and her energy livened. 'It's better than whatever you were going for before, but that's not to say it's right for you.'

'I see,' he said, slowly. He leaned back, but kept his eyes on hers.

'I doubt that,' she said, raising an eyebrow, refusing to look away.

'One for you,' said Cleo, as she placed a drink in front of Marcus, 'and one for you.' She threw Anita a questioning look as she put down her drink.

'And one for you,' came a deep, rich voice that took them all by surprise. A dark hand placed Cleo's drink in front of her. Cleo looked up at the tall man with cropped dark hair and cavernous brown eyes, and her mouth dropped open.

It was Anita's turn to raise an eyebrow. 'Will you join us?' she asked, motioning to a spare chair.

He hesitated, his energy uncertain.

Cleo responded for him. 'Of course he will. No one in here is half as interesting as us.'

The man looked a little embarrassed, but inclined his head and sat. 'Thank you,' he said.

'I'm Anita, this is Marcus, and that's Cleo,' said Anita, barely able to stifle her smirk at Cleo's obvious interest in the man.

'I'm Edmund, and I know who you are,' he said, intelligent eyes flicking between them.

'Most people seem to these days,' said Cleo, her interest abating. 'How can we help you?'

Anita gave Cleo a chastising look.

'What?' said Cleo. 'He's obviously here for a reason, so we might as well get to the point.'

Edmund paused, looking Cleo over before responding. 'She's right,' he said, 'I am here for a reason.'

'Yes?' prompted Cleo, when he didn't immediately continue.

'I'm your new handler, from the Institution.'

'Great,' said Anita, looking at the ceiling. 'What do you want?'

Edmund gave Anita a long, penetrating look. 'They warned me you might be hostile,' he said, 'but I don't understand why you think we're on different sides?'

'Really?' said Anita. 'You can't think of, oh, I don't know, one or two reasons why I might not trust you people? Maybe something to do with Helena lying to me for years about my parents? Or maybe because Helena lied to me, to get me to steal something that didn't belong to her? During that debacle, I wound up getting tortured to protect her secret. Would one of those suffice as a reason?'

'You did try to steal the cylinder,' said Marcus, his hurt voice cutting across Anita's alcohol fuelled rant, knocking the wind from her sails.

'Marcus, I...'

'Don't.' He looked at her with hard eyes, rising to his feet and leaving the carriage, his energy crushed.

Anita's head crashed into her hands. 'Great,' she said, lifting her eyes and rounding on Edmund. 'Now, what do you want?'

'I want what you want,' he said. 'I want to find the Relic and return it to the Gods for real, so we can guarantee energy stability. I'm going to do everything I can to help you achieve that.'

'Why are the Institution helping us? Why not try to find it on your own?'

'You know why,' he said.

She looked blankly at him, and he narrowed his eyes.

'Because you opened the cylinder in your mind.'

* * * * *

Anita left the bar. How did they know she'd opened the cylinder? She'd told no one but Cleo… But she wouldn't give him the satisfaction of asking.

'Anita, wait...' Edmund's voice trailed after her, but she ignored it. He didn't follow.

She made her way to Marcus' compartment, cursing that she hadn't come clean before. She knocked lightly on his door. 'Marcus, it's me. Please let me in.'

After a few silent moments, she heard the lock disengage. The handle turned, and the door popped open a crack before Marcus' footsteps retreated. She pushed the door wide and entered, feeling uncertainty both in his energy and her own.

'I'm sorry. I meant to tell you. I just haven't found the right time.'

'Is that all?' he said, perching on the edge of a table, looking at her with fiery features.

'Marcus, please, this isn't the time for us to fight.'

'Then what is it the time for?'

She walked to the bed and sat, gripping the wooden edge so hard her knuckles went white. 'We have to work together,' she said, looking up at him, imploring him not to make it difficult.

'We tried that before, and ended up destroying the temples, along with hundreds of lives.'

'That's not fair,' she said. 'I know you're angry...'

'... why's Edmund here?' he said, cutting her off.

Anita looked away. 'Because I opened the cylinder in my mind, and somehow the Institution found out about it.'

'You did it?' he said, his energy rising, then faltering. 'You told them before you told me?'

Anita hit the side of the bed with her hands. 'I told nobody but Cleo. I have no idea how they found out.'

'Maybe you placed your trust in the wrong person.'

'You think Cleo told them?'

'She seemed happy with the idea of a new handler, so maybe her loyalties lie with them.'

'I would never, for a second, question her loyalty. She would never betray me like that. But while we're on the subject of betrayals...'

Marcus hung his head. '... Anita.'

'Yes?' she said, launching to her feet. 'Shall we talk about how you beat me up during the Chase?'

'You tried to steal from my family,' he said. His eyes were hard as stone as they met hers, not conceding an inch.

'I did not. Helena told me I was recovering something your father had stolen from her. She told me it would help with the energy, and I believed her. When I realized she'd lied, I put it back.'

Marcus' shoulders slumped, and he looked away, saying nothing for some time. 'I'm sorry,' he said. 'I should never have helped Gwyn during the Chase. I was angry and hurt and... I loved you.' He blurted the words, seeming to take even himself by surprise.

Anita stilled and their eyes met, moments of silence ticking by, a tense energy stretching across the gap between them.

'I still love you,' he whispered, longing thick in his voice, his eyes searching hers.

Anita's energy rose, desire creeping through her as she drank in Marcus' familiar features. She didn't think, couldn't think. Her body moved by itself, taking steps towards him.

He responded at once, rushing towards her and pulling her into his arms. Their lips met, whatever dam that had been holding back their energy collapsing before the force that surged between them. Relief and comfort and lust washed over her, Anita's mind knowing nothing but sensation. His hands went to her face, hers to his back, each pulling the other closer, kissing deeply, relaxing into the familiar feel of their bodies pressed together. Burning guilt seared through her, but a treacherous part of her wanted him, needed the comfort of his touch.

His lips moved to her neck, and he pushed her back towards the bed, lowering them down onto its surface. The press of his weight stole every ounce of focus, her body screaming for more. His hands searched for a way to reach her skin, but the contact of his fingers under her clothes broke something in Anita. She had to stop him; it had already gone too far.

Her body went rigid, hands static in Marcus' hair. She pushed his lips away. 'We can't do this,' she whispered, breath ragged.

He rested his forehead on hers. 'Why not?' he said, pulling back to look at her, moving his hand to her face, caressing her cheek.

Energy swirled across her skin where his fingertips stroked her. She closed her eyes, forcing herself to focus, refusing to get lost in his touch.

She pushed him back and sat up. 'I can't deny I have feelings for you,' she said, before biting out words he wouldn't want to hear. 'But I'm in love with Alexander.'

'Alexander's dead,' said Marcus, gently, sitting next to her, taking her hand in his.

'I don't think so,' she said, pulling herself free, putting distance between them. 'I think I would feel it. We meditated so much together that his energy started to mix with mine. But everything feels just as it did before.'

'That could be wishful thinking,' said Marcus.

'It's not; I know it's not, and I have to find him.' She stared at the floor. 'I'm sorry, Marcus.' She lifted her eyes to his. 'I didn't mean for this to happen, it's just… everything that's going on...'

'... we've all been through a lot,' he said, his energy resigned. He took several deep breaths before he spoke again. 'I'll help you look for Alexander if that's what you want. We don't know if we can trust the Institution or the rebels yet, but I do trust that you and Cleo want the same thing I do: to return the Relic for real. To set up a democratic system, one that ensures energy stability once and for all.'

'Thank you,' she said, relief flooding her. She couldn't imagine losing Marcus too. 'You should know, after the announcement, I'm going to the Wild Lands.'

'Why?' Confusion captured his features. 'I thought you wanted to help?'

'I plan to help. I'm going to find the Magnei.'

'What? Why? How do you even know about them?'

'Because that's what I found out when the cylinder in my mind popped open. The location of the Magnei in the Wild.'

* * * * *

Anita, Cleo, Marcus, and Edmund sat around the rustic wooden table in Cleo's warehouse apartment, sipping tea and eating late-night dark chocolate gingers.

'Tell us everything,' said Marcus.

Everyone directed their attention to Anita, who frowned.

'I've already told you. I was meditating, I realized why I couldn't get the image of Gwyn falling over out of my mind, and I dropped the cylinder. It bounced back up and unfurled in mid-air, right in front of me. I don't know what finally caused it to open,' she added, sensing the question about to come forth from Cleo's lips.

'And you saw nothing written on the inside of the cylinder?' said Edmund.

'No,' said Anita, 'but I knew how to find the Magnei, and that they can help us return the Relic for real.'

'How will they do that?' asked Marcus.

'I don't know,' said Anita. 'I can't explain it. I just… felt it.'

'You *just felt it*?' teased Cleo.

Anita shoved her. 'Yes. It was like the image of the Relic came into my head and then an image of the Magnei, and then a feeling that it was all going to be alright.'

'Maybe they've got the Relic and have already sent it back?' said Edmund. 'How do you know they're not sorting it out on their own?'

'I don't for sure,' said Anita, a tinge of frustration creeping into her tone. 'It was clear that they could help us, but it felt like they needed us as much as we needed them.'

'So, the plan is we find them?' said Marcus.

'The plan is for Cleo and me to find them. You need to stay here, to ensure the rebels do what they've promised,' said Anita.

'You can't go by yourselves,' said Marcus. 'Where are they, anyway?'

'The Jungle,' said Anita.

'The Jungle?' said Marcus. 'The Jungle?' he said again, looking at Anita as though she were mad. 'Nobody goes there; it's too dangerous, and so far away.'

'It's probably not that dangerous. I think the Magnei drive people away to keep the world from knowing they're there.'

'And I'll be with them,' said Edmund.

'You'll be what?' said Marcus, looking at Anita in protest.

'No, you won't,' said Anita. 'We only just met you.'

'But an extra pair of hands could be useful,' said Cleo.

'Not if they stab us in the back,' said Anita.

Edmund frowned. 'The Institution wants energy stability, and the only way to ensure that is if we return the Relic to the Gods. This is our best lead; I need to come.'

'How do we even know the Institution sent you?' asked Anita.

'Ask Melia, she'll vouch for me.'

'I don't like this at all,' said Marcus.

'Marcus, you're the only one with an army to rival the rebels,' said Anita. 'If they go back on their word, you're the only one who can make sure a democratic system is put in place; your role is not in question.'

'Who put you in charge?' said Marcus.

'My mother, when she planted that damn cylinder in my head,' snapped Anita.

Marcus exhaled, but said nothing.

'Edmund, you can come with us if Melia confirms who you are,' said Anita. 'But don't think that means you're our handler. I'm not a member of the Institution.'

'Understood,' said Edmund, sitting back in his chair.

'For Gods' sake, are you really going to do this?' said Marcus.

'I don't think we have much choice,' said Anita.

'Then take Sol and a few of my guards with you.'

'No,' she said. 'We don't want to attract attention, and it would look suspicious if half your private guard suddenly disappears. Not to mention, we don't want to turn up on the doorstep of the Magnei looking hostile.

They're the most powerful among us, and we need to make a good first impression.'

* * * * *

Draeus and Rose read the brutality on the ground before them. All around was tranquillity itself, a reward for the senses. Water lapped gently at the shore, the air filling their lungs with the smell of salt and pine. The isolated beauty was breath-taking, but so were the remnants of death, still plain for anyone to see.

A shudder ran through Draeus as his energy responded to the disturbance. The Institution had discovered the massacre days ago, and the bodies had been burned. But the absence of bodies didn't make the blood stains any less shocking.

There was no sign of the Relic, and no clues where it had gone. They looked around, careful to take in every tiny detail of the sheltered cove where the group sent to retrieve the Relic had set up camp.

Only once satisfied he'd memorised every detail, Draeus walked deep into the cove, to examine the spills of blood that stained the sandy ground there too. 'The attack started here,' he said, turning to face Rose.

'How do you know?' she asked.

'They entered from the back and used the rocks as cover. See? Back here? They could have easily slit the guard's throat and pulled him behind the rocks before anyone noticed.'

Draeus turned his head and walked a dozen paces forward, to where two rust-red stains colored the sand. 'Two of the guards huddled around the fire, here,' he said. 'They were taken out in unison.'

'Because the disturbance is so clean?' asked Rose.

58

'Yes, that, and because the fourth patch is down by the water, meaning the guard there heard nothing that made him leave his post.' They walked back to the fourth and final intrusion in the sand.

'Seamless,' said Rose, grimly.

'Yes,' said Draeus, taking one last look around, 'and meticulously planned. If it was passing opportunists, then they knew what they were doing.'

'You think it was more likely someone we trusted? Someone who knew about the plan?'

'Or someone who overheard one of us talking about the plan. The guards were probably taken out before the Relic even arrived, given two of them were sitting by the fire. It seems strange that someone would risk killing four people—and leave them with their valuables—unless they knew what was coming.'

Rose looked out across the water. 'So, what next?'

'None of the trading post owners have got wind of a shady package. So I suppose we head to the Cloud Mountain and see Timi, assuming he's still alive. He knows more than he should about the criminal underworld, so maybe he can help.'

'I doubt he'll share with us.'

'Maybe not, but we can sniff around a bit while we're there.'

'Helena's convinced he's hiding something,' said Rose. 'It would be so good to catch him out.'

CHAPTER 5

'Citizens,' Matthew's voice rang across the great expanse where the temples had once stood, 'I address you today with a mix of sadness, regret, and promise.

'We know that the Descendants' rule has not made for a prosperous environment for everyone. We have known for decades that the Descendants cared more for lining their own pockets than fulfilling their duty to the world. And when they finally took action, at last returning the Relic to the Gods, they brought about death, disaster, and injustice like never before.

'That is the source of my sadness and regret,' he said, letting the words sink in, 'for we, the revolutionaries, have been planning our coup for some months. We've been gathering support and resources in the Wild, planning how we should proceed. If we had acted sooner, maybe, just maybe, we could have averted this cruel tragedy.

'However, we considered the return of the Relic a crucial step towards equality, and now, with the final source of Descendant legitimacy ended, a new era can begin.'

Shouts of agreement came from the crowd and Matthew looked into their eyes, showing them he meant every word.

'This is the promise I offer: the Relic and the Descendants will no longer hold sway over us. We are free to craft a new type of society. A society where we elect our leaders, where we take energy stability seriously, and where anyone, no matter their background, has the chance to lead us, as one, united people.'

The crowd applauded. Matthew paused, waiting for the noise to die down before continuing, visibly buoyed on the crest of their approval. He explained the proposed structure, and they listened, hanging on his every word.

Joshua, Matthew's right-hand man, leaned towards Gwyn, who sat next to him in the front row. He was almost shaking with excitement. She was no reader, but Gwyn could feel it.

'I take it you're going to run for a seat?' he asked, conversationally.

'Yes,' said Gwyn, turning her head and sizing him up, raising an eyebrow. He was quite delicious, in a funny sort of way, his intense green eyes set off by floppy blond hair. He was the kind of person who noticed people, who scrutinised them to work out what they wanted. But did he use that skill for good or for evil? 'Are you?' she asked, not considering, until now, that it was a likely prospect.

He smiled. 'That would be telling,' he said, winking at her. 'If I were to, we'd be seeing a lot more of each other.'

She held his gaze as her head raced to work out what he meant, her eyes going wide when she realized. 'My seat?' she said. 'You're going after my seat?'

'May the best man win,' he said, flashing her his charming, vote winning smile.

'Oh no,' she replied, the delight of a challenge lighting her up from within. 'It'll be a woman.'

'... however, it will not be easy.' Matthew's voice cut across the exchange between them, their encounter ending as they turned their attention to him once more. 'There is a great deal for us to put right before we can return to stability. But this new structure is our best hope, giving equal chances and prosperity to all.'

'But what about the Descendants and councillors?' asked a sceptical voice in the front row. 'Are we to believe they're going to give up all they have without a fight?'

'I'm glad you mentioned that,' said Matthew. 'Gwyn, Marcus, will you please join me on stage?'

Gwyn and Marcus made their way up the steps to where Matthew stood, Joshua giving Gwyn's hand a quick squeeze as she got up. Gwyn's energy lurched, half angry, half intrigued, but she acted as though nothing had happened. She took her position on the stage, resolutely not looking his way.

'Marcus, Gwyn,' said Matthew, 'could you respond directly?'

'Of course,' said Marcus, getting in before Gwyn could. 'I know this may come as a shock to many of you, especially those who have lived a life governed by men like my father, and his father before him. However, the remaining Descendants, that is, Gwyn and I, are wholeheartedly behind Matthew's plan to bring about Democracy.

'It is our view that for too long, there has been a gaping divide in our society. I pledge publicly, now, as I have already done in private, that my personal army is at the disposal of Matthew and his men. They are to help ensure a fair election. We want nothing more than to bring about energy stability, and for everyone to have an equal chance to thrive.

'We are deeply sorry for the terrible disaster that took place here, but we must not let our loss be in vain.

Gwyn and I fought to fulfil our vows to return the Relic. Now that we are free from it, we must make it count.' Marcus looked to Gwyn, and she took over.

'We've already disbanded the ruling council, and I'd like to echo Marcus' words. We are entirely supportive of this new era in our history. Indeed, to show how fully we are behind the new system, I intend to stand for election. This is not, as some of you may think, a ploy to remain in control; I have no interest in becoming our leader. Instead, it is a demonstration of my desire to be a part of creating a new world, of which we can all be proud.

'Unlike in the past, those living in my constituency now have the power to decide if they would like me, or someone else,' her eyes flicked involuntarily to Joshua, 'to represent them. I will support the decision, whatever it is, without question.

'I plan to convert the Body residence here, in Kingdom, into a home for children who have lost their parents, either because of the Relic return, or otherwise. It is my view that everyone should have a safe place to call home. I hope to make this a reality for many vulnerable children, who do not have a home today.'

The crowd applauded vigorously, Gwyn again catching Joshua's eye, who gave her a congratulatory look. Her opening parlay had been effective; he was going to have to step up his game.

* * * * *

'So, what's the deal with you and Marcus?' asked Cleo, her tone full of concern.

'What's the deal with you and Edmund?' countered Anita, hoping to throw her off. 'You seemed pretty cosy at your place the other day...'

'He's hot,' said Cleo, with a shrug. 'Nothing wrong with a bit of flirting.'

'Flirting...?' said Anita, suggestively.

'Oh, stop,' said Cleo, 'nothing's happened, and nothing will; I can't stop thinking about my mystery man. Melia's confirmed Edmund is who he claims to be, though. Now, stop trying to deflect, and tell me what's made things weird between you and Marcus.'

'It's good Melia's confirmed he's from the Institution,' said Anita, ignoring Cleo's dictate and moving to a new pile of books. They now had access to rooms in the archives that had previously been locked away, and were helping to work through the books and other artifacts. 'At least we don't have to worry about him being an imposter any longer.'

'Anita, I'm serious.'

'Oh, fine,' she snapped. 'We kissed.' She slammed closed a book with such force that a little cloud of dust swirled up in protest.

'Careful,' said Cleo, 'they've only just let us in here. They'll throw us out if they think we're trashing the place.'

'I feel so guilty; I can barely look at Marcus. I shouldn't have done it, but he was there, and we kissed, and it felt good… at least for a second. But Alexander's got to be alive, and I don't want to give Marcus false hope.'

'You let him kiss you?' said Cleo.

Anita gave her a warning look. 'Nothing really happened; I stopped it before it could.'

'But it would have otherwise...'

'... thanks for stating the obvious,' said Anita, pacing to vent her frustration.

'We might never find Alexander,' said Cleo, her voice full of compassion. 'You should prepare yourself for that possibility.'

'How can you say that?' she said, rounding on her best friend.

Cleo held up her hands in peace. 'I'm not saying he's dead, but where could he be? If he fell into the hole under the temple... well, you know as well as I do, there's no hope. But if he got away, why hasn't he come back?'

'Maybe he was hit on the head and can't remember who he is,' said Anita. 'Or maybe he was kidnapped. A Descendant's a valuable prisoner.'

'For what? Nobody's ransomed him, and surely, if he'd hit his head, someone would have recognised him and brought him back? Anita, I'm not trying to be cruel, but what if he's alive and doesn't want to come back?'

'Why wouldn't he?' she said, taking deep breaths to remain calm.

'I don't know... for any number of reasons. Maybe he feels too guilty about what happened to face everyone, or maybe he's found a lead about where the Relic is and is following it, or maybe he just wants to start again, away from the crazy life he had here.'

'Away from me?'

'I didn't mean that.'

'Maybe not, but the fact is, if he's still alive, free, and in command of his mind and memories, and choosing not to come back, he's also choosing not to come back to me.'

'You've got to admit it's a possibility,' said Cleo.

'I know he would come back for me if he could.'

'How?'

'I can't explain it,' said Anita, 'but we meditated together so much, it's like our energy became intertwined, like it was easier to function when he was there, like we were part of each other. I know it sounds crazy, but he felt it too. He would come back for me.'

'Feeling that way led Alexander's mother to her death. She meditated so hard and for so long trying to find his father, that one day she just didn't come back.'

'I'm hardly doing that,' said Anita.

'No, but you've been meditating a lot, obviously trying to find his energy. Just be careful, and remember that at some point, you need to live your life.'

Anita huffed. 'Can we please talk about something else? Like, for example, all these documents we need to get through before we leave for the Wild…'

They searched for anything that would give them clues about the Magnei, or how to return the Relic for real. So far, they'd found nothing concrete, only insignificant details.

Most of what they'd found bolstered Cleo's suspicions about the way the Relic had been discovered. The research group had mysteriously deviated from their planned route, with no obvious explanation, and had stumbled upon the Relic, apparently by accident. It all seemed like too much of a coincidence.

'Look here,' said Cleo, picking up the next manuscript in the stack. 'It's a draft of the original speech. The one telling the world about the Relic discovery and prophecy.'

'Gods!' exclaimed Anita. 'That's from the seven hundreds!'

'I know,' said Cleo. 'Amazing!'

'What does it say?'

'A lot of it's too faded to read, but the prophecy's still here. It says: *We, the Gods, give to the people of the world this Relic, as a trial, not only of your ingenuity, but your spirit. We made you, in our likeness, and now we send a test for our creations. Visionaries will return this Relic to us. From that moment, the energy will be forever stable, and you will be free.*'

'Visionaries? Not Descendants?' said Anita, surprised.

'I think the Descendants were called Visionaries for a while,' said Cleo, 'right back at the beginning. Maybe the meaning is the same?'

'Maybe,' said Anita sceptically. 'But why have we never heard that term before? And why don't they ever use this version of the prophecy in ceremonies?'

'Don't know,' said Cleo.

'Because it could undermine the Descendants' authority?' said Anita.

'I suppose, but not if Descendants and Visionaries are one and the same.'

'But what if they're not? The Descendants must have changed the wording, which casts doubt on their legitimacy.'

'Gods,' said Cleo. 'Even if it's all totally innocent, I'm not sure we should share this too widely.'

'My word,' said Anita. 'It's serious if you're saying things like that.'

'It is serious. I get why they locked all this stuff away... What do you think would happen to the energy if suspicion got out about the Descendants' legitimacy?'

'I doubt it would be good,' said Anita. 'But... what if it doesn't have to be the Descendants who return the Relic? What if there are other criteria we don't understand?'

'One problem at a time,' said Cleo. 'Maybe the academics, or the Institution can shed some light.'

'Maybe,' said Anita, doubtfully.

* * * * *

They continued to work their way through the materials in the archives for the next week, making headway with only a fraction the artifacts before admitting defeat. Anita had to return to Kingdom to give an energy update, and they would head into the Wild—to the Magnei—from there.

'Someone needs to work through what we couldn't,' said Cleo, addressing the Institution members who had gathered in the private dining room of the boutique Rochester Hotel in Kingdom. 'We did what we could in the time we had, but there's so much more we haven't even touched.'

Cleo and Anita told the small party what they had found. Edmund, Marcus, and Melia were the only Institution members Anita recognized, with Rose and Draeus still in the Wild Lands.

'Well, I'm afraid I can't cast any light,' said Melia, 'but the potential ramifications are mind blowing.'

'If it really does mean that anyone can return the Relic,' cautioned Anita.

'Of course,' said Melia, 'but we can't let this rumour get out. The truth wouldn't matter; people would jump to conclusions without encouragement.'

'We're hoping the Magnei will be able to help,' said Cleo.

'We all hope that,' said Melia. 'Unfortunately, only the Gods know if our hopes are well founded.'

'Any news on the location of the Relic?' asked Anita.

Melia shook her head. 'No, nothing. Rose and Draeus went to the Salt Sea. It looks as though the attack there was well planned and pre-meditated. In all likelihood, whoever stole the Relic knew what they were looking for.'

'We were betrayed,' said Cleo.

'Or overheard,' said Melia.

'The former is more likely,' said Marcus.

Melia gave a non-committal shrug.

'So, what next?' said Cleo. 'Dad and Rose have gone to the Cloud Mountain? What do you think they'll find there?'

'I don't know, but the mountain seems to have been unaffected throughout, so there must be something going on up there… When are you leaving?'

'Straight after the meeting with Matthew and his people,' said Anita. 'I'm giving an energy update, and we'll slip away after that; everyone will assume we're heading back to Empire.'

'But who will monitor the energy while you're gone?' asked another Institution member; a short girl with auburn hair.

'Nobody,' said Anita, 'or at least nobody properly. Marcus will continue to take readings, but there's not much anyone can do from the observatory, other than watch how things unfold. The Magnei, on the other hand, could finally give us some answers.'

'You really think they can?' asked Marcus, still not happy that he had to stay behind.

'Yes, I'm sure of it,' said Anita, giving Marcus a firm look.

* * * * *

Anita and Marcus walked the short distance to their usual meeting spot with the rebels. Sol was unusually absent, and Marcus was agitated, clearly holding something back. Anita stopped abruptly outside their destination and turned to face him. 'What is it?' she said to his back, as he kept going.

Marcus stopped, turning slowly, and walking back to where she stood, standing so close she almost took a step back. He placed a hand on her cheek, his thumb caressing her cheek bone.

Anita opened her mouth to speak. 'It's okay,' he said, before she could, 'I'm not going to kiss you. You've made your feelings on that clear. But I'm worried about you going into the Wild, just the three of you, with no proper security. It's too dangerous.'

'Marcus,' said Anita, reaching up and placing her hand on top of his before removing it from her face, 'we've been through this. We need to move quietly and swiftly, and we don't want to look hostile when we arrive. We'll be safer if we look like traders than if we travel in a bigger group.'

'I...' Marcus searched for words, but she cut him off, pulling him towards the meeting room.

'Marcus, it's settled. I appreciate your concern, but we're going, as planned. Now come on, or we're going to be late.'

They entered the meeting room to find everyone else already there, sipping on herbal teas and eating biscuits the housekeeper had made for them.

'Let's start,' said Matthew. 'Anita, we're all dying to know what happened to the energy after the announcement.'

'Of course,' she said, taking the seat opposite Matthew, 'but I'm afraid it's not the news we were hoping for.'

Matthew's shoulders slumped at her words. 'Well, we knew it wouldn't be easy,' he said. 'Please, go on.'

'There was an immediate spike in the energy after your speech,' she said. 'It was pronounced, almost taking the energy back to pre-crisis levels—that is, the level before Christiana's death. However, several hours later, it came crashing back down for no apparent reason. Since then, the energy has been fluctuating, and the fluctuations are huge. It swings up to higher levels than before, but then comes careering back down.'

'But the fluctuations to higher levels surely show we're on the right track,' said Joshua. 'We just need to prove that we genuinely intend to do what we've said we will.'

'That's one hypothesis,' said Anita, 'and I hope it's that simple. Unfortunately, it's unlikely to be so. Emotion drives the energy. The trust people had in our old system was shattered. We need to build trust in a new one, and that takes time.'

'But you think it will bounce back?' asked Gwyn.

'I can't say for certain,' said Anita, 'but I don't see any reason why it shouldn't, under the right conditions.'

'And we're doing all we can to put those conditions in place,' said Matthew. 'Thank you, Anita. We will continue with our current plan to hold the election in two months. It'll be tight, but it seems best we use the momentum we've got and hope that helps with the energy. Joshua, where are we with planning?'

* * * * *

Draeus and Rose were five miles out from the base of the Cloud Mountain, each driving an energy truck full of supplies, when they ran into the first group of guards. The guards stopped and questioned them, their cargo examined thoroughly before they were allowed to proceed, and two surly men accompanied them for the rest of their journey.

They passed several other roadblocks as they grew closer to the mountain, each more severe in its fortification. They had to stop at every one and explain the reason for their visit. The guards ushered them through without incident, and they eventually made it to the mountain's base, from where they were allowed to proceed to the top unaccompanied. They left the supplies at the bottom; someone else would haul it all to the top.

They had inquired why security was so high, but the guards—several of whom Rose recognised as having once served Austin—met their questions with stony silence.

'That was an unexpected reception,' said Rose, as soon as she was confident they were out of earshot. She was already out of breath from the climb.

'They've certainly stepped it up a bit,' said Draeus, his eyes alight.

'Those guards used to belong to Austin's army,' said Rose. 'They must be the men and women who defected when Marcus took over.'

'Amber,' said Draeus, darkly. 'What in the world is Timi doing, aligning with her?'

'He had little choice if he needed this kind of force; not exactly easy to come by.'

'No.'

'The question is,' said Rose, 'why does he feel he needs all this protection? Assuming it's Timi who's up there.'

'The place still feels weird, even more so than last time.'

'I agree,' said Rose. 'It feels like there's some kind of buzz all around us, like there's something in the air itself.'

'We won't get a straight answer from Timi, or any of the others.'

'You'll have to distract them; buy me time to do some digging around.'

They reached the top the following day. Amber and two cronies were waiting for them, a broad, simulated smile across her face.

'Draeus, Rose,' she said sweetly, 'what an unexpected pleasure to see you both. I thought you would leave, after dropping the supplies at the base, given our people are bringing everything up.'

'Timi is one of my most valuable and respected customers,' said Draeus. 'It would be unthinkable for me to come all the way here and not express my gratitude face to face. And, of course, to discuss if there's anything else I can help with.'

Amber's smile became fixed. She paused a beat too long before responding. 'I'm so sorry, you haven't heard?' she said. 'We haven't seen Timi since the Relic return, and if you haven't either, then our worst fears must be true.'

'We know he's here,' said Rose, crossing her fingers. 'Please stop the theatrics and take us to him. It's Institution business.'

'Institution business?' said Amber. 'We don't recognise that organisation here. In fact, we consider them to be treasonous. If you don't want to be locked in one of our cells, then taken back to Kingdom by force, I suggest you leave at once.'

'Treasonous?' said Rose. 'Haven't you heard what's taken place in Kingdom, since the Relic return? The rebels are creating a new, democratic world. I'm afraid they don't feel the way you do about the Institution. So I guess it'll have to be by force.'

Rose squared up to Amber. 'I've known you for more than a decade. I know you have to do what you have to do, but we're not willingly leaving this mountain until we've seen Timi.'

Footsteps rang out behind Amber, and a man dressed in a black monk's robe—who had been standing out of view by the door—motioned for Amber to step aside. 'Please come with me,' he said, his voice soft and aged, 'I will show you to Timi's chambers, so you can see for yourself.'

They climbed the precarious steps to the very top of the mountain, then ducked through the concealed passage that led to the bare and unwelcoming chambers belonging to the Spirit Leader. Awaiting them was a sight neither of them had expected.

'Timi?' asked Rose, taking a tentative step forward. 'Is that you?'

A man sat in the centre of the room, hunched over, head bowed, all hair scorched from his head, terrible burns afflicting every visible piece of flesh.

The man sat motionless, as though he were meditating, waiting several moments before he raised his eyes to them. It was undeniably Timi, his eyes alert and calculating as he smiled at his guests.

'Rose, Draeus,' said Timi, formally, moving his arms to the side and bowing his head in sarcastic welcome. 'To what do I owe the pleasure of your company?' He motioned for them to take a seat.

'What happened to you?' asked Rose, taking in the burns. 'Did this happen in the temples?'

'Obviously,' he said harshly.

Rose's eyes went wide at his tone.

'I was close to the front, and during the action, my robes caught fire. Luckily, one of my monks pushed me to the floor to extinguish the flames. He got me to safety through the Body Temple.'

'Why didn't you stay in Kingdom?' asked Rose. 'Why leave without a word?'

'Look at me,' said Timi, pretending to be shocked. 'I needed urgent medical care. There are very few in this world whom I trust to administer such care. But, aside from that, I didn't know the cause of the disaster. What if it had been an attempt by the rebels to kill us all? I left as much for my protection as for the healing skills we have here.'

Rose stifled a smirk, while Draeus, as usual, was an impenetrable wall of impassiveness. 'I doubt you'd be top of their hit list,' said Rose, trying to keep her disdain to a minimum.

'One can never be too careful,' said Timi. He could easily read the contempt in her energy, even if she hid it from her tone. 'We do important work here; it's essential that's continued.'

'Like what?' asked Draeus, casually.

'Like things we don't discuss with those from outside the mountain.'

'Is that why you need all the security?' asked Rose, knowing he'd never willingly tell them what he was up to. 'Whatever you're doing can't be good if you need this kind of protection. And why did Amber make out you were dead?'

'It's dangerous to jump to conclusions,' said Timi, hotly. 'What we're doing here is ground-breaking; it will help us all, eventually. In the meantime, we can't let some new regime seize our work and ruin everything we've achieved. Amber does what's needed to protect us.'

'If it's for the good of everyone, why keep it secret?' asked Rose. 'And I can't think of anything we need so desperately, aside from a way to return the Relic. Are you working on that?'

'Heavens no,' said Timi. 'I'll leave that to the rest of you.'

'You haven't heard anything regarding its location?' said Draeus.

'No,' said Timi, confused. 'You've lost it?'

Rose shrank in embarrassment, silently cursing. 'It was taken by force,' she said, 'by someone who knew about our plan. We were betrayed.' She held Timi's gaze, not accusingly per se.

'Who?' he asked. 'Who was it?'

'We don't know,' said Rose.

'Leads?'

'Nothing,' said Rose. 'Its continued presence in the world is still unknown by the public. And nobody's tried to blackmail us… yet. I can't think of any other motive, other than someone wanting to sell it to a private collector, but we can't find anything down that route either. Can you think of anything we may have missed?'

'No,' he said, meeting her gaze.

'Any thoughts on how we could track it down?' she asked.

'Nothing immediately springs to mind, but I'll let you know if I think of anything.'

'He's ready for you,' said Amber, from the corner.

It startled Rose and Draeus, although Timi had clearly known she was there. Timi looked angry, either at her presence, or her words.

'That will be all, Amber,' he said fiercely, watching with stormy eyes as she turned to leave.

'Visitor?' asked Rose.

'Not exactly,' said Timi, 'but I have to go.'

'What about the Institution?' asked Rose, as they stood. 'Why haven't you been in touch with the leadership?'

'I wondered how long it would be before they sent someone looking for me,' he said. 'I want nothing more to do with that organisation. Being a member has brought me nothing but trouble, and most recently, almost got me killed.' He gestured towards his scarred skin. 'In any case, I have more than enough here to keep me occupied. I simply don't have time to do their bidding.'

'So that's it? You're going to walk away when the energy is more unstable than it's ever been before?' said Rose.

'As I said, the work we're doing here will help everyone. I'm serving the people better by devoting my time to that. Now, I really must go. Amber will see you out.'

CHAPTER 6

'Do you think he'll be there?' asked Cleo, in hushed tones, not wanting Edmund, who she'd been flirting with outrageously, to overhear.

'Probably, unless he's otherwise engaged,' said Anita, rolling her eyes; they'd already had this conversation a thousand times.

'And you're sure it was him at the temples, during the Relic return?' said Cleo.

'Do we really need to go through this again?' said Anita, frowning. Cleo gave her a look that confirmed they did, and Anita sighed. 'Fine. Yes, I'm one hundred percent sure it was him, and I got the impression he knew what was about to happen.'

'Because he said the words, *you know.*'

'Exactly.'

'And then you left him and started running to the front.'

'Yes.'

'Why didn't he try to stop it? I'm sure if he'd known, he would have.'

'And that analysis of his personality and motives is based on... what exactly?' asked Anita, with more hostility in her tone than she'd intended. 'Two fleeting interactions?'

'Yes. I'm an excellent judge of character,' said Cleo, haughtily.

'I think this one's a stretch, even for you.'

'Well, I disagree.'

'Then why didn't he try to stop what happened?'

'Maybe it was *meant* to happen.'

'*Meant* to happen? Since when have you been into determinism?'

'I'm not. But maybe the Magnei know things we don't, and maybe he had to let it happen for some reason we don't understand.'

'Cleo, what's got into you?'

Cleo looked away. 'I know this is going to sound crazy, but I think I love him.'

Anita looked at her for a long moment. 'You've only seen him a couple of times.'

'I know, I know. But… I've never felt like this before.'

There were stranger things than love at first sight, but… 'He might not be there,' she said gently. 'And we don't know if he's a Magnei for sure.'

'A girl can hope.'

They'd camped as close to their destination as they'd dared the previous evening, not wanting to alert the Magnei to their presence. They were now packing their things and preparing to make the final short walk to the place where the cylinder had told Anita the Magnei would be.

The Jungle was nothing like any of them had imagined. They'd been told stories about it since they were children; ghost stories and horror stories and tales of children disappearing, never to be seen again. In the flesh, it was serene, undisturbed, and full of beautiful birds and flowers. If children had truly disappeared here, surely it was because they hadn't wanted to leave.

The trees were huge, old, and well spread out. They looked as though they'd been crafted for climbing and tree house building, fat branches growing wide and low. Anita had given into the childish impulse to climb one the previous evening, reaching the top and spying the Magnei settlement in the distance. She'd quickly dropped to the ground, a shiver of uneasy energy running through her at the sight.

'Ready?' asked Edmund, slinging his backpack over his shoulder and walking to where Anita and Cleo sat.

'As we'll ever be,' said Cleo, accepting his offer of help to don her own pack.

They walked through the woods in silence, tension rising, the air around them seeming to grow thick with energy as they approached. Cleo and Edmund realized something here was strange, but for Anita, as a reader, it was like a sensory overload. A barrage of energy waves swirled all around her, hitting her skin and mind, the hair on her arms standing on end, the sheer magnitude of it causing her to struggle to focus on anything but the energy.

'Are you okay?' asked Cleo, noticing Anita's distractedness.

'Yeah, I'm fine, just finding it difficult to separate the energy around us into distinct units,' she said, shaking her head, trying to clear the fog. 'Can't you feel it?'

'It feels different; like I'm lighter, almost floating,' said Cleo, moving her arms to the sides and testing the air.

'You might be able to,' said Anita, remembering her lessons with Alexander, which seemed like eons ago now. 'Maybe that's one of their cool tricks.'

'Ooh, I hope so,' said Cleo excitedly, flapping her arms as though imitating a bird.

'I'm pretty sure that's not the way to do it,' laughed Anita, finally getting her senses under control.

By the time they reached the entrance to the settlement—two enormous, ancient trees with branches that formed an archway—Anita had worked out a way to push the energy to one side. Although it was draining, at least she could focus.

They approached the village, which was eerily quiet. The only figure was an old man dressed in earth-coloured clothes, standing right in the centre of the archway.

'I trust your journey was not too arduous,' he said briskly, shirking any kind of conventional greeting. He didn't wait for an answer, instead, turning to usher them through more trees, to a beautifully ornate village hall.

Cleo looked at Anita, as though she might know what was going on. Anita shrugged, as surprised as Cleo at this strange reception.

Their journey had been arduous, and they'd had some close calls, but since reaching The Jungle, they hadn't given any of that a second thought. There was only room for anticipation and excitement in their minds.

The hall looked almost as though it were part of the trees themselves, branches both disappearing into the building and arching in regal stretches above its roof. Wildly intricate carvings covered the walls, punctuated by stained glass windows, and one door, large and imposing, which swung outwards to admit them as they approached. Anita took a deep breath. Here goes nothing, she thought, as she stepped from the tranquil light-filled clearing into the dingy space beyond.

* * * * *

Anita entered first, with Ed and Cleo stepping through the door in her wake. She peered around as her eyes struggled to adjust, then felt a wash of familiarity as she recognised the room. She'd doubted it from the outside, the beautiful, natural building entirely at odds with the space inside, but she'd known from the design of the windows, and the shape of the door, and now she was inside, she felt like she'd come home.

The hall from her mind played out before her. Whereas inside her head it was devoid of life, now, in the real world, it was full to the brim. People packed the space, every inch full of humanity, balconies bulging with life.

Every pair of eyes fixed on them as they cautiously entered. Anita scanned the room, taking in the people the eyes belonged to. They looked normal; clean, tidy, and dressed in what looked like old, worn, but ordinary clothes. They looked interested in their visitors rather than hostile, neither apprehensive nor afraid.

When she read their energy, Anita realized the barrage she'd experienced outside the settlement had evaporated entirely. The energy in the room felt normal, as did the energy of the people themselves, albeit more intense than she'd expect from the average Kingdom- or Empire-ite.

Anita felt a rush from behind her, Cleo's form moving at speed past where she stood. Cleo went to a slight man with longish hair, who had launched himself towards her from a throne at the front of the hall. He and Cleo met halfway, the man gathering her to him before reaching down with his lips, kissing her passionately, not a moment's hesitation at the presence of an audience.

Anita frowned and bit her lip, confusion and embarrassment marring her thoughts. Ed's collapsing energy snapped her out of it. She gave him a comforting look before turning her attention to the thrones, and who sat atop them.

Her mouth dropped open, her breath hitched, her energy lurched. Her brain struggled to process the information provided by her eyes. She took steps forward, needing to get closer, to be absolutely sure, blinking to force her eyes to focus in the dim light. The woman turned her head away from the couple, still locked in a fierce embrace, and calmly took in Anita's approaching form. She smiled warmly, the same smile Anita had seen almost every morning of her life.

'Cordelia?' she whispered, all the noise she could force from her body. 'What are you doing here?'

Cordelia stood and walked to where Anita was now rooted, her body disconnected from her thoughts. Cordelia raised her arms wide and enfolded Anita, as she had done a thousand times before.

'Anita,' said Cordelia, her voice steady and commanding, 'I'm so, so happy to see you.'

* * * * *

Anita, Cleo, and Edmund sat on a low bench to the right of Cordelia's throne. Cordelia had offered refreshments, which they'd reluctantly accepted, not wanting to appear rude.

It had become apparent that the hall was an audience chamber, and Cleo's mystery man, Bakko, along with Cordelia, presided over events. Anita had asked why they couldn't talk in private, without the entire village watching on; she had so many questions that she burned to ask. Cordelia had replied that there were no secrets here.

After what felt like an endless preamble, Cordelia turned to Anita. 'Anita, my dear, why don't you tell us why the three of you are here, and how we can help you.' Anita was about to begin, when Cordelia added, 'It's wise to remember you're in a room full of very skilled readers; honesty is the best policy.' She said it jovially, but a steely undercurrent laced her tone.

Anita nodded, gathering her thoughts, her mind still reeling from the shock of Cordelia's position.

'As you presumably know,' said Anita, looking pointedly at Cordelia—did she know her grandmother at all? 'My mother was a Body Descendant.' A ripple of angst flowed out across the energy of the audience, and Anita hesitated, wondering why.

'She planted a brass cylinder in my mind, which was given to her by the Spirit Leader.' The energy settled, so she continued. 'I didn't know it was there until I started meditating with Alexander, and found it in my centre. Alexander thought it best to destroy the cylinder from the outset. He said cylinders were often weapons, planted by hostile forces.

'So I tried to destroy it, but it protected itself, running away to the most hidden place in my mind.' She glanced around the room. 'It took many weeks to find where it was hiding, but eventually, we found it. Then came the challenge of trying to open it. Nothing worked.' She looked over to Cleo, her mouth almost falling open at the brazen looks between her and Bakko.

'And that's where everyone always goes wrong,' said Bakko. His head snapped towards Anita as he stood.

'Excuse me?' she said, not realising he'd even been listening.

'People try to prise them open, force them open, bend them to their will to make them reveal their secrets, as though trying to prove their dominance over the object in their mind,' he said, prowling the space between them. 'In reality, brass cylinders, just like people, respond better to other types of persuasion: coercion, coaxing, coaching, encouragement, seduction...,' he let the word linger as he looked at Cleo, who blushed in an uncharacteristic show of embarrassment. 'How did you eventually get it to open?'

'To be honest, I'm not sure,' said Anita, looking Bakko up and down, trying desperately to understand him. 'Dumb luck, I think. I was meditating by myself at the time of the Relic return—the cylinder would kick anyone else out as soon as I touched it, so that was the only way. My mind wouldn't focus, and I kept thinking about what was going on in the temples. It suddenly clicked into place what was going to happen when they returned the Relic, and I dropped the cylinder. Instead of rolling away, as I'd expected, it bounced back up and unfurled right in front of me. Then I knew the information it had been hiding.'

'Ah ha!' Bakko laughed, leaning against a stone column. 'Jealousy,' he said, with relish. 'You had a covetous one.'

'I had what?'

'You mean it was jealous that Anita cared more about what was going on at the temples than figuring out how to open the cylinder?' asked Cleo.

Bakko looked at her warmly. 'Exactly, my little Mind, exactly.'

Cleo smiled up at him.

'Speaking of the temples,' said Anita, a note of hostility edging into her voice, 'why didn't you stop it?'

Bakko whirled away and sat back on his throne. 'Not for me to interfere, I'm afraid. We observe, we don't influence.'

'Even when you knew it would result in so much death?'

85

'What did the cylinder tell you about us?' he said, with a snap of his fingers, forcing the weight of attention back onto Anita.

'It told me the Magnei were the ones who could undo the mess we're in; that you alone had the power.'

'No, it didn't,' said Bakko, impatiently. 'It told you the Magnei alone could undo the hold of those in power, that we alone could unlock the light.'

'What did you say?' asked Anita, shocked.

Cordelia gave Bakko a look, clearly of the opinion that he had overstepped. He sat back and signalled nonchalantly to Cordelia: the floor was all hers.

'We should take this one step at a time,' said Cordelia, firmly.

'But, Philip's note...'

'In time, Anita, we'll get there. But first, why did you come here?'

Frustration raged through Anita's energy, but she played Cordelia's game, knowing this was the fastest route to what she wanted. 'Because I thought the Magnei might be able to help us send the Relic back for real.'

'Why did you think that?'

'Because of the cylinder; it pointed me here.'

'And why do you want to return the Relic?'

'Because I've seen the damage energy instability can do. As long as the Relic is in the world, there's a risk people will find out. If that happens, the energy could collapse entirely.'

'And what is it you think we can do to help?'

Anita took a deep breath. 'I'd hoped you could tell us what we have to do to send the Relic back for real, and that you might help us find it. But I think I know who these people really are,' she said, motioning around her, 'and if I'm right, you can only help with the first step in the journey. Even then, because of what we've done so far, you might not even be able to help much with that.'

'Who do you think they are?' asked Cordelia.

'Siblings,' she said, with conviction. And as the words escaped her lips, the energy in the room went wild.

* * * * *

The chamber's mute attendees erupted into snarls and hisses and jeers. Cordelia had only to stand to put a stop to it, then decreed they all leave. 'You know why the visitors are here. As is our custom, we will let our visitors rest a while before we agree what should happen next. Please carry out your duties until we summon you.'

They all left, every single one, and although their energy remained indignant, not one person raised an objection. The last person exited, and the doors swung closed, the loud *thunk* floating across the room. The tapestries, which were identical in every detail to the ones in Anita's mind, swallowed the noise.

'That's better,' said Cordelia, 'now we can talk properly.'

'Why couldn't we before?' asked Anita, warily, standing from the bench and walking around the room.

'Because it's not the way we do here things,' said Cordelia. 'We seldom get visitors, and when we do, everyone has a right to know who they are and why they're here.'

'What do you do here?' asked Anita, keeping some distance between them, looking up at the balcony, taking in every detail to try and spot differences from the place in her mind.

'As you said, we are siblings, or more precisely,' she said, seeing the confused look on Edmund's face, 'siblings of Descendants and their offspring.'

'Descendants can have more than one child?' asked Cleo, her energy soaring at the discovery.

'Since the very first,' said Cordelia. 'I myself am from a line that can be traced back to the very first Descendants. The older brother of the second Body Descendant, to be exact.'

'So, the line was broken from the start?' asked Edmund.

Bakko scoffed. 'The line was never intact. The whole thing is a farce.'

'What?' said Anita. 'How could that be?'

Cordelia gave Bakko another look. He shrugged and rolled his eyes. 'Carry on,' he said, 'but I only speak the truth.'

'In the beginning,' said Cordelia, 'the Gods created the world and people in it. They created the people in their image, each with a predisposition towards one of the three skills.'

'So far, so familiar,' said Cleo, impatiently.

'The people lived as you would expect; they had triumphs and problems, famines and feasts, squabbles and pacts, but for the most part, they got along together, leading perfectly pleasant lives with perfectly stable energy.

'The Gods watched for a while, until the Body and Spirit Gods got bored. They moved onto other things together, a close relationship developing between them. The Mind God, Theseus, became obsessed with the world they had created, but also resented the friendship between the other two. He could have joined the other Gods and left this world alone, but he chose another path, as Minds often do.

'He became obsessed with power and status, resolving to become the only God remembered by the world, and determined to destroy his fellow creators. But, to achieve that, he needed superior power. The Gods' personal energy, their power, was equally matched, but Theseus devised a way to steal some of the others' for himself.'

'How?' asked Cleo, hanging on Cordelia's every word.

'When the Gods created the world, they put an equal amount of energy into it,' said Cordelia, 'using that energy to create everything we know. For Theseus to succeed, he would need some of that energy for himself. So, he created the Relic and used it to syphon energy out of the world and into him, slowly, one small measure at a time.'

'So the Relic itself makes the energy unstable?' asked Anita.

'Yes,' said Cordelia. 'It went on for years without the other Gods noticing. As I said, they had shifted their attention to other things. They eventually realized something was wrong, and it didn't take long to get to the bottom of what that was.'

'So they put the prophecy into the world,' said Cleo, 'to tell the people to get rid of the Relic? But why didn't the Gods retrieve it themselves and stop him that way?'

'The Gods do not influence what happens here,' Cordelia replied. 'It would have broken the agreement they set up at the start.'

'But Theseus had already broken that agreement,' said Cleo, indignantly.

'The other Gods would have been just like him if they had broken the agreement as well. Instead, they tried to banish him to the edge of their realm.'

'I'm sensing that didn't go so well,' said Anita.

'No. He'd already gained a lot of power from the Relic and was stronger than the other Gods expected. He escaped into the world and has been causing havoc ever since. His power is not at its most impressive here, but his strength is not to be underestimated.'

'And the other Gods?' asked Edmund. 'What happened to them?'

Cordelia sighed. 'Theseus pulled them here too, and they can't go back until the Relic is returned.'

'And the longer that takes, the more powerful Theseus becomes,' said Cleo, 'because he's still stealing energy from the world?'

'Exactly. The Body and Spirit Gods,' said Bakko, smiling at Cordelia, Anita desperately trying to understand their relationship, 'put the prophecy into the world, and a group of academics found it, along with the Relic.'

'I knew there was something strange about that discovery,' said Cleo, triumphantly.

'The original prophecy proclaimed that anyone could return the Relic,' Bakko continued, 'but Theseus changed it, so the people thought it was only the Descendants who could send it back.'

'A couple of hundred years before the time of the Relic discovery, three dominant families, one Mind, one Body and one Spirit, had formed an alliance,' said Cordelia. 'They used their combined resources to set themselves apart from everyone else, hoarding power. 'A group of academics had been trying to fight them, but the three families were too powerful, and claimed to have been put in charge by the Gods. Of course, it was all rubbish, but Theseus saw in this an opportunity to make sending the Relic back even more difficult.

'He tipped off the three families about the Relic discovery, and they changed the prophecy, making it say only they could return the Relic. The families announced the prophecy to the world, cementing their dominant position, and their greed meant they never tried to return the Relic. Theseus has been sucking energy out of the world ever since.'

'What happened to the academics who found the Relic? Or others who knew the truth about the prophecy?' asked Edmund.

'Those who could be bought were made into councillors and rewarded handsomely for their silence. Anyone who threatened to reveal the truth didn't survive long enough to try,' said Bakko.

'What about the Gods?' asked Anita. 'Where are they and why haven't they done anything?'

Cordelia smiled. 'They've been trying to find the Mind God. They think he's been living inside the Minds of other people, to help keep secret his identity, and to preserve his energy. They believe he was occupying Austin, but since Austin's death, he's disappeared.'

'That would explain it,' said Anita.

'Explain what?' asked Cleo.

'When I killed Austin, it felt like a burst of energy escaped from him just before he died. I thought little of it, but… could that have been Theseus escaping?'

'Most probably,' said Bakko. 'Unfortunately, we have only ideas as to where he could be now.'

'And the other Gods?' asked Cleo. 'Where are they?'

'The Gods formed an underground resistance movement. A group to whom the Institution can trace its origins.'

'The Body and Spirit Gods are behind the Institution?' asked Cleo.

'You could say that,' said Cordelia.

'But where do you two, and this place, fit in?' asked Edmund, his energy impatient, to Anita's surprise.

Cordelia looked evenly at Edmund. 'We're here to protect those who the Descendants would have otherwise killed, and we support those who seek to ensure energy stability.'

'The same goal as the Institution,' said Anita, suspiciously.

'Yes,' said Cordelia.

'And everyone in the Institution looks to you for their orders?' asked Anita, sensing Cordelia and Bakko's true positions were more than mere onlookers.

'Yes,' Cordelia repeated.

'Hang on,' said Cleo. 'You run the Institution, Cordelia?'

'I suppose I do,' she said, her features neutral.

Cleo's mouth fell open as she turned her head to look at Anita. 'All the time, right under our noses!' she exclaimed, before her features turned distrustful. 'Did you know about this?'

Anita threw her best friend a dirty look. 'No, of course not. How did you hide it?' she asked Cordelia.

'It wasn't hard,' said Cordelia, with a shrug. 'When I was younger, I made sure I stayed under the radar, and now, preconceptions about women my age mean nobody would ever think to suspect me. And, seeing as I've never attracted attention, nobody keeps tabs on my movements.

'You never thought to question the long walks I would take Thorn on, or the long lunches I would have with friends. And if you didn't, why would anyone else? As I said, a woman of my age, who seemingly cares only for her dog and baking cakes, attracts not even a second thought.'

'Amazing,' said Cleo. 'I never suspected a thing.'

'Not your finest hour,' mocked Bakko.

Cleo threw him a menacing look.

'But you still haven't told us where the Body and Spirit Gods have been hiding,' said Anita, looking between Bakko and Cordelia, her energy rising. 'It's you two, isn't it?'

Cordelia and Bakko sat still, the great hall silent, as though the room itself waited for what would come next. Bakko turned to Cordelia before disappearing in a blur. A gust of air hit Anita as he sped past, the door to the hall swinging shut.

When the dust settled, Cleo was missing, and panic filled Anita. 'What just happened? Where has he taken her?' she demanded. 'What's going on?' Her voice sounded shrill in her ears.

Cordelia descended the steps to stand next to Anita, placing a familiar hand on her arm before trying to pull her into an embrace. Anita pushed her forcefully away, putting several paces between them.

'You're right, I'm the Body God,' said Cordelia, hurt in her voice, 'and Bakko is the Spirit God. My real name is Tatiana, and Bakko's is Jeremiah. I possess Cordelia's body, the real Cordelia, who's from an illegitimate line of the first Descendants. She and I share this body, as we have since she was a little girl. Bakko, on the other hand, walks in his godly form here. It leaves him vulnerable to attack, but also enables him to use his power more freely than Theseus or me, hence his little trick just now.'

'Where has he taken Cleo?' Anita asked, adrenaline still coursing through her.

'He probably just wanted to talk to her, away from prying ears; he's surprisingly taken with her.'

'How could you keep this from me all this time?' asked Anita, pain spilling into her words. 'You've always pretended to despise the Institution, and here you are, running it.'

'I never wanted to lie to you, and it was a shock, even to me, when Elistair turned up on my doorstep with you in his arms. It was a risk, taking you in. I knew you'd attract attention, but I loved Jeffrey, as though he were my own son, and you were all I had left of him.'

'What do you do here and how have you kept yourselves hidden all this time?' demanded Edmund, rudely cutting across the moment, his energy betraying his frustration.

Cordelia fixed him with a stern look. 'The energy of those who come here is potent; the families who seized control all those years ago could only do so because they were so powerful, and their descendants are no exception. This, coupled with the unique training Bakko and I can offer, means we have a talented pool of people here who work on research problems.

Our goal is energy stability, and anything we learn through our research, we filter back to the mainstream academics in Kingdom and Empire, via the Institution. We research a whole range of energy topics, as well as tracking Theseus, of course.'

Silence settled over them, Anita's mind reeling.

'The cylinder in my head never contained the answer,' said Anita, 'only more questions.'

'I really meant the cylinder for your mother,' said Cordelia, wistfully. 'With everything that went on with her generation of the Institution and Descendants, we hoped they would return the Relic.'

'But she misinterpreted the message and gave it to me instead,' said Anita.

'As far as we can tell.'

'What do we do now?' asked Anita. 'How do we find the Mind God, and how do we return the Relic for real?'

'I'll tell you the same thing I told Philip when he worked it out,' said Cordelia.

'Philip's note for Alexander? You're the one behind it?'

'I know nothing of a note.'

Anita took a moment to remember the exact wording. 'It said, *Alexander, remember the lessons from Philip & Fred. Be a good scholar. Jeffrey will help you unlock the light. Destroy this note when you have memorised what I have said. I have faith in you. Philip*'.

Cordelia smiled. 'Yes, that was essentially my message to him.'

'But what does it mean?' asked an exasperated Edmund.

Cordelia sighed, her irritation plain. 'Be a good scholar is the first half of the old saying that truth is not always what it seems. I was referring to the illegitimacy of the Descendants' claim to being the only ones who could return the Relic. To find out how to return it, we need as many heads as we can get. I was hoping Philip would get the message out.

'The bit about Jeffrey refers to my son,' said Cordelia, pausing, 'he was the only one I ever told about this place, including the true identity of the people here. If the people refused to believe the revelation about the Descendants, the proof could be found here, and Jeffrey could lead the way.

'The Philip & Fred bit were Philip's nicknames for two famous authors who wrote children's stories. In the last story they wrote, they brought all of their heroes and heroines together to fight off an attack from an evil God...'

'... it was a message to Philip, that everyone had to work together to return the Relic?' asked Edmund.

'Yes,' said Cordelia.

'But he never worked it out,' said Anita.

'He worked it out,' said Cordelia, 'he just didn't have the courage to tell the world the truth. To be fair to him, he'd recently lost his son in the fire that killed your mother, and worried that Alexander would get caught in the crossfire. Still, I was disappointed.'

'Why don't you send the Magnei to Kingdom or Empire and tell the world the truth?' asked Edmund.

'The Mind Descendants spy on us. We tried once to get a group through, but not a single person survived the trip, and we don't have an army at our disposal. The spies stationed near here have disappeared recently though, so I'm assuming Marcus has stopped the practice.'

'Meaning, you could come out of hiding?' said Anita.

'We could,' said Cordelia, hesitantly, 'and indeed, we might, but I first want to understand the new lay of the land in Kingdom. The world has had a significant shock, and I don't want to be responsible for more upset. Tell me, what's happened since the temples collapsed? Our information flow has been patchy since that day.'

* * * * *

Cleo jolted to a halt and opened her tightly shut eyes to a cascade of weeping branches fanning out above her. They were densely packed and covered in white blossom, unusual given the time of year. Her disorientation was complete until Bakko's face appeared above her, and her senses finally registered the ground pressing against her back.

She sat up quickly, blood rushing to her head, Bakko's hand shooting out to stabilise her. A jolt of energy passed like electricity between them, and Bakko's hand sprang away in response, confusion clouding his features as he approached with caution for a second touch.

'You've never felt that before?' asked Cleo, surprised.

Bakko shook his head, saying nothing as his hand made contact with her skin. This time, instead of a jolt, a tingling sensation radiated out from where they touched. 'You have?' he asked, Cleo surprised at his sudden lack of certainty.

'Well, not personally,' she admitted, 'but Anita has, and she told me about it.'

'Interesting,' he said, back to his usual cryptic tone as his hand slid up her arm, skimmed her shoulder, then rested over the pulse at her neck.

Cleo shivered at the sudden flood of energy radiating through her, her toes going fuzzy when it reached them. He took her wrist, leaving the hand at her neck, and wrapped his fingers over her pulse there too. The energy intensified further, building through her blood.

'Mirror my hands,' said Bakko, softly. She hesitated, looking into his eyes, searching for reassurance. 'Trust me,' he urged, compelling her with insistent eyes to touch him.

Cleo did as he said, reaching her fingers to the places where she could feel his blood pumping at the surface of his skin, and instantly the sensation changed. No longer was his energy moving from him to fill her. Now, their energy flowed back and forth between them, and through them, intermingling, exploring. Cleo closed her eyes and cleared her mind, comprehending nothing but the tide of energy that matched her heartbeat.

Bakko touched his mouth to hers, an explosion of sparkling force peppering her skin. She opened her mouth to him, caressing his lips with hers, their energy rising still higher as the kisses deepened.

The contact seemed to lift them, throwing them upwards, Cleo impulsively pushing her mind into Bakko's, searching for… something.

He willingly let her in, and she knew this was a space that, in over a thousand years, not a single other person had explored.

He pulled his lips from hers, compelling her to open her eyes inside his mind. She did, holding his gaze for a moment more before dragging her focus to their new surroundings.

It was like they were hovering between the ground and the sky, flying, but at the same time connected to the earth.

The place was unlike anything she had seen before. 'This is your centre?' she asked, looking around at the collage of water, air, and earth that filled the vast expanse of his mind. It shifted as she took it in; mountains forming and falling, new rivers springing from the ground, building momentum as they snaked their way downwards. They cut through the earth, bringing life to all kinds of wonderful plants and flowers, that, in an instant, came to life, the very pinnacle of beauty, and then shrivelled and died, as though they had never been at all. Seas rose and fell, great forests covered new ground, only to be pushed back like an army in retreat.

Bakko watched as she took it all in. 'In a way, this is my centre,' he said, stroking the hair back off her face. 'But we Gods don't have a centre as you do, and our minds are not segmented like a young person's. We have only one vast space, and the scope of it is greater than that of any other you will know.'

'So, it's true then? You're a God?' she said, not quite believing it could be possible.

'Yes.'

'That explains a lot,' she said, shrugging before turning her attention back to the landscape. 'So, when a centre comes together, is it like this?' She'd never meditated with anyone who had passed that landmark.

Bakko shook his head, looking indulgently in her eyes, the play of a smile on his lips. 'No,' he said, running his hand down her arm until his fingers reached hers. 'Most people lack this scale and scope. A centre is the only true reflection of a person's subconscious. It lays your soul bare, so even a casual observer could learn your secrets in a second, could know you better than you know yourself, if they only knew how.

'To my dismay, most people haven't discovered the art of meditation, or maybe they're afraid to try. Most centres are narrow and protected places, rigid in form, like a barricade against the outside world, defending all that person holds dear.'

'You say that like it's a bad thing,' said Cleo, running her fingers over his.

'Not bad,' he said, 'just… limiting. Change is the only enduring force we know. Those with closed, protected minds try to secure a wall around their fleeting and familiar existence, seeking to block out uncertainty, trying to force all energy to stand still.'

Cleo nodded. 'Is that so wrong?'

'Of course not,' he replied. 'But those who embrace and revel in the true reality are the ones we need to find; they're the ones who will help us return the Relic.'

'Because they're the ones who are open to discovering new things?'

'Partly that, and partly because their energy flows more freely, which strengthens it, and makes it more potent. It takes a lot of effort to maintain the status quo. If you're concentrating on that, there's less energy to focus on the future.'

'And your energy is entirely free?' she said, a note of disappointment creeping in. 'That's what we're looking at?' She turned her head away from him to take in, once again, the shifting patchwork all around.

'Almost,' he said, grasping her fingers and pulling her with him. 'You see down here?'

Cleo couldn't see a thing, a blur of colour and light filling her vision as they moved at lightning speed through his mind.

'This curious area has taken root of late,' he said, setting her down at the edge of a cluster of four or five trees. It was difficult to tell their true number, as their roots had grown above the surface, all tangled together. 'There used to be a forest surrounding this place, but these trees were left behind when it went. Can't imagine why,' he said, mischievously.

He pulled her forwards, through a gap in the roots, into a domed cavity. Shafts of butter gold light spiked through from every angle. Pelts of fur, a deep, rich brown covered the floor.

Bakko pulled Cleo down onto the warm furs, serenity embracing her as she lay in his arms, looking up at the mesh of roots above. 'See,' he said, kissing her lightly on her hair, 'my barricade against the changing forces all around.'

She smiled and snuggled closer before kissing him, her hand sliding under his shirt. 'Well, if nothing is permanent,' she said, carefully tracing the muscles of his chest, 'then we must take full advantage while we can.'

* * * * *

They reconvened in Cordelia's quarters, one of a network of small tree houses spread out across the forest. The platform had just one room, with a sloping ceiling, and a balcony at one edge. Inside was a bed, a desk, a makeshift kitchen, and a small table, but they sat outside on the balcony, where several strips of wood perched precariously atop two trestles, with wooden benches either side.

They sipped smoky tea and ate banana bread, Anita delighted to discover that Cordelia's baking tasted as good here as it did in Empire.

'Come back to the city with us,' said Anita. 'The only way people will believe the truth is if they see evidence. We'll go back, tell the rebels about the prophecy, use the Magnei as proof of the Descendants' longstanding deceit, and find people to help us figure out a way to return the Relic.'

'You're not worried about the effect that will have on the energy?' asked Edmund, his scepticism palpable.

'I don't see we have much choice,' said Anita. 'We thought we were buying ourselves time by pretending to return the Relic, but really, we've done the opposite. We've given Theseus more time to syphon off energy, which will make the world more unstable. We have to bring this out in the open and asked for help… Maybe we should have given the people more credit from the start.'

'The Magnei could work with the academics,' said Cleo. 'That might speed things up.'

Bakko's impatient energy bubbled to the surface. 'We need to focus our search. As I showed you, Cleo, some people have minds that can help us, and some people do not.'

'What do you mean?' asked Anita, eyeing Cleo.

'He showed me that a person's mind is open to new discoveries, or it's not,' she said. 'Some people use their energy to hold onto all they know, others free their minds from constrictions and conventions, and let their energy take them wherever it wants to go. Bakko means we should seek those with open minds to help us; we need visionaries and creative thinkers; they stand the best chance of finding a solution.'

'How do we find these people?' asked Anita.

'Simple,' said Bakko. 'We stage a challenge.'

'Like a Chase?' said Anita.

'Exactly,' said Bakko, 'but this one will focus on Mind rather than Body skills. We need someone who can think like the Mind God to have a chance of expelling him from this world.'

'So, your plan is to go back to Kingdom, tell the rebels the truth about the Magnei and the prophecy, then ask them to announce a challenge, before they've even held the election?' asked Edmund. 'Lunacy.' His eyes darted to Bakko's hand on Cleo's.

'Who said it had to be before the election?' said Cleo, her tone hostile, but Anita felt her guilt. Cleo removed her hand from under Bakko's. 'In fact, there's no reason it can't be immediately after the election, as a celebration to mark the occasion.'

'Which gives us less than a month to get back to Kingdom, convince the rebels, and prepare the challenge,' said Edmund.

'We never said it would be easy,' said Cleo.

'It seems sensible,' said Anita, reading Cleo and Edmund's energy, and trying to move them on before things descended into a fight. 'Unless anyone has any better ideas?'

She paused, but no one spoke.

'However,' she said, 'the other obvious problem is that we don't know where the Mind God or the Relic are. We could find a way to send them back, but have to search for years before we can make it happen.'

'We'll keep our ears to the ground,' said Cordelia. 'He'll turn up eventually, and we might already know where he's hiding.'

'Where?' asked Anita, frustrated that Cordelia was only now sharing this news.

'The Cloud Mountain seems an obvious location,' said Cordelia. 'Communications from Timi have ceased entirely since the temples collapsed, but there's been no announcement regarding a new Spirit Leader. If Timi were dead, or missing, they would have selected someone to take over by now.'

'Draeus and Rose were on their way there when we came out here,' said Anita. 'We should find them; they may have information that could help.'

* * * * *

'We're done here,' said Cordelia. 'Go now, please. We will leave first thing in the morning. Bakko, please see to the preparations.'

'As you wish,' he said, raising an eyebrow at his fellow God.

'Anita,' said Cordelia, holding her back and waiting for the others to file down the spiral wooden steps before speaking. 'I... I'm sorry.'

'I should hope so, after lying to me for so many years.'

Cordelia paused. 'I wasn't talking about that,' she said, continuing before Anita could respond. 'I mean, about Alexander. I tried to get to him, but others whisked him away before I could.'

'What?' she said, stunned. 'What do you mean? You saw him after the temples collapsed?'

'It was during the collapse, but he was nearing the exit. I didn't see him again once the temples were down, but I didn't hang around.'

'He didn't fall down the hole by the Mind Temple.'

'Not unless he turned around for some reason, but there was so little time, I don't think he could have.'

'He's alive,' she said, one weight lifting, only for another to settle.

'I'm sure if he could have contacted you, he would have,' said Cordelia, reading her mind.

'Then you think he's in danger?'

'There are many plausible explanations. In my experience, it's unwise to jump to conclusions.'

Anita couldn't bear to talk about Alexander, so she asked Cordelia about something else that had been bothering her. 'Have I ever been here before?' she said, taking Cordelia off guard. 'Or my mother, or Peter? Did either of them come here?'

'Not as far as I'm aware,' she said, shaking her head a little as she spoke. 'Why do you ask?'

'Do you know the places in my mind?' said Anita, instead of getting straight to her real question.

'We've never meditated together, and I make a point not to barge uninvited into people's minds. You've never told me, so I'm afraid I have no idea. Is one of them somewhere here?' she asked, her interest piqued.

'Yes,' said Anita, slowly, wondering for a moment if it were wise to tell Cordelia the truth, before dismissing the notion; the women had raised her, after all. 'It's the Great Hall,' she said, watching for Cordelia's reaction.

'The Great Hall?' Cordelia repeated, visibly shaken. 'The Great Hall of the Magnei? The one here?' she said, her voice urgent.

Anita nodded. 'And I'd very much like to know why.'

Cordelia sat down on one of the benches, motioning for Anita to join her. 'Anita, the Great Hall is the only unnatural structure the Gods built in this world. It was here from the very beginning, used by the first people to worship their creators.

'Over the years, people started to worship only one or other of us, and eventually worship was split into the three distinct temples you're familiar with today. The Great Hall is no longer used for worship; the Magnei are a secular people. They blame the Gods for their being ostracised from society, so we use the hall for meetings and events. How it became a location in your mind, I cannot say. What causes something to take root in a person's mind is a mystery, even to us Gods. We made sure of it at creation, so free will was assured.'

'So you can't help me,' said Anita.

'I'm not sure anyone can,' she replied. 'Some things are meant to be a mystery, even to the Gods.'

CHAPTER 7

Anita, Edmund, Cleo, and the two Gods, Cordelia and Bakko, travelled swiftly towards Empire. Anita was determined to get back to check the observatory's readings, and Cleo was keen to visit the archives. They were nearing the border between the wilderness and the farming district, when they came across Draeus and Rose at a trading post.

It was a bizarre building to match the equally curious district. Everything was upside down, with bedrooms downstairs and communal spaces above. The rooms were decorated with strange furniture, from boat hulls as beds, to tree stumps as seats, to artwork made of cutlery, and each room was a different shape and layout. It was odd yet somehow chic, the owner an eccentric with exacting standards.

Upstairs was one vast open plan area. Floor to ceiling windows overlooked an enormous lake, and the setting sun cast the room in a golden orange glow.

Anita stared out across the lake, tracking the sun's ponderous movements through the sky. She revelled in the few precious minutes to herself, before the others came upstairs and the relentless pace took hold once more.

She felt energy approaching from her right, from one of three staircases that popped up into the room, each entirely different from the others: one spiral, one basically a ladder, and the other a somewhat understated, glass-sided affair. She resisted the urge to turn and see who was there, holding onto the tranquillity of the scene before her, but when her senses told her who it was, she whirled around to greet him.

'Marcus?' she said, surprise clear in her tone. 'What are you doing here?'

'It's a nice joint, this one,' he said, light-heartedly, 'unlike so many of those glorified shacks that call themselves trading posts. I thought I'd come out for a couple of nights off,' he said, the devil-may-care Marcus of old taking Anita by surprise.

'Have you been spying on me?' she said, a warning flaring in her voice.

Marcus stepped towards her. 'No, I promise I wasn't spying on you, but the lack of information was driving me mad, so I thought I'd come and look for you. I will admit I sent a few scouts out ahead of my group, and they reported back where it looked like you were heading, but I have absolutely not had people following you,' he said, his most charming smile dancing from his lips to his eyes.

'Come on,' he said, spreading his arms wide and gathering her into an embrace, 'don't pretend you're not happy to see me.' He moved his hands to her arms and pushed her far enough away to kiss her cheek. His face remained close, one hand moving to her chin, his mood flirtatious as he positioned his eyes above hers, so she had to look at him.

His energy lifted and her cheeks flushed.

'See,' he said, triumphantly, kissing her temple, 'you missed me too.'

He broke away as the others clattered up the stairs. He chose a big, comfortable armchair and lounged back into its depths. He called to the waiter to bring him a whisky and some nibbles, Anita taking a seat opposite, in a smaller armchair by the roaring open fire.

Once Marcus had greeted the surprised group, and Cleo had sent Anita several covert eyebrow raises, Anita filled them in on what they'd found in The Jungle. Draeus, Rose, and Marcus' mouths fell open when they learned Cordelia's identity. Cleo laughed out loud at her father's confusion; it was so out of character.

Anita brought them up to speed on their plan, before urging Draeus and Rose to share news from their own explorations.

'Well, I can't pretend what you've just told us isn't a tremendous shock,' said Draeus, visibly shaking away his disbelief before telling them about the killings at the Salt Sea and their trip to the Cloud Mountain. 'Timi's there, but he seems more odd than usual,' said Draeus, shooting sideways glances at Bakko and Cordelia.

'How so?' asked Cordelia, leaning forward in her seat.

'He was seriously injured in the temple collapse,' replied Rose. 'He had burns all over him, his hair mostly gone, but there was a nervous edge to him I've never seen before. He's surrounded himself with security. Amber has people everywhere, and we were escorted wherever we went. He's more secretive about what's going on up there than ever, and he got rid of us as soon as he could.'

'To get to the mountain, you have to go through military checkpoints, and they're letting virtually nobody up the mountain itself,' added Draeus.

'And he's left the Institution,' said Rose. 'Says he no longer wants anything to do with it, as he has more important things to focus on.'

'He wouldn't give you any details as to what that was, I take it?' asked Cleo.

'No,' confirmed Draeus, 'just that it was ground-breaking, that it would help everybody, and that it had nothing to do with returning the Relic.'

'He considers the work he's doing more important to the world than finding the Relic,' added Rose. 'He said the security is to stop the rebels from destroying everything he's worked so hard to achieve.'

'Did you ask him about the Relic?' asked Anita.

Draeus nodded. 'He says he has no idea where it is, nor does he have any idea how to find it.'

'And you believed him?' asked Cleo.

'If he was lying, he did so convincingly,' said Draeus.

'When you say he was nervous,' said Cordelia, 'what specifically made you think that, aside from the security?'

'He couldn't wait to be rid of us,' said Rose. 'Amber came to get him shortly after we arrived. She told him someone was ready to see him, and he became… twitchy. I don't know if it was because, in that moment, Amber revealed how close she is to him, or because he worried she would let something of consequence slip, but he left at speed, which is most unlike him.'

'What do you think?' Cordelia asked Bakko.

'Difficult to say,' he replied.

'What do you mean?' asked Anita.

'Whether he's being inhabited by the Mind God,' said Cordelia.

'Can you inhabit someone without their permission?' asked Cleo.

'Yes, it is possible,' said Bakko, 'but it's much easier with a willing host.'

'How so?' said Cleo.

'A hostile takeover takes a great deal of energy to maintain. You always have to be on your guard, worried about whether the host will try and make it known to others you're in there, or try to expel you, or even kill themselves to escape you. The host is fighting a constant battle for control, albeit one they're extremely unlikely to win.'

'It's possible Timi's being inhabited against his will?' asked Anita.

'Anything is possible,' said Cordelia, 'but I don't think he would have been nervous if that were the case, as Theseus would have been in control. What's more likely is the Mind God is at the Spirit Mountain, either in his godly form, or inhabiting someone else, and Timi was worried Rose and Draeus would find out.'

'We have no way of knowing that for certain,' said Bakko.

'But if Theseus is there, it stands to reason the Relic is also,' said Cordelia.

'So, what next?' said Rose, never one for resting on her laurels.

'We go back to Empire,' said Anita, 'tell the world the truth, ensure the elections go ahead as planned, and figure out a way to return the Relic.'

'Using people from the Mind challenge we're going to set up,' added Cleo.

'Oh, is that all?' said Marcus, flippantly.

'And how do we find the Relic?' asked Rose.

'We have to get into the Cloud Mountain, and have a good look around, without Timi, Amber, or anyone else knowing we're there,' said Draeus, surprising the others with this deviation from his usual sensible self.

'Impossible,' said Rose. 'You saw the security.'

'I saw it, but I'm also willing to bet they haven't lavished as much security—if any at all—on the dark side of the mountain.'

'The dark side of the mountain?' said Cleo, rounding on him. 'What do you mean?'

Draeus bowed his head and took a deep breath before facing his daughter's demanding eyes. 'It's where your mother and I used to live, before she went mad. Or at least, that's what I thought was happening. There's a back way into the Cloud Mountain from there.'

* * * * *

Cleo slumped back in her seat. 'What?' she said, softly, shrinking under the pressure of everyone's eyes. An awkward silence descended on the group. 'Tell us what you know,' Cleo finally said, steely determination locking back into place.

Draeus looked around, finding he had the rapt attention of all present. He gave a little nod, resigning himself. 'Your mother and I met when I was a young trader in the Wild Lands. I used to travel far more widely than I do today, to all the places too dangerous or too remote for others to want to venture. I found items to trade beyond the wildest dreams of the others in my business: spices, flowers, crystals... and my reputation flourished. If you wanted something different, or difficult to find, I was the one you came to.

'As my reputation grew, the requests became more and more outlandish. A councillor requested I venture to the dark side of the mountain and bring back a type of mushroom that was rumoured to grow there. I was cocky, never having failed before, and I accepted without a second thought. I went, and found it to be a barren, desolate place, with little sunlight to bring life. Green sludge and fungi were the only things that grew.

'I resolved to complete my job quickly and leave as soon as I could. I climbed to the high caves, where the councillor said I would find the mushroom. I was on my third or fourth cave, when, to my astonishment, I pulled myself up over the ledge, and found a wall of glass across the cave mouth, complete with a sliding door.

'My first thought was that I was hallucinating, that the fungi I had climbed past was making me delusional. Then a beautiful young woman came out, and I thought I must have slipped and fallen to my death; she was an angel sent to take me to the Gods.' Draeus paused, smiling at the memory. 'But when I asked her if this was so, she slapped me sharply across the face. She said it was to snap me out of whatever craze had overtaken me, then instructed me to get up off the floor and come inside at once.

'We fell in love. Several years went by, and I travelled back and forth to the cities, continuing to trade. Joselyn… your mother,' he said to Cleo, 'continued to work out there. I didn't know what she was doing. She was secretive, and I never thought to mind not knowing. But, as nothing grew on the dark side, Joss would sneak into the mountain and steal food and other supplies. I have no idea how she found the way in. I don't think anyone in the mountain knows about it, but somehow, she discovered a chink in the mountain's armour.'

'What happened next?' asked Cleo, sensing her father was coming to the end of his story, leaving so many questions unanswered, the searing pain of betrayal cutting through her insides.

'Later, Cleo,' he said, with pleading eyes, before returning his attention to the others. 'So, you see, I know there's a back way into the mountain. I suggest I go to Joselyn's cave, use the tunnel, and find out more about what's going on inside.'

'If you're going, I'm coming too,' said Cleo, adamant, desperate to know the woman she'd thought was dead, ignoring Bakko's placating squeeze of her hand.

'Cleo, it's not safe,' said Draeus. 'We don't know what we'll find there.'

'What do you mean *we*?' she demanded.

'I think Anita should come with me,' he said, holding up his hands before Cleo could respond. 'Anita has Body and Spirit skills which will be invaluable, and you have phenomenal Mind skills, which are needed to set up the Mind challenge.'

'Someone else can do that,' said Cleo, her insides bunching, ready to explode with fury.

'Who?' said Draeus. 'You and Bakko are the only ones who fully understand what you're trying to achieve, and Bakko's a Spirit, not a Mind.'

Cleo looked at Bakko, considering for a second, then quickly rejecting the possibility that he would let anyone else see the inside of his head. 'Fine,' she said, knowing she was defeated, 'but as soon as the Mind challenge is over, I'm coming to join you.'

'I'm coming with you,' said Marcus, 'and my bodyguards too.'

Anita looked as though she might protest, then shrugged her agreement.

'That's settled then,' said Rose. 'We'll go back to Empire, help ensure the elections go smoothly, tell the world the truth about the Descendants, and set up the Mind challenge. Draeus and Anita will go to the Cloud Mountain, and find out what's really going on there. Now, if you don't mind, I think that's enough for one day. I'm going for a dip in the lake.'

* * * * *

No one questioned Rose's decision to swim in the dark, and they all dispersed back to their rooms, all aside from Cleo and Draeus. They stayed, sitting in silence for some time.

'Why didn't you ever tell me about her?' asked Cleo, imagining what else her father might have lied to her about. 'What happened?'

'Cleo,' said Draeus, then paused, struggling to find the right words. 'I always planned to tell you, but I could never work out how.'

Cleo's face was hard and dispassionate. She was too angry to give him the reassurance he obviously craved. 'Is she still alive?'

Draeus looked away. 'I don't know,' he said, his shoulders slumped with shame.

'You don't know?'

'As I told the others, your mother was secretive, and I didn't think to question it for a while. We met under insane circumstances, and she'd been living in the cave for years; I was caught up in the thrill of it all. She was extraordinarily intelligent, devouring the books I brought out for her, picking through the intricacies of the political news I'd heard, outwitting me at every turn. But she was also eccentric, with radical views. After a while, she started to scare me.'

'How so?' asked Cleo, softening a little.

Draeus met Cleo's eyes. 'She thought the Gods walked among us, that they were stealing energy from the world, that the Descendants were illegitimate, and that we had to overthrow the status quo to prevent disaster.'

'She was a genius? And you didn't believe her?' Cleo spat, disgust thick in her tone.

'Cleo, even you must admit, in isolation, it sounds crazy. I thought she'd gone mad. It started as a single comment here or there, but by the end, the ideas consumed her. She was obsessed, single-minded about expelling the Gods from this world.'

'So you left her,' accused Cleo. 'You didn't believe her, were too scared to open your mind, and ran away.'

'No,' said Draeus, forcefully. 'I tried to understand where it had all come from. We lived in the middle of nowhere. She saw not a single person other than me, so how could she have known all this?'

'And?'

'She got defensive, saying I had to trust her, that the likes of me could not comprehend her work. For a while, I tried to understand, to give her the space she asked for, but it ate away at me. I had no secrets from her, nor would she have tolerated it if I had. It came to a point where I couldn't live with the imbalance. I tried to make her understand, but she was firm in her resolve; she would rather lose me than share her secrets, so I left, and haven't been back to this day.'

'You told me she was dead,' said Cleo, tears welling up in her eyes.

'I didn't know what else to say. She may well be dead… discovered sneaking into the mountain. Maybe she's still there, devising the answer to this puzzle. Or maybe she's found another location to call home.'

'Or maybe she has the answer. What if she's already discovered a way to return the Relic, and no one believes her?'

'Cleo, she lived in total isolation. Even if she found the answer, who would she tell?'

'And where do I fit into all of this?' asked Cleo, upset that her name was yet to be mentioned.

'I moved back to Empire, and one day, eight or nine months after I left the mountain, you turned up on my doorstep. I'd only just returned from a trip into the Wild, and there you were, tiny and helpless, only a couple of months old, with nothing but a note to confirm who you were.'

'What did it say?'

'It said, *Find here our legacy, of which we can both be proud. All my love, Joselyn.*'

Cleo took a deep breath, blinking back tears. 'What was she like?'

He smiled indulgently at his daughter. 'She was like nobody I had ever met, nor like anyone I've met since. Full of exuberance, entrancing, determined, volatile. I wonder now if she was a Magnei; I'm sure her energy was powerful beyond what she showed me. She had an intense personality that many in polite society wouldn't have tolerated.'

'How do you mean?' asked Cleo.

'It was like her intelligence blinded her. It was only important to say whatever followed logically in her mind; no empathy, no regret, no compromise. Things were right or wrong, black or white. Greyness scared her.'

'You think that's why she lived alone?'

'In part, yes, but also because her work demanded it. But then, I don't know what that work really was.'

'Do you think she's still there?'

Draeus shook his head slowly. 'I have absolutely no idea.'

* * * * *

The two Gods, Cleo, and Rose arrived back in Empire, still pondering the mystery of where Edmund had gone. They had parted ways from Anita, Marcus, and Draeus at the trading post, the plan for Edmund to return to Empire with them. However, the night before they'd planned to leave, he'd disappeared.

They'd enquired with the trading post owner, who'd told them he'd checked out and gone on his way. They'd searched for him high and low nonetheless, to no avail. They'd delayed their departure for a day, to see if he would turn up, but when he didn't, they'd left and headed for Empire, full of questions.

They went their separate ways on the outskirts of Empire, not wishing for anyone to see them travelling together, in such a conspicuous group. Bakko and Cleo headed to the archives, Cordelia went home to retrieve Thorn, her springer spaniel, from a neighbour, and Rose went to find Gwyn, to learn the latest news on the rebels and the election.

As it turned out, it wasn't hard to locate Gwyn. She was running for the temple area seat in the election, and she announced her presence everywhere she went. Rose found her holding court outside the Body Temple. A crowd of loyal followers gathered around her, lapping up every word she spoke.

Gwyn saw Rose, who inclined her head towards Temple Mews, Empire's prestigious shopping street. Rose went to sit in a café and waited for Gwyn to appear.

Gwyn joined her ten minutes later, happy for the break. The endless barrage of questions and accusations from voters were wearing her resolve a little thin.

Rose relayed the stories from the Wild Lands, filling her in on the Magnei, Cordelia and Bakko, and the trip Anita, Marcus, and Draeus were now on to the dark side of the mountain. She told her of their suspicions about Timi and the Mind God, and then asked for news of goings on in the cities.

'Wow,' said Gwyn, pausing before starting her own story, her mind reeling. 'It's so farfetched, I'm not sure I should believe you! It's all been very boring here, by comparison. The rebels moved to Empire a few days ago, once they'd done all they could to patch up Kingdom. Matthew says he wants to make a clear break from the rule of the Descendants, and seeing as they ruled from Kingdom, he thought Empire a better base for the future government.

'Election plans are going off without a hitch, and the people seem quite excited about the new system. Matthew's popularity is growing by the day. A few of the old councillors have started a rival party, which I think is good for Matthew's overall vision, but they don't seem to be gaining much support. I'm campaigning for the temple area seat here, but I'm up against an old Body councillor, as well as Joshua, Matthew's right-hand man.'

'Do you think you'll win?' asked Rose.

Gwyn shrugged. 'It's difficult to say. I have strong support, but so does Joshua. People associate me with the old system, and Joshua with the new… it could go either way.'

'Has there been any trouble?' asked Rose.

'Not really. Matthew's been holding open meetings to demonstrate the transparency of the new system. A few councillors have been giving him a hard time, but other than that, nothing I know of.'

'And everything's ready for the election? All the logistics are in place and robust?'

'Yes, it all seems very well organised. Marcus left his chief bodyguard, Sol, here to run the logistics, and he's done a good job. They've gone out to all the trading posts and local community halls and encouraged everyone to register. They've issued polling cards and have enlisted volunteers to run the polling stations, who will also count the votes. And they've organised a second, central count of votes, to ensure there's no vote fixing.'

'Sounds well thought out,' said Rose, nodding her approval. 'We just need to fit in the Mind challenge now.'

'And that's where I come in?' said Gwyn. 'I was wondering why you were here…'

Rose looked a little sheepish, taking a large gulp of her marshmallow laden hot chocolate. 'We had hoped, given the relationship you have with Matthew and his team, that you would try and convince them.'

'You also want me to persuade them that announcing the truth about the Relic return is a good idea. Am I right?

Rose nodded.

'That will take more doing. They've established themselves as a bastion of truth and transparency. Should they make that announcement, they would either have to lie to the people about their prior knowledge, or admit they've been withholding the truth. Neither is a happy position.'

'I know,' said Rose, 'and it's regrettable we've ended up here, but I can't see another way, not without perpetuating existing lies, or creating new ones.'

Gwyn took a deep breath. 'I'll see what I can do; that's all I can promise.'

* * * * *

Matthew stood and started pacing, his feet moving of their own accord, barely noticing he'd left his desk. They were in his office inside an old council building. It was worn and tired, with hardly any natural light. The leather adorning the top of the beaten up desk was battered and holey, the furniture drab and depressing.

Gwyn had made fun of him for his choice of office, but he wanted to stay grounded. Surrounding oneself with opulence was a sure-fire way to fail in that endeavour.

'You want me to announce to the world that the Relic still exists?' said Matthew. 'Was this the plan all along? Convince me not to say anything at first, then tell me later I should announce it to the world, undermining my messages of honesty?'

'Of course not,' said Gwyn. 'If you like, blame the Descendants and say it's only recently come to light. I'll lose my seat for sure, but it will protect you and your party.'

'Until it comes out that I lied to protect a lie.'

Gwyn shrugged. 'You also need to tell them the Relic's dangerous; it's syphoning energy out of our world. We need all the help we can get to return it, once and for all.'

'And you want to stage a new sort of challenge, to find those who might be able to help?'

'Yes.'

'But you can't tell me what that will entail.'

'No. As I said, Bakko and Cleo are working on it.'

'And the people arriving from the Wild Lands are relations of the Descendants? And I should use them to illustrate the Descendants' long-term deceit.'

'Yes,' Gwyn confirmed, staying silent as Matthew mulled it over.

'You'll be out of the running as soon as the message is out, you know that?'

'That may well be so,' said Gwyn, 'but as you're always at pains to point out, there are more important things than winning the election; the truth, for one. Not to mention, the energy continues to drop steadily, with no other explanation. The mood of the people is higher than it has been for months, food rationing is working well, and everyone's excited about the prospect of a new political system. Yet the energy still falls.'

'After the elections, the energy will pick up,' he said, but he could hear the uncertainty in his own words.

'That's probably not true, and if the energy is still troublesome after the election, there's a simple path for anyone who wants to cause unrest.'

Matthew's shoulders slumped. 'When do you suggest I make the announcement? Before or after the election?'

'I think it should be as soon as possible,' said Gwyn. 'You can't win the election based on a lie and then reveal the truth just after you've won.'

'But if we tell them now, the whole thing could fall apart.'

'Look, all you have to do is stand up and say that new information about the Relic has come to light. Tell people it's still in the world and is being used for evil. Tell them the first Descendants twisted the prophecy, and that anyone could be the one to send it back. Use the Magnei to show that the pure bloodlines of the Descendants have always been a myth, and show them the original prophecy Cleo found in the archives.

'Say that you will not give in to this new difficulty, but will, in an open and inclusive way, seek the help of others to find the answer that will save us. To kick off the search for those who can help, you will hold a Mind challenge straight after the election, and encourage anyone with immediate ideas to come forward as soon as possible.'

'You make it sound so simple,' said Matthew, cynically.

'I don't think it's simple, but it has to be done. I'll almost certainly lose, and you may have to be replaced, but the new system will endure, and we'll be a step closer to fixing the energy crisis. It's the right thing to do, Matthew; you know that as well as I do.'

* * * * *

Gwyn looked up at the energy projection Joshua had set up outside the Body Temple in Empire. He'd summoned her here for a debate, announced it to the world, and left her with little choice but to attend. She already regretted coming, but she couldn't leave now; the sizeable crowd had already seen her.

Matthew's face appeared on the projection, the place becoming silent as he began his address. 'Citizens,' said Matthew, a ripple of excitement running through the crowd at this new greeting, 'today, I must share grave news…'

Rushing filled Gwyn's ears as she listened to Matthew tell the world she was a liar and a fake, that her old life was nothing but a fabrication, that her parents and friends were liars too. He went even further than she'd expected, admitting that he'd known for some time that the Relic return was a hoax.

The crowd would turn on her. They would find her wanting, they would reject her, pelt her with venomous words… and maybe other things. Gods, she had to get out of here. But… how? And where would she go?

'… the Mind challenge will take place after the election,' said Matthew. 'It is an opportunity for us to come together, as one people, united behind a single goal: to free ourselves, once and for all, from the destructive influence of the Gods.'

The broadcast came to an abrupt end, taking Gwyn by surprise.

The crowd didn't seem to know what to do, the mood uncertain. Joshua wasted no time. He stepped up in front of the gathered mass, a grave look on his face.

Gwyn couldn't focus. She had to think, to snap herself out of it.

'You see,' Joshua shouted, 'even when the Descendants told us they were finally trying to do their duty—to return the Relic—they were still, in fact, lying.' He roared the word with relish, rounding on Gwyn, daring her to respond.

Gwyn stood still, willing her brain to come up with an escape route. There was no way out. She took a breath, then stepped up beside Joshua. As she turned towards the crowd, she scanned their faces, and, miraculously, years of training slipped back into place. Her mind cleared, and she lifted her head. She squared her shoulders, gravitas slipping around her like a cloak.

'Bravo,' said Gwyn, barely loud enough to be heard, so the crowd had to quieten to catch her words. 'Bravo,' she repeated. 'Matthew makes an announcement, the implications of which are widespread and grave, and Joshua here,' she said, turning, gesturing in his direction, 'without delay, gleefully presses his advantage. But,' she said, emphasising the *t*, then pausing, letting the tension within the crowd build until the air was charged and heavy, 'what he has neglected to mention, is that Joshua also knew of the Relic's continued existence. Joshua was at the meeting where it became known, and Joshua,' she looked back to the audience, her palms open, pointing at the sky, 'chose, like Matthew, not to make that information public.'

Joshua tried to speak, but she continued before he could get started. 'Do you not remember,' said Gwyn, addressing the crowd with authority, 'the situation in which Matthew found himself when he first arrived in Kingdom? Destruction. Confusion. Loss. Plummeting energy. And he decided—right or wrong—to keep secret that the Relic was still in the world.

'However, now that we are on the right track, he has laid himself at your feet, and told you the truth. He's gone beyond that, even. He's admitted he does not possess the solution, that to solve this problem, we need to work together.' She let the thought sink in. 'What more could you ask of a leader than that?'

Gwyn turned to face Joshua, inviting him to respond, but he had nothing to say. The crowd dispersed, sensing the show was over, and Joshua came closer. He stood between her and the audience and took hold of her chin, ferocity hard and cold in his eyes. 'Do not think, for even a moment, that you shall find victory here,' he said. 'This seat is mine, and I will not let you stand in my way.'

* * * * *

Cleo and Bakko had been living an almost entirely secluded existence since returning from the Wild. They'd spent their days between the archives and Cleo's apartment, gleaning what inspiration they could from past Mind research, and talking through challenge formats. They meditated together whenever they could, wandering each other's minds, finding it a fruitful way of coming up with ideas for the challenge, at least, before the inevitable distraction of the other became too great.

They'd made significant strides with the challenge, only a few finishing touches to go before they were ready. The tingles of energy had provided inspiration, along with countless articles in the archives, research into all three disciplines, and of course, Bakko's mind.

Now, as the justification for their secluded existence was coming to an end, they savoured every last precious moment. Light poured into Cleo's bedroom, the curtains wide open, to let in not just the sun, but also the perfect view across the river. She wished they could hide here indefinitely, watching the landscape.

'The energy's been surprisingly stable since the announcement,' said Cleo, lifting her head from Bakko's chest to look into his eyes. He smiled and stroked her glossy hair.

'Cordelia will have a view as to why that is,' said Bakko, after a long pause. He often did that, Cleo left wondering if he'd heard her before he would come back with some cryptic response, his brain having had four or five steps of conversation with itself first.

'How very banal,' mocked Cleo, his response this time seeming to do no more than answer her comment.

He pulled her to him and kissed her. 'Sometimes I get distracted by your beauty,' he said.

'Liar.' She shoved him, playfully.

'We have to go,' he said, kissing her one last time.

'Fine,' she said sulkily, 'but as soon as it's over, we're coming straight back here.'

CHAPTER 8

Anita and Marcus looked around them, their expressions full of disbelief. The place was barren and foreboding. Nothing grew. The landscape was a greyish black from the rocks and boulders strewn as far as the eye could see. To say the going underfoot was tough was an understatement, each step bringing with it the threat of a sprained ankle. The sky was clear yet grey, the sheer-faced mountain rearing up before them, keeping them in perpetual shadow.

Draeus had insisted that Marcus' bodyguards remain at the boundary to the dark side, only a few hundred metres from where they now stood, but seeming a lifetime away, across the treacherous ground, and obscured by the curve of the mountain. They were on their own, the three of them, as they approached Joslyn's cave.

They reached the rock face and looked up, Draeus pointing out the best route to climb. 'Wait for me before you enter the cave,' he warned Anita. 'Joslyn may be Cleo's mother, but she's formidable, and she might not be pleased to see us.'

Anita agreed, then set off in the lead, her movements nimble and confident as she navigated the route Draeus had shown them. She reached the top, having barely broken a sweat, and took in the strange glass wall across the mouth of the cave before her. She almost disregarded Draeus' instruction to wait, but a cry from below pulled her back from temptation.

She looked over the edge to see Marcus' feet dangling free, arms stretched above him, hands clinging to the rock. His face was ashen as he struggled to get both his emotions and limbs in check.

He regained his footing, but Anita could feel his terrified energy, so guided him to the top. She helped him over the lip, and he sprawled on the floor, energy racing.

'I will never fathom why you enjoy such terrible past times,' he said, once he'd finally got his thundering energy under control.

'It's the danger,' she said, offering him a hand to help him to his feet.

'You're crazy,' he said, holding her hand a moment too long.

She raised an eyebrow, their faces close. 'One of us is,' she said, pulling away as Draeus swung up onto the ledge.

'Right,' said Draeus, suddenly business-like. 'Follow me, and let me do the talking; this may not be easy.'

Draeus took a deep breath and marched up to the door, knocking fiercely. They waited for almost a full minute, disappointment infecting their energy, when a figure appeared on the other side of the glass. The door slid open, and a waft of spiced air flooded out, an intoxicating warmth wrapping around them, beckoning them.

Joslyn, eyes not leaving Draeus, motioned for them to come inside. She closed the door behind them, and motioned towards a rough sort of table, which looked as though someone had carved it out of the cave itself. The seats were upturned food crates with worn wool-stuffed canvas pouches perched on top. Anita lowered herself onto one, Marcus sitting close by her side.

'Not you,' said Joslyn, with a slight shake of her head, still looking at Draeus. Her accent was thick with notes of the Wild. 'You can help make tea.' She turned to an ancient-looking metal stove and placed a kettle of water on top.

Anita stared at the woman, struck by her resemblance to Cleo. They didn't look the same, as such, but more that there was a deeper, more innate resemblance of movement, presence and energy. There was a clear family resemblance. They both had long, sleek, black hair, a petite frame, and olive skin, but there was something else she couldn't quite put her finger on, something that made Anita feel she and Joslyn were already friends.

'Now,' said Joslyn, approaching the table with a pot stuffed full of leaves, 'what explanation do you have for this impolite disturbance?' She poured the tea, and Anita and Marcus waited, expecting Draeus to answer.

He said not a word.

Anita opened her mouth to respond, but Draeus shot her a sharp, warning look, which caused it to close of its own accord.

Joslyn smiled. 'At least I don't have to listen to some tittering, half true explanation,' she said, handing around chipped clay mugs. 'Of course, I already know why you're here,' she said, taking a seat and indicating to Draeus that he should too. 'It's not difficult to imagine.'

'Delicious tea,' said Draeus, taking a deep sip.

Joslyn nodded. Her energy—strange in ways Anita couldn't begin to understand—took an upward turn at his comment. They sat in silence for many minutes, each sipping their tea. Anita couldn't help but feel awkward, wondered what the hell was going on.

'At least you're not bombarding me with useless questions,' said Joslyn, approvingly. 'You never were one for idle chatter,' she said to Draeus, her expression that of a lioness testing her prey. Draeus met her eyes but said nothing, features neutral, as was his energy. They sat like that for what felt like an eternity, Draeus and Joslyn's eyes locked together. Anita dared not even look around, for fear of doing something wrong.

'Fine, enough of this,' said Joslyn, eventually, springing up from her chair and pulling Draeus behind her. 'You two, come,' she said, not looking back over her shoulder as she headed further into the blackness of the cave, candles appearing to light their way.

They entered a sizable circular chamber. A bed covered in furs sat at its centre, white drawings, words, and symbols covering every inch of wall.

'I don't have the answers to many of your questions,' said Joslyn. 'But I can share my progress.'

Anita, frustrated by all the strangeness, almost opened her mouth to ask a question, but Marcus, standing ever close, seized her hand before she could. Anita spun towards him, ready to unleash her irritated energy in his direction instead.

'Young love,' said Joslyn, not even looking at them. 'So full of delicious volatility, don't you agree, Draeus?'

Draeus said nothing, but turned to Anita and Marcus, giving them a stern look that made them shrink like naughty children. Anita snatched her hand away and folded her arms in front of her.

'Good for you,' laughed Joslyn. 'Hard to get; my favorite tactic too.' She still faced away from them.

Anita scowled but stayed quiet; Joslyn was obviously a reader, so she focused on getting her energy under control.

'What can I tell you?' said Joslyn, before launching into a volley of information. 'All you seek is in the

Cloud Mountain, including some things you don't yet know you're looking for,' she said, with a smile. 'They have stepped up security, so it's difficult for me to get in and out without detection; I must be careful to keep my entrance secret.

'They have created a whole, prosperous town inside the vast mountain crater; food grows, men and women work, and not only spiritual people, but practical ones also. They have brought together the most skilled craftsmen from across the world, the most skilled everything, in fact. Anything they can't produce, they buy. People pay a fee to come and live here. Timi makes coin trading their creations, along with the rare and natural things that grow here.

'The energy is strange; it has become so over recent months, uncomfortable, for someone like me, that is.'

'A reader, you mean?' asked Anita, not able to contain herself any longer.

Joslyn whirled around and fixed her with cool, deep eyes. 'A reader?' she mocked. 'Is that what you call it? You ignorant people who know nothing of what you have inside you? You think you either have or don't have, as simple as that? When in fact, it's like light, or sound, or love, or anything else worth a second thought; a spectrum. You will find it uncomfortable in there too, of that I can assure you.'

Anita wanted to say more; to complain she hadn't answered her question, but she thought better of it, waiting for Joslyn to continue without further interruption.

'Let me think,' said Joselyn, pondering, 'what else would you want to know? Oh yes, of course, how to actually return the Relic…'

Joslyn paused and walked to a section of drawings on the wall. 'Look familiar?' she asked, this time looking expectantly at them, waiting for an answer.

'They're replicas of the drawings and inscriptions that were found alongside the Relic,' said Marcus.

'Indeed,' said Joslyn. 'I've deconstructed them; the only clues the Mind God left as to how to return the Relic.'

'What?' said Anita. 'The Mind God created the inscriptions? Not the Body and Spirit Gods?'

Joslyn looked confused. 'What have those two got to do with anything?' she said, almost venomously. 'That useless pair haven't done a single thing to help. You realize they could put an end to this tomorrow, if they overlooked their ridiculous *no meddling* rule? Did you know that?' she demanded.

'They implied as much,' admitted Anita.

'Then, of course, two useless Gods, who refuse to do anything to help the world they created, did not put the images and inscriptions next to the Relic. No. The Mind God did this himself. He, like every Mind, is arrogant but playful. He put these alongside the Relic to help us send it back, but by setting the Descendants apart, as the only people who could return the Relic, he knew few people would concern themselves with investigating too closely. Not to mention, the Mind God, Theseus, occupied Austin—and his father before him—so could put a stop to Relic research whenever it suited him.'

'You think someone was getting too close for comfort? That's why they banned Relic research?' asked Marcus.

'Of course,' she snapped, 'why else?'

'But you continued your work,' said Anita. 'Have you made any headway?'

Joslyn shot her another sharp look. 'Of course I've made progress, but I don't have the answer, if that's what you're hoping for.'

'Walk us through it,' said Draeus.

'Draeus, it's important to understand I didn't tell you this all those years ago, because I was only just starting my research. When I told you small snippets, you thought me mad. If I'd shared it all, you'd have left without delay.'

'Maybe,' said Draeus, 'I guess we'll never know for sure. Please continue,' he said, after a moment of silence, motioning to the drawings and refusing to meet her eyes.

'Let us start with the drawings,' said Joslyn, seemingly unconcerned by Draeus' discomfort. 'The first is of three people around a vaguely circular blob of blue-ish colour, which most have taken to refer to the three Descendants around the Relic. We now know this is ridiculous, as the Descendants are a hoax, so we may look more objectively at the drawing.'

Joslyn talked, but Anita couldn't concentrate. Her eyes roamed across the drawings of people and symbols. She only heard snippets, 'Three people… blue is the color of energy… it's floating, indicating they're raising it up…'

'… or an indication that energy should be used to return the Relic?' said Marcus, snapping Anita back into the moment. Joslyn ignored him. 'Above this scene are three symbols, which people have historically assumed to represent the Gods, however, this is an assumption based on nothing but conjecture. The symbols—a triangle pointing down, a triangle pointing up, and a diamond—do not appear in any other literature concerning the Gods. This does not mean they do not represent the Gods, just that there is nothing I can find to support the notion.'

'One to ask Cordelia and Bakko,' said Anita. Marcus nodded his agreement.

'The illustrations seem to depict three people sending the Relic, or some energy, skyward, towards the symbols waiting above,' said Joslyn. 'This much is in line with the prophecy, although there is some uncertainty as to who these people are, their gender, their skills, and indeed, whether it is three people, or whether the three are being used to depict a crowd.'

'The questions just keep on coming,' said Anita, almost under her breath.

Joslyn shot her another look, but kept going. 'So, let us turn our attention to the inscriptions: *look to the light*, *knowledge is power*, and *she who dares will surely triumph*. Commonly, these are considered to be motivational messages to the Spirit, Mind, and Body Descendants respectively. Again, now we know this is fiction, we must look objectively at what they could mean.'

Anita zoned out again, turning to take in the rest of the room. '… return should be done in daylight… although maybe metaphorical… but *knowledge is power*… makes me think literal… maybe some weakness of the Mind God to be exploited…'

Anita finished her scan of the cave walls; a depressing place to live, with no natural light.

'The third saying,' said Joslyn, 'indicates a woman will be instrumental in returning the Relic, although it also implies a single person, which contradicts the images. It implies an element of personal risk. They may know how to return the Relic, but until they take a leap of faith, there will be no triumph.'

Joslyn's diatribe ended. It appeared she'd achieved little in the decades spent searching for an answer. Joslyn's eyes found Anita, piercing her as though she could sense Anita's thoughts.

'You may think I have uncovered little,' said Joslyn. 'To think this would be to misunderstand the nature of the problem, and to underestimate the number of stones that I have turned.'

'But it doesn't give us much to go on, other than what we already know,' said Anita, sounding negative, although not meaning to. 'What do we do next?'

'You venture into the mountain and see what you can glean,' said Joslyn. 'There are new people in there who you know far better than I. They might give something away that we don't already know.'

'What are they doing up there?' asked Marcus. 'Why build a new town and bring all these people here?'

'Utopia,' she replied. 'They have resources beyond imagination, and now they have a God, the Relic, and all the energy this brings with it. Albeit they don't realize the Mind God is taking the lion's share for himself.'

'Their intention is to leave the rest of the world to die?' said Anita.

Joslyn shrugged. 'I do not know the Mind God's true intentions, but there may be one inside who does.'

* * * * *

The light was pure and clean, a riot of otherworldly colour, as it skipped through thousands of tiny crystals and out across the floor of the new temple. Three people worked diligently in its centre, lifting with reverence a rock-like object, and placing it on a sculpted metal plinth made especially for this. This temple was of a new design. Instead of three parts, one for Mind, Body, and Spirit, this had only one circular area, enclosed on all sides by a curtain of crystals, and open to the sky above. At its centre sat the finishing touch they had all been waiting for. Finally, the Relic was in its rightful home.

Anderson, Bella, and Edmund took a step back and admired their work. 'It's magnificent,' said Edmund, marvelling at the way the light illuminated the Relic's every nook and cranny.

'It certainly is,' said Timi, stepping into the circle, pausing a moment, a look of admiration on his face. 'He'll be pleased,' he said, before his eyes locked onto Edmund. 'I heard you'd made it. What news?'

Edmund met Timi's gaze. 'As I told the others,' he said pointedly, this the fourth time he'd repeated his story, 'they're coming to the mountain, to the dark side, where there is, apparently, another way in. They'll use this back entrance to spy on us. They know there's something strange about the energy in the mountain, and they suspect both that the Mind God is here, and that you have the Relic. They suspect the Mind God is using you as a host, Timi.' Edmund paused a moment before adding, 'Is that true?'

Timi fixed him with an impervious look, clearly with no intention of revealing the truth.

Edmund huffed. 'Very well. They have announced to the world the truth about the Relic return, as well as the truth about the Descendants, which I'm sure you already know. They plan to stage a Mind Challenge to find those who could help solve the problem of how to return the Relic for real. This will take place immediately after the election, but again, I'm sure you already know this.'

Timi nodded. 'Nothing else?' he asked, suspicion clear in his tone.

Edmund shook his head. 'No, that is all,' he said, his attention wandering back to the Relic as a change came over the temple. Edmund was no reader, but even he could tell there was a surge of energy coming their way. He looked towards the entrance, the hair at the back of his neck standing on end, a mix of trepidation and excitement filling him.

He was almost disappointed when a tall, well-built man with blond hair entered the circular space; he'd expected something… more. The man walked to the Relic and placed his hand upon it, stroking it affectionately, as though it were a pet dog.

'It's perfect, is it not?' said Anderson, carefully observing the man's movements.

'It is perfect,' replied Alexander, although his face remained neutral. 'Everything went exactly to plan.'

* * * * *

Marcus and Anita made their careful way through the small hole at the back of Joslyn's cave. It was low to the ground, and they had to crawl on hands and knees to fit through.

'Follow it to the fork and then keep left,' said Joslyn, as they disappeared into the unknown. 'Make sure you stay silent all the way; you never know who might be listening.' She said the words more to herself than to the others, who had already rounded the first bend.

They crawled in silence, Anita at the front, moving as quickly as she could, a light strapped to her forehead to illuminate the path. The floor was cold and unforgiving, and they had bruises on their knees in no time, but it wasn't far to the fork, so they pressed on in comradely silence. They did as they had been told and turned left, feeling the ground almost immediately slope upwards, the tunnel becoming pebbly, slowing their progress as they picked their way along.

'There's light up ahead,' whispered Anita, eventually, 'only another minute or two and I think we'll be there.'

Marcus grunted his acknowledgement.

They reached the end and waited for several minutes, listening intently, adrenaline pumping, their senses heightened, before they snuck out into the back of an enormous, dingy storeroom. They stood up and looked around, Anita surprised by both the sheer scale of the place and the breadth of resources. Racks and racks of metals, rocks and fabrics, not to mention the food, of which there appeared to be enough to satisfy an army for a decade.

'I guess this explains why Timi's monks haven't been affected by the rationing,' said Marcus quietly, brushing dust from his legs.

'I guess so,' said Anita, taking in every detail, wasting no time in the hunt for the door. The room was chilly and poorly lit, and aside from the colossal quantity in storage, there seemed to be nothing special about it. Anita was pondering the purpose of it all, when Marcus' hand shot out and pulled her towards him, spinning them into a side row.

'Shhh,' Marcus whispered in her ear, holding onto her when she tried to move away. 'Listen.'

Anita listened and recognised the far-off sound of muffled voices. 'A little dramatic,' she whispered, using the hand that had come to rest on his chest to push them apart. They moved towards the voices, close enough to hear words, which, to their disappointment, concerned only the supplies the two men had been sent to retrieve.

Marcus and Anita waited for a handful of minutes until the men had everything they needed. When they left, a dull *thunk* reverberated through the store as they pulled the hefty door shut.

'Looks like we found the way out,' said Anita, heading quickly towards it.

'Anita, wait,' hissed Marcus, catching up with her as she reached the door, grabbing her arm. 'Before you throw that door open, what's the plan here?'

Anita turned to face him. 'That's more your style than mine,' she said, putting her ear to the door and listening intently, focusing every ounce of concentration on detecting nearby energy. 'It's clear,' she said, finally satisfied there was no one there.

She reached out to the door handle, pressed down the lever, and gave it a solid tug, the heavy wood moving ponderously towards her. She opened it just a crack and peered carefully through the gap to see what lay beyond.

'Wow,' she said, almost involuntarily, as she took in what lay before her. She'd expected to emerge in some dark corridor, that they would have to sneak around to find anything significant. The reality was altogether different. She found herself gazing out over what she could only describe as a small town; houses, shops and people bathed in soft light from the open crater above.

'We're in the crater?' asked Marcus. 'I had no idea we were up that high.'

'I know,' said Anita. 'Strange.'

The crater was enormous. The storeroom was positioned at its edge, set apart from the town, presumably quarried out of the mountain itself. It was also set slightly above the level of the buildings, meaning they had a good vantage point to spy on the whole place.

The town was bustling; sounds and smells wafting on the light breeze up to where Anita and Marcus hid, people going about their business as though this were any normal community. On the far side of the crater, the land was being farmed; crops and orchards growing happily, people working in the fields. But to the right of where they stood, on the edge of the crater, was a tall cliff. On top of the cliff sat a curious, decadent structure.

They took in the spectacle for a moment in silence. 'It looks like some kind of temple,' said Marcus eventually, eyeing the winding stone steps that snaked to the top.

'That would make sense, given the whole place is angled towards it… are those crystals all the way around?' said Anita, not quite believing her eyes.

Marcus gave a low chuckle. 'I think so,' he said, taking in the structure. 'I take it that's our new destination?'

Anita smiled but gave no answer. Instead, she heaved the door open a little further, and slipped through.

* * * * *

Anita headed toward the temple, Marcus left with little option but to follow in her wake.

They headed around the edge of the crater, using the scattered boulders as shields. Anita moved quickly, meaning Marcus trailed behind, taking care not to make a sound. He caught up to her near the bottom of the cliff, Anita having paused to study the temple from a closer vantage. 'I wonder what they could possibly want a temple like that for,' said Anita, sarcastically.

'You think it's up there?' said Marcus, ducking down to keep out of sight.

'If it's here, yes,' she said, excitedly. 'It's as likely a place as we're going to find.'

'We can't just waltz up those steps; the entire town would see us.'

'That's why we're going round the back,' said Anita, making a break for it across a gap in their cover. Marcus took a deep breath before propelling himself behind her.

'Round the back?' he asked, having reached the safety of another boulder, his back pressed against it. The jagged coolness provided a strange sort of comfort.

'It's the only place that's not overlooked. If you follow the edge of the cliff around, you can see there's space behind.'

'I'm not blind,' he snapped. 'But you're not seriously intending to climb a sheer cliff face, with no idea what's at the top?'

Anita frowned. 'Of course,' she said, as they reached the base of the cliff. 'Don't worry, you can stay at the bottom and keep a lookout if you're scared to come up with me.'

Marcus raised his eyebrows. 'Aside from the way I feel about climbing, I don't think having a lookout is a bad idea. Or, at the very least, I can try to make it back to the cave if you get caught.'

Anita shrugged. 'Very well.'

'Here will do well enough,' said Anita, when they made it to the back of the strange structure. She scoped out the climb, determining her route, then nodded. 'Wish me luck,' she said flippantly, grasping hold of the cliff.

'Wait,' said Marcus, placing a hand on her arm and pulling her back from the face. 'Seriously, Anita, be careful.' He paused, trying to make the gravity of his words sink in. 'Make sure you come back down here in one piece.'

Anita half smiled, softening a little. 'I'll be fine. I've climbed things far more difficult than this and come back alive. And you be careful not to strain yourself, sitting down here keeping watch.' Her eyes twinkled as she lifted off, beginning her climb.

'Funny,' said Marcus, 'very funny.' He settled down to watch and wait.

* * * * *

Anita climbed quickly and easily, this face no more of a challenge than the cliffs in Empire, where she'd frequently trained. However, when she reached the top, she paused, concentrating all her energy on trying to work out what was going on above. She strained her ears and focused her energy field, but everything was silent and still. She waited a few more moments before lifting her head and peering over the top, apprehensive about what she would find, and surprised to see a curtain of crystals between her and the space beyond.

The curtain circled right around the outside of the cliff, forming, from what she could make out, a huge open space inside. She couldn't see any movement on the inside either, so, steeling herself for surprises, she hoisted her body easily over the lip, crouching like a cat on the edge, waiting carefully for any reaction her presence might provoke.

To her relief, everything stayed still and quiet. She crept silently toward the barrier of crystals, keeping low to the ground, every movement carefully considered. She reached the crystals and lay flat on the rocky floor, tentatively reaching out with her hand to make a small hole through which she could see. She was careful to make only small, slow, delicate adjustments to the crystals, only too aware that any shift in light would draw immediate attention.

She moved her eyes to the hole, shocked to see people talking intently inside, a wash of energy and sound suddenly hitting her. Her energy leapt, adrenaline flooding her as she watched for a reaction, preparing for a hasty retreat. When no one noticed her, she looked down and took several deep, long breaths, slowing her pulse, before looking up once more.Her eyes found three figures. Two of them she recognised immediately. That double-crossing runt, thought Anita, as she took in a tall, skinny, red-haired form: Anderson, the Relic expert. Her mind raced through the implications. Had he been the one who'd betrayed them after the Relic return? Was he working for the Mind God all along? Or for Timi? Is this where his wife, Bella, had really been? Not looking after her sick mother?

The second figure was Timi, which was less of a surprise, given he ran the place. She pushed all thoughts of them to one side, forcing herself to focus on their conversation.

'Everything is ready,' said Anderson, addressing the other two with something akin to reverence. Anita couldn't tell for sure if the third figure was a man or a woman, as they were wearing a cloak and the hood was up, but, given their height and broad shoulders, she guessed it was a man. 'I've arranged it, just as you stipulated. The ceremony will take place exactly as you planned.'

'Good,' said the man in the cloak, a tickle of dread pooling in Anita's stomach.

'Yes, very good,' said Timi, nodding at Anderson, although his face remained a steely mask of contempt.

'I aim to please,' said Anderson, sounding… resentful… 'Now, if you'll excuse me, I have other things to which I must attend.'

Anderson made to leave, and Timi followed him. 'I'll leave you alone with the Relic awhile,' said Timi, something akin to fear in his voice. 'See you at supper.'

The third man turned away from Timi's departing figure, circling slowly towards where Anita hid, and her breath caught in her lungs. She was dimly aware of the Relic behind the man, who had been shielding it from view. But the sight of the thing that had caused all this mess barely even registered. Something far more powerful clutched her insides.

She watched as the man turned, in what seemed like slow motion. As he lowered his hood, revealing a mess of dishevelled blond hair. Anita's energy exploded, a million feelings radiating out of her, hitting him like shards of razor glass. She thought she saw him wince, but he kept turning, electric blue eyes scanning the crystals, seeking.

He found her and his features contorted, as though he were in pain, but his energy remained resolutely neutral. She froze, half of her wanting to jump up and run into his arms, the other half gripped by terror.

'What are you doing here?' asked Alexander's familiar chocolate voice.

Anita stared at him for a long moment, confusion turning to anger at his imperviousness. 'That's it?' she demanded, not stopping for a second to think. 'You disappear. I think you're dead or held captive. Now we're finally reunited, and you ask me that?'

Anita felt suddenly ridiculous, lying on the floor. She climbed to her feet, on the inside of the crystals, and took a step towards him.

Alexander's mouth twitched, and a shadow flashed behind his eyes, but he remained absolutely still, adding fuel to Anita's fire. 'Nothing?' she raged. 'You have nothing at all to say to me?' A plea crept into her voice, and she thought she saw something soften in his eyes.

'What are you doing here?' Alexander repeated, impatiently.

'I could ask you the same question,' she said, her tone still hostile, but uncertainty crept in.

Alexander said nothing, his body language cold and aloof, features uninviting, and Anita realized he was… different. His energy was strange, and his eyes lacked depth. She studied them, finding them cold as stone; none of Alexander's complexity on display.

'Alexander, what's going on?' she asked.

No words came to his lips, but his features twitched once more. She was about to ask him if he was okay, when his body convulsed. He collapsed to the floor, legs crossing underneath him as though he were about to meditate. He looked up at her, his familiar soft eyes finally meeting her own, but they suddenly snapped shut, a frown taking hold of his face until they opened once more, all tenderness snuffed out by a look of pure evil.

Anita recoiled, whirling away from him, racing back through the crystal curtain and over the side of the cliff. She expected to see him appear at the top, or for him to call others to apprehend her. But the place remained silent and still, as though she'd imagined the whole encounter.

She climbed to the bottom, Marcus' concerned form hovering nervously. 'What happened?' he asked, unease seeping out of him.

'We have to get out of here. Now,' she said, grabbing his hand and pulling him behind her, flying back the way they'd come.

'Anita, what's going on? Were you discovered?'

'You could say that,' she said, only just loud enough for him to hear. 'I'll tell you everything when we're back in the cave. Now stop asking me stupid questions, and run.'

* * * * *

They made it back to the cave without incident, Anita's energy almost back under control by the time they tumbled out of the tunnel and onto Joslyn's floor.

'Gods, what happened?' asked Joslyn, rushing over and helping Anita to her feet. 'Your energy is wrecked.'

'Thanks,' said Anita, bitterly.

'Seriously,' said Marcus, pushing himself to his feet. 'What the hell happened up there?'

Joslyn led Anita to the bed and forced her to sit, Marcus following, crouching in front of her. He looked over her limbs, making sure she hadn't suffered an injury, then hooked her hair back off her face and looked directly into her eyes. 'What happened?'

Anita met and held his gaze a moment before responding. 'The Relic's up there, and so are Timi, Anderson, and Alexander,' she said, matter-of-factly, 'and they're planning something… some kind of ceremony.'

'Hang on,' said Marcus. 'Alexander's up there?'

Anita looked from one of his eyes to the other and then dropped her head. 'Yes. Along with Anderson, Timi, and who knows who else.'

'Anita,' said Marcus, gently, 'what happened?'

She relayed the story, leaving out no detail, and then waited for the inevitable barrage of questions. To her surprise, it didn't come.

'Spineless bastard,' said Marcus, not being specific about which of the three, in particular, he was referring to.

'All of them,' said Joslyn, nodding her agreement, 'hiding away in a mountain fortress.'

Anita's hackles rose. 'We don't know what's going on yet,' she said. 'They could be there against their will for all we know. Timi seemed scared, and Alexander's energy wasn't like it usually is. I told you, he was making weird facial expressions, and then collapsed to the floor.'

'You think the Mind God is using Alexander as a host?' asked Joslyn. 'Not Timi?'

'I don't know,' said Anita, shaking her head then launching herself to her feet. 'But I think Alexander wanted me to meditate with him; I think that's what he was trying to signal to me.'

'If he were being used, that would make sense,' said Joslyn. 'Alexander's centre would remain his and his alone, even if he were a host. The Mind God could force his way in, but Alexander could probably keep him out for a time.'

'It's worth a try then,' said Anita. 'I'll go back up there after the sun has set, and try to make contact.'

'You'll what?' said Marcus, rounding on Anita. 'You can't be serious? It's obviously a trap.'

Anita shook her head. 'I don't think so. And even if it is, it's not like we have a better plan.'

'Anita,' said Marcus, slowly, 'have you stopped to consider the possibility that Alexander's the one behind all this? You said the other two feared him. He didn't seem to be under guard, and surely a powerful Spirit isn't a natural host for the Mind God?'

'Of course I've considered it,' she said, trying to keep emotion out of her voice. 'But we have no other option. The Mind God continues to syphon energy out of the world. We have no plan, and no idea what to do next. If we can get to Alexander, we'll have someone on the inside.'

'You expect us to believe that's really why you want to do this?' said Marcus, hotly.

'Yes.' Anita spat the word, anger boiling inside.

'I could go instead,' he said. 'I'm doubtless more objective.'

146

Anita laughed a cruel laugh. 'Objective? In what world are you that, when it comes to the two of us?'

Anita felt the word 'us' rip through Marcus' energy, and guilt chased away her anger.

'The two of you?' he said, squaring up to her. 'Where has *he* been since the world collapsed? Where was *he* when you were a prisoner? Why's *he* still up there now, even after you stood two feet in front of him?'

Anita looked down, letting the dust settle. 'Marcus,' she said, placing her hand on his arm, 'I'm sorry, but I've got to do this.'

'Obviously not as sorry as I am,' he said, snatching his arm away and storming out.

'I do love a lover's tiff,' said Joslyn, delighted, clapping her hands together in glee.

'We're not lovers,' said Anita, firmly. 'I see now where Cleo gets it from.'

Interest shone in Joslyn's eyes. 'Cleopatra is like me?' she asked.

'Yes. She's the go-to person in Empire for gossip of any kind, and she loves nothing more than a bit of melodrama. She most certainly does not get that from Draeus.'

'No,' agreed Joslyn, 'he's a bit of a stick in the mud with all that. Too discrete for his own good. Tell me more about her; I want to ask Draeus, but I... I know I won't say the right words.'

'Well,' said Anita, 'where to start? She looks a lot like you. Her skin's a bit lighter, but she has your features, and long dark hair, just like you. She flits through life, chasing gossip and boys. She loves getting dressed up, gets overexcited about parties, and works at Draeus' bar in Empire. She runs the place really, which she enjoys, because it's where everyone goes to gossip. She's...'

'... she's the cleverest, most devious, most calculating person I know...,' came a deep, male voice from the entrance.

They whirled around to see Draeus, back from taking a message to Marcus' bodyguards.

'... and I'll be damned, but I can't control a single thing she does,' he finished, stepping fully into the cave.

'No one can,' said Anita, with a smile, walking past Draeus to the exit. 'Everything alright with the message?'

'All fine,' he said, and Anita left them alone.

CHAPTER 9

The election had gone as well as anyone could have hoped, at least for everyone except Gwyn, who had lost to Joshua. Matthew's party had swept to victory, and Matthew was now ensconced as the inaugural President. Many former councillors had won seats, especially in Kingdom, but a good injection of fresh blood had made it into the world's politics. With a new leader at the helm, the air in Empire was abuzz with possibility.

'We're all set?' said Rose, walking up the steps in front of the new parliament building in Empire, looking from Bakko to Cleo with apprehensive eyes.

'As we said,' said Cleo, impatiently, 'we're ready to go.'

'And you've included the Relic inscriptions, as per the note from Draeus?' Rose pressed, not taking the hint.

Cleo huffed. 'Yes, we have included that modification. It wasn't difficult.'

Bakko sent a nudge to the edge of her energy field, letting her know he felt her pain.

'Okay then,' said Rose, 'let's talk Cordelia through it.'

Bakko's eyes flashed with annoyance. Like he, the Spirit God, needed permission from Rose to speak to his fellow God. This time Cleo sent him a nudge, and he grasped her hand as they entered the impressive new construction.

The building was a mix of traditional and modern; intricate carvings combined with swathes of glass and steel. It had an established yet progressive feel, light exposing every nook and cranny of the huge circular debate hall. The offices on the higher levels were cosy and inviting, in stark contrast to the previous halls of power.

'How did they build this so quickly?' said Cleo, marvelling at the ornate stone carvings that wrapped over the edge of the nearest pane of glass.

'Enough people with a strong enough desire to see it done,' said Bakko, running his hand over a section of particularly intricate stone leaves. They moved around the edge of the building, taking it all in, until they came across Bakko's fellow God. 'Cordelia, good to see you.'

'Likewise,' said Cordelia, 'and it's good to see you two as well.' She nodded in Cleo and Rose's direction.

'Let's get to it then,' said Bakko, wishing this formality over, so he could retreat back to seclusion with Cleo. 'I take it we're in here?' He entered the main hall without waiting for an answer.

'Welcome,' said Matthew, walking towards them with open arms. 'Thank you for coming. This way,' he said, gesturing towards the dais in the centre of the round chamber.

The room was filled with an array of newly elected people, their energy excited and upbeat, the new system still novel and enticing.

A few detractors sat with crossed arms, their negative energy permeating the general buoyant enthusiasm. It hit Bakko's energy field like a barrage of irritating pins.

'Ladies and gentlemen,' said Matthew, gesturing around with wide, open arms, 'it is with great pleasure that I present to you, Bakko, the Spirit God, and Cleo, daughter of the renowned trader, Draeus. They come to us today with a plan to find those who can help return the Relic. Please welcome Bakko and Cleo.' He waved a hand in their direction, then took his seat in the front row.

Bakko and Cleo stood a moment, letting all eyes settle on them, each taking in a different segment of the room. They let the pause reach almost awkward proportions before Cleo spoke, her voice quiet and intense. The audience leaned closer, so as not to miss a word.

'You all know the truth now,' she said. 'About the Relic, the Descendants, the old system of rule.' She paused, picking out the most sullen politicians, meeting their brooding eyes. 'And you're aware of the ongoing consequences of ignoring the Relic return. Which is why tomorrow is a pivotal day in our fight to stabilise the energy, and you,' she let the word hang, 'are crucial to our success.' Cleo stopped talking, looking to Bakko, who continued.

'The Mind challenge will take place where no person has before set foot,' said Bakko. 'We will hold the event in the central chamber underneath the temples, here, in Empire, around the pool of water that grounds the energy there. The Magnei have, from preliminary challenges, interviews, and energy tests, already picked the nine Minds who will compete.

'While the challenge takes place beneath the temples, we will hold a festival above. We will fill the temples with music, food, dancing, and games. It is of extreme importance, for the success of the activities below, that we have a well of positive energy for contestants to draw upon. The people above won't be able to see the challenge, but they must remain in high spirits for the duration. This is where all of you come in.'

'You must create a party atmosphere and keep the place filled with people,' said Cleo. 'For as long as it takes.'

'And how long will that be?' asked one of the politicians.

'Could be hours,' Bakko said, shrugging. 'Could be days.'

'You want us to keep a party going for days?' scoffed an ex-councillor.

Bakko's eyes flashed. 'Will that be a problem for you?' he asked, the room like a vacuum as they awaited his answer.

The man bowed his head and shook it, not meeting anyone's eyes, not able to find a voice to reply.

'Good,' said Bakko, turning in unison with Cleo and heading for the exit.

'Aren't you going to tell us about the format of the challenge?' asked Joshua, his tone demanding.

Cleo kept walking, but Bakko stopped and looked over his shoulder. 'No,' he said simply, then followed Cleo out of the room.

* * * * *

The following day, an hour before noon, the politicians diligently arrived at the temples in Empire. A sizeable crowd already milled outside, expectant and excited. The contestants—all aside from Cleo—waited nervously in the rooms below, which had, until recently, belonged to the Body Descendants.

The band was setting up, and traders prepared food, meat turning on spits, the delicious smell wafting through the air. Bars had been dotted around the temples, plentiful and well-stocked, and games had been set up for those with a competitive side.

'Everything ready?' asked Cordelia, standing in the open space of the Body Temple.

'Yes,' said Cleo. 'As ready as it's ever going to be.'

Cordelia nodded. 'I'll see you down there,' she said. 'I'm going to prepare.'

'See you there,' said Bakko, clasping Cordelia's shoulder as she passed him, before she descended through the hole in the floor.

Bakko looked around, satisfied there was little more they could do to ready the place, and weary of the growing mass of energy all around. 'Come with me,' he said to Cleo, turning in the direction of the Spirit Temple, moving towards it at speed. Cleo followed, careful not to be obvious about it; they were trying to keep their relationship secret from the public.

Bakko descended into the quarters that had previously belonged to Alexander—his belongings yet to be removed—and waited impatiently for Cleo to join him. She descended the stairs, barely thirty seconds behind him, but he sprang forward to meet her, lifting her down the final few steps.

'Finally,' he breathed, kissing her with urgent intensity.

Cleo responded enthusiastically. 'We've only been here a few hours,' she teased, between kisses.

'A few hours too many,' he said, pulling her backwards, to a beaten-up old leather sofa. 'It's intolerable.' He sat and pulled Cleo down with him. She sat across his lap, legs out along the rest of the sofa. Bakko leaned back into the leather, taking a deep, restorative breath. 'That's better,' he said, as Cleo wriggled down to lie along the sofa, putting a pillow in his lap, then resting her head.

'Too many energy signatures?' asked Cleo.

Bakko absent mindedly stroked her cheek, then pushed her hair back off her face. He nodded. 'I can't stand it all the time; I'm not used to it.'

'So, you'll go back to the Wild after the challenge?' Cleo asked, her tone hesitant.

Bakko smiled. 'I don't know,' he said, taking her hand and pulling it to his lips. 'Where do you intend to be?'

'I suppose that depends,' she said, matching his playful tone.

'Oh? Upon what does it depend?'

Cleo turned suddenly sombre. 'Bakko, seriously, what will happen to us? If we return the Relic, won't that mean you'll have to leave this world too?'

'There are always ways,' he said, distantly.

'Like what?'

'Like, let's not talk about it now. We've got a big day ahead of us, and… if anything turns sour, promise me you'll get out of there. I won't be able to protect you...'

'… I know. We've been through this a thousand times,' said Cleo, swatting away his hand and sitting up.

'Cleo,' he said, halting when he saw her face. He met her flaming eyes, then hesitantly placed his hand on her cheek.

She looked at him defiantly, then bowed her head, blinking her anger away. She sank back into the warmth of his embrace, burying her head in his torso.

'Cleo,' he said again, faltering a moment before finding his resolve.

She turned her head to meet his eyes.

'I love you,' he said. 'I've never loved anyone, and I will fight until my dying breath for us to be together. I will find a way.'

* * * * *

154

Noon arrived, loud and unwelcome, and feet thundered in the temple above where Bakko and Cleo lay. The temples' central council chamber had been removed entirely, meaning one could now walk freely from one temple to another. They had kept the very centre point clear, ensuring the hole in the floor remained uncovered, connecting the sacred pool below to the sky.

'Time to go,' said Bakko, gently prising her to her feet. He led her into the tunnel at the back of the room, and they walked in silence through the dark.

'Good luck,' he said, squeezing her hand as they reached the door to the Mind quarters.

'You too,' she said, kissing him one last time before they were sucked into a world full of others. She pulled away, took a deep breath, and walked confidently into the room that held the other contestants. Bakko watched her go.

Cleo looked around the room, taking in the eight other contestants, none of whom she recognised. Four women and four men, spread across a wide range of ages, from a boy who could have been no older than thirteen or fourteen, to two older contestants, who must have been at least eighty. One looked to be around Cleo's age, the rest older, with the look of smug self-satisfaction about most of them.

We'll see how smug you are once we're in, thought Cleo. But a knot of anxiety gripped her stomach as she tried to work out which of them represented the biggest threat. Of course, it was impossible to tell; she didn't know their capabilities.

Cordelia had been most insistent that Cleo shouldn't have any advantage over the others, and Bakko had agreed. He had been unwilling to bend the rule, even a little. So, frustratingly, Cleo was in the dark about her fellow contestants. Of course, she knew a great deal about the challenge itself, having been instrumental in its construction, but she didn't know everything, nor did she know how much the others had been told. Maybe they had a good idea of what they were heading into as well.

'Ready?' asked a politician helping to run the challenge. 'It's nearly time for you to go up there and wave at the crowd.' The woman's tone was irritatingly perky. 'Remember to smile,' she added. And, as if they might not have understood, she smiled and waved her hand in energetic demonstration.

Right on cue, the stone in the roof that sealed the chamber slid aside, and Matthew's excited voice floated down from above. '... so, without further ado, ladies and gentlemen, please welcome our contestants!' He said the words in a crescendo, hyping the audience to ever greater levels of animation.Wild applause met them as they climbed the steps into the light of the temples above. Cleo raised an involuntary eyebrow; at least the energy levels were high enough. She tried to block out the noise and concentrate on what they would face in only a few short minutes.

Matthew introduced them all. Cleo waved as he called her name, but she barely heard his words, forcing herself to focus her mind, thinking of nothing but the challenge ahead.

'The challengers will enter the minds of the Gods,' said Matthew, mysteriously, 'where they will work to solve a puzzle laid before them. The first to solve the puzzle will be crowned champion.' He took a moment to revel in the excitement.

'There is no second place,' said Matthew, a hush falling. 'The challenge could take hours or days, and it is the job of us all,' he said, waving a sweeping hand across the crowd, 'to maintain a lively atmosphere of celebration up here, ready to welcome our victor.'

A cheer went up from the crowd.

'So, with no further delay, let us wish our contestants the very best of luck, and send them to their challenge.'

The audience roared, stamped, and clapped as the contestants filed down through the floor. The stone slid back into place, muffling the cacophony overhead.

Two more politicians ushered the contestants to the central underground chamber, their movements thick with fear as they hovered before the door. 'Send them in, then leave,' came a quiet, penetrating voice from beyond. The politicians jumped to obey the command of a God.

Cleo hung back as the rest of the challengers entered, watching their faces carefully as they ventured into the unknown. She felt her own pulse rise as she followed them, a wash of energy hitting her like a force field as she stepped through the door.

Inside, the room was almost dark, only a few flickering candles lighting the way. It was unnaturally still and calm, and the challengers spread out in a circle around the pool, each moving to their own spongy mat and sitting down.

The Gods were in the very centre, sitting back-to-back, holding hands on both sides. They had their eyes closed, floating above the pool of water, and acted as though they hadn't noticed the room's new occupants.

Cleo hadn't been expecting this. She wasn't sure what she had been expecting, but the sight of Bakko and Cordelia sitting on the water was curious, captivating and distracting.

'Sit or lie on your mat, whichever you wish,' a quiet but powerful voice said, without either Bakko or Cordelia moving a muscle. They all did as they were told, each contestant fixated on the Gods, tense, and excited to see what would come next.

'When you are ready, begin your meditation,' said the voice, which Cleo thought might belong to Cordelia. 'Push your energy towards the pool, and you will arrive where you're supposed to.' The voice ceased, and the room went still. They waited for several long heartbeats, to see if the Gods would say anything further, but, met with stony silence, they lowered themselves into meditation, one by one.

Cleo opened her eyes inside the meditation, and found herself in the familiar landscape of Bakko's mind. The impossible expanse of continuous change rolled out from where she stood, and a familiar shiver of warmth ran up her spine. Concentrate, she told herself, as she looked around for the first step of the challenge that she had helped devise.

Although she knew the theory behind the tasks ahead, she didn't know the exact details of how they would manifest, nor the order in which she would have to face them. Her eyes found the other contestants, who had gathered just down the slope from where she stood. They were looking around, bewildered, and she moved towards them, thinking maybe they'd found the first clue.

She reached them to find she was wrong. They were simply overwhelmed by what they saw around them, this unlike any mind they had meditated to before. They heard a rumbling behind them, and turned in unison to see a great, edgeless mirror appear out of the ground. It stood fifteen feet in the air and reflected the colossal, changing landscape behind them, wispy clouds drifting across the calm blue sky. Words appeared across the mirror, and the group took several steps forward to see what they said.

'*Why are you here?*' read the youngest contestant. 'It's asking us to tell it why we're here?' he said, incredulous, as though this were the easiest thing in the world. He didn't wait for an answer, but stepped up to the mirror, and said in a loud, clear tone, 'I'm here to win the Mind challenge.'

They waited expectantly for something to happen, and after a few moments, more words appeared in the mirror. 'Set yourself free,' read one of the women. 'As in the saying, *the truth will set you free?*'

Cleo was in the dark, like the rest of them. She had been expecting something different, and a twinge of annoyance crept into her energy.

'Maybe we need to tell it why we're here, aside from the obvious,' said a middle-aged man. He stepped up to the mirror and said, 'I'm here because my wife recently found out I was having an affair with her best friend. She told me if I didn't enter, and win, she'd divorce me. The only way to save my marriage is to win this challenge.'

As well as raised eyebrows and hidden smiles, his words also caused the mirror to change in appearance. The reflection blurred, then went pitch black, and a tunnel became visible beyond.

'Great,' said the same woman, 'let's go.' But, as she tried to step through the mirror, a shock wave hit her. It threw her to the ground, and then she vanished into thin air.

'Kicked out of the meditation,' said one of the others. 'I don't think she was supposed to step through.'

'I guess that would be me,' said the cheater, gingerly stepping towards the mirror. He reached out a hand and felt the boundary of the tunnel, his features a knot of anxiety. He breathed a deep sigh of relief as his fingers crossed the threshold, his body following them through into the tunnel beyond. He immediately disappeared from view, the hole closing, a flawless mirror blocking their way once more.

The rest of the contestants stepped up to the mirror and gave their reasons one by one. Cleo was careful to lag behind, both so she could learn a bit about her competition, and also because she didn't want them to know why she was really here. The old couple went through next, without incident. They were here because they were husband and wife, had lived long lives together, and had run out of entertainment. The challenge had presented a great opportunity for them to do something exciting, and they had leapt at the chance.

Then came another of the middle-aged women. 'I'm here to make a name for myself,' she said sheepishly. Nothing happened. 'I am,' she protested, looking around at the others. 'I'm here to become famous.' Again, the mirror remained a mirror.

'Let me try,' said a portly, officious woman around the same age. 'I am here because I'm the best Mind I've ever met. If anyone can win this challenge, it's me.' Self-assurance dripped from her, but the mirror remained resolutely in place. 'It's broken,' she said, as though this were the only explanation.

'Or maybe only the first three are allowed through?' mused a man around the same age as Cleo. He stepped up to the mirror. 'I'm here because I've always had a crush on Cleo. I knew she would be here, and knew this would be a chance to impress her.' The mirror instantly changed to black, and he stepped through without a backwards glance.

'Well, I guess it's not broken,' said Cleo, going a little red.

'Apparently not,' said the youngest contestant, shooting her an infuriating look as he stepped up to the mirror once more. 'I'm here because there's a girl I'm trying to impress too. Nothing turns a head like a

160

champion,' he said honestly, and the mirror changed for him too.

Cleo shrugged. Given the two remaining women had already had a go, she stepped up to the mirror. 'I'm here, firstly, because I want to help save the world, and secondly because I'm in love with Bakko.' The mirror changed to black, and she turned to look at the other two. Something told her they were going to have a hard time getting through. She turned and stepped into the black, a jolting rush of energy dragging her forward.

She landed in a crumpled heap on a bed of soft green moss, trees rearing up all around her. The other contestants were on their feet, looking around in bewilderment. 'Where are we now?' asked the guy with a crush on her.

'I have no idea,' she said. Although she'd known truth would be a component in the challenge, she didn't know the mirror would be its execution. It was all very different from what she'd thought it would be like.

They were wondering what to do next, when a creaking, cracking sound whipped through the air around them. Six wooden doors rose in a semi-circle from the ground. Each door was distinct; short, tall, narrow, wide, one with a stained-glass window, one with a brass knocker, one with a letterbox, several with rounded tops, one with a strange triangular top, but they each had a unique number, from one to six, somewhere on their surface.

They were taking in the doors and wondering which to approach, when a voice boomed out in Cleo's head. 'Take the others through door three,' it said, evaporating as quickly as it had appeared. She looked up to see five startled faces, and walked towards door one.

'What are you doing?' asked the young boy. Your door, thought Cleo, smugly.

'Just having a look at what we're dealing with,' she said. 'I'm Cleo, by the way. I've just realized we haven't even introduced ourselves.'

'I'm Rupert,' said the young boy, giving a half wave.

'Wilan,' said the guy with a crush on her.

'I'm Glen, and this is Patsy,' said the old man, motioning to his wife, who was ignoring them, scrutinising the doors.

'Desmond,' said the cheater, walking up and examining door two. 'Were you all given a door to lead the others through as well?' he asked, casually, working his way down the row of doors.

'Were we supposed to reveal that?' asked Wilan, bunching his hands.

'Nobody said we couldn't, I suppose,' said Glen, taking a seat on the moss and watching his wife move slowly from one door to another.

'Who has which door?' asked Cleo. 'Mine was door one.'

'No, mine was door one,' said Rupert, rushing to door one, presumably to reinforce his claim.

'Maybe everyone is in this situation,' said Cleo, looking to the others. 'Which doors were you?'

'Two,' said cheating Desmond, shrugging.

'Five,' said Patsy's husband, Glen.

'Six,' said Wilan.

'I wasn't given a door,' said Patsy, continuing her minute inspection.

'So that's two for door one,' said Cleo, 'and nobody for doors three or four.'

'Bit strange Patsy's the only one without a door,' said Rupert, his youthful voice thick with suspicion.

Patsy frowned. 'Bit strange there are two people claiming to have been given door one,' she replied. Her tone was even, but her eyes were hot.

'I don't think so,' said Desmond, cutting across the tension as he inspected doors three and four. 'It's not surprising the Gods have given us something that's not straightforward. The question is, what's different about these two doors?' he asked, looking at the doors suspiciously.

'And it's basic Mind education to question everything,' said Wilan, joining Desmond by the doors. 'Even something like an explicit instruction from the Gods.'

Patsy half smiled as they all crowded around the two unclaimed doors. At least I know who my competition is, thought Cleo, studying the doors closely, along with the others.

Door three was the most plain of the lot; it had a rounded top, a handle, and a shiny brass number three in an odd location at the bottom of the door. Conversely, door four was ornate, with every possible embellishment, including a section of beautiful stained glass across the top. The number four was large, silver, and had elaborate serifs. The ensemble screamed of stately decadence, whereas door three was understated and peasant-like in comparison.

'Nothing conclusive,' said Desmond.

'Maybe we should go through door one then,' said Wilan, trying to sound casual, but falling a long way short. 'Two of us were told to go through that door, so maybe the answer is as simple as that.'

'The Gods have set us a challenge,' said Glen. 'That explanation seems a little mundane for an event of this magnitude.'

'I agree,' said Patsy, nodding at her husband's words. 'The answer has to lie somewhere in these two doors.' She looked studiously at them. 'Door three seems hopeful,' she said, then paused, trying to draw out her competition: Cleo.

'Why?' Wilan asked, ruining Patsy's attempt. 'Door four is so much more ornate.'

Patsy couldn't hide the slight purse of her lips.

'And the glossy, flashy option is rarely the path to enlightenment,' said Desmond, looking pointedly at Wilan's expensive clothes, slicked back hair, and gleaming shoes.

'There's nothing wrong with taking pride in one's appearance,' scowled Wilan, shooting a sideways glance at Cleo to see her reaction.

Feeling the weight of attention turn towards her, and not wanting to reveal her cards too early, she deflected. 'Glen, you haven't said much. What do you think?'

Patsy's eyebrows went up just a fraction. Game on.

'Honestly, I don't know,' said Glen, shooting a glance at his wife. 'But if I were to take a punt, I'd go for door four. It is my experience that, no matter how much we try to fight it, appearance is important, and door four is the most finely crafted of them all.'

'See,' said Wilan, pointedly. 'It's settled.'

Cleo knew she had to make her move, with momentum swinging towards door four's cause. But just as she was opening her mouth, Rupert jumped in.

'Well, I don't know about the rest of you,' he said, 'but the Gods told me to go through door one, and that is what I intend to do. Cleo, Patsy, I think you should come with me. Cleo, for obvious reasons, and Patsy, because you weren't given a door, and there's strength in numbers.'

The group looked curiously at Rupert, who was all puffed up with youthful gusto. Cleo was preparing to dismiss him, when, to everyone's surprise, Patsy said, 'Great; I'm right behind you.' She walked confidently towards Rupert and sent Cleo a meaningful look.

Cleo caught on immediately. 'Okay,' she said. 'Go on then, Rupert.' Urgency peppered her words. 'Lead the way.'

Rupert couldn't believe his luck, and yanked the door open with excitement, rushing through into the blackness beyond. Cleo and Patsy halted as soon as he disappeared, throwing each other a *thank the Gods he's gone* kind of look.

A loud noise erupted from the open doorway. They looked apprehensively into the black space, and, moments later, the door spat Rupert back out, slamming shut behind him. Rupert landed in an undignified heap on the floor, emitting a loud string of expletives before disappearing into thin air.

'Fail,' said Wilan, with a grin, looking to Cleo for approval.

'And then there were five,' said Desmond. 'So, what are we going to do?'

All eyes turned to Cleo. She paused a moment, deciding what to say. 'It's clearly between doors three and four,' she said, slowly. 'The choice we have is between something flashy and something simple. We have very little to go on, other than that, but, in my experience, flashy things are usually so in order to divert attention from something rotten underneath. Things that are plain and straightforward tend to be just that.'

'You make a compelling case,' said Wilan, stepping behind Cleo. 'I agree; door three it is.'

Desmond laughed at Wilan's sudden change of heart, but said, 'Okay, I'm with you.'

'I'm afraid I can't agree,' said Patsy, her palms spread upwards as she gave a shrug. 'It's got to be door four. An occasion such as this needs pomp and ceremony. Door four is the one for us.' She said it as though it were a fact, indisputable, obvious, and entirely out of their hands.

'I'm with Patsy,' said Glen, getting to his feet and standing behind his wife.

'Well, I guess there's only one way to find out who's right,' said Wilan, stepping towards door three. 'Hopefully see you on the other side,' he said, swinging the door open and stepping through. They waited, half expecting to see him returned to them, as Rupert had been. Nothing happened.

'That settles it once and for all,' said Desmond, following Wilan confidently through the frame.

'Come on,' said Patsy, taking Glen's hand and pulling him towards door four. 'There's more than one way to skin a cat.' Glen looked wary, but he was obviously loyal to his wife. They stepped through the opening, and Cleo was suddenly alone. A profound silence settled around her. With the others gone, she felt the peculiarity of the energy, the atmosphere almost snapping with electric tension. She took a deep breath, then stepped through door three.

* * * * *

Cleo emerged to find herself on a ledge, halfway up a cliff, overlooking a millpond sea. The sun was enormous as it set on the horizon, casting spectacular rays of shimmering orange light across the water. She was alone, none of the others anywhere to be seen, her only companion a chalkboard attached to the rock behind her.

'So, it's just you and me,' came a quiet voice from the edge of the cliff, making Cleo jump violently. She turned to see who was there.

'Patsy,' said Cleo, breathing a sigh of relief as she took in the old woman.

'We were the only two who persuaded others to come through our doors,' said Patsy, with a mischievous grin.

'You played it well,' said Cleo, returning the smile.

'Likewise,' said Patsy. 'You were very convincing. So, what do we have next?' She stepped up to the chalkboard. 'Hmmm,' she said, prompting Cleo to take another look.

'Triangles,' said Cleo, surprised, taking in the crude drawings that had appeared. 'There was nothing there when I looked a minute ago.'

'Well, something there now. Male energy,' said Patsy, indicating to the triangle pointing upwards. 'Female energy,' she said, gesturing towards a triangle pointing down. 'And the diamond represents joined energy.'

Cleo's energy rose with excitement. 'You know what these symbols mean?'

Patsy laughed. 'Of course. Well, I know what the ancient tribes of the Wild think they mean, anyway.'

'Ancient Wild tribes?' asked Cleo, hardly able to contain her interest.

Patsy rolled her eyes. 'It's such a shame they don't teach proper history in schools any longer,' she said, huffing a little. 'Back in a time before the Mind, Body, and Spirit Gods were worshipped separately, the people were split into only two groups: those who lived together in the cities, and those who lived in the Wild.

'Those who chose the Wild lived a nomadic, tribal existence, always moving from one place to another, trading with other tribes. They lived to conquer their energy. It is said that—alongside the furtherance of their skills—they looked for those with whom they could join their energy. This required not only practice, but compatibility, and willingness from both sides. A fleeting touch might reveal you'd found a match, but you had to trust the other. Trust them enough to put your life in their hands.'

'What do you mean?' asked Cleo, bursting with questions. 'How could a touch reveal if your energy is compatible? And what do you mean, about putting your life into their hands?'

Patsy frowned. 'Tingles,' she said. 'Have you ever felt them?'

Cleo said nothing, reeling at this news. She nodded in a way that both confirmed she had and encouraged Patsy to continue.

'When you meditate with a person who gives you this sensation, you literally share your energy with them. This heightens your abilities, especially if that person is stronger in another discipline, but it also leaves you vulnerable. The other is able to sap some, or all of your energy, and keep it for themselves. In the most extreme cases, people have taken every last ounce from another, and found them dead and cold when they emerged from the meditation, whether they meant to or not.'

Cleo shivered, realising the power Bakko had knowingly had over her, and the power Anita, Marcus, and Alexander had unwittingly had over each other.

'However,' continued Patsy, 'if you can find someone with whom you are compatible, and also able to trust, you can join your energy together, giving you the kind of power you could never hope to achieve alone.'

'But how would that help anyone? What's the point, when you would be asleep in the outside world, unable to do anything with it?'

'It's possible to half wake from a meditation,' said Patsy, shrugging. 'Back before it was considered bad form to do so, people did it all the time. It's a sensation like extreme focus, concentration, and clarity of thought, all mixed into one. When two people join their energy, they're able to do things they can't by themselves.'

'Wow,' said Cleo, stunned by the thought of what else might be out there, that had been forgotten about, or purposely cut out of modern life, or hadn't yet been discovered.

'There's been a dumbing down in recent times, of course,' said Patsy. 'It's a travesty, if you ask me.'

'I think I agree,' said Cleo, still reeling. 'What do we do now? Do you think we're supposed to join our energy?'

'No,' said Patsy, smiling knowingly. 'These signs mean other things too. For example, you would send them to someone, if you wanted to challenge them to an energy dual.'

Cleo made sense of the words just as Patsy's arms went wide. Her eyes closed, frown lines appearing on her forehead as she fanned her arms forward in a vigorous motion. There was nothing Cleo could do. Even if she'd known she was in a dual, she didn't know how to wield her energy. Could she block? Deflect? Turn her opponent's attack back on itself?

Patsy's energy hit Cleo hard in the chest, knocking her to the ground. Beautiful blue sky filled Cleo's vision, before everything went black.

* * * * *

Cleo awoke to find Bakko's face above hers, her head throbbing, vision blurred. 'I got kicked out of the meditation?' said Cleo, her voice ringing in her ears.

'Not exactly,' said Bakko.

'No. He pulled you out,' said Cordelia's furious voice.

169

'But Patsy had me beaten,' said Cleo, 'fair and square. I don't know how to dual with energy.'

'We do NOT interfere,' spat Cordelia.

'He didn't. He just sped up the inevitable and prevented me from getting a pummelling for no reason,' said Cleo, leaping to Bakko's defence. She looked to him for confirmation that this was truly what had happened. He gave a slight nod, and she relaxed. 'The outcome would have been exactly the same if he'd left me in there.'

'You don't know that,' said Cordelia. 'You have no idea what Patsy would have done next.'

'Where is Patsy?' asked Cleo, trying to move them to less dubious ground.

'She's being crowned victor, to the raucous appreciation of the crowd. Next, she will give the winner's interview, where she'll tell everyone what happened in the meditation. After that, all the challengers will take part in the presentation of prizes,' said Cordelia, as Bakko looked deep into Cleo's eyes, searching her soul.

'At least I know how to send the Relic back now,' said Cleo, sitting up, 'and neither of you two breathed a word of it. Clever of you to include someone with Patsy's knowledge in the challenge.'

'You haven't a clue the implications of what she told you,' said Cordelia, her tone barbed.

'Enough,' said Bakko, turning on Cordelia. 'You're furious with me, and you're taking it out on Cleo. If you want to fight with anyone, fight with me, later, when this is all over. For now, we need to make sure that Cleo's fit for the prize ceremony, so I'd appreciate it if you left us alone.'

Cordelia's rage burned across the room, but she left.

Bakko brushed his lips across Cleo's. 'I was worried about you,' he said, stroking her cheek. 'If you'd felt Patsy's energy… she's dangerous. Her opening punch was a fraction of what she could have done; I couldn't risk her harming you.'

'I know,' said Cleo, reassuringly. 'I don't think she would have hurt me—unless I'd tried to stand in her way—but there was nothing I could to do to fight back. I was a lamb, and she was a wily old fox. I would have surrendered if it had gone any further.'

'Really?' said Bakko, surprised.

'Of course. I can't see any advantage of refusing to realize when I'm beaten.'

'How wise you are,' he said, pulling her to his chest.

'I'm annoyed the challenges manifested in different ways to how I thought they would though,' she said.

'It was Cordelia,' he said. 'She insisted we change everything, so you didn't have an advantage. But it didn't work out badly, and we tested the same core Mind principles you and I agreed on.'

'Truth, persuasion, knowledge, and reason,' Cleo said, realising he was right. 'And as I said, at least I know how to return the Relic now.'

'Oh?' asked Bakko, amused. 'And how is that?'

'Anita felt tingles with both Alexander and Marcus, and they each represent one of the Mind, Body and Spirit disciplines. If what Patsy said is true, they need to jointly meditate, merge their energy, half wake, and then send back the Relic together.'

'And how do you propose they go about doing that?' he asked, not unkindly.

Cleo's shoulders slumped, and she let out a long breath. 'I don't know. But at least it's a step in the right direction.'

'If you say so.'

'You are so infuriating,' she said, giving him a shove.

'We do not interfere,' he said, pulling her back into his arms.

CHAPTER 10

Once the sun set, Anita returned to the crater, having told only Joslyn her plan. She made her way through the tunnel, into the storeroom, and then out into the fresh night air, the town's small buildings lit up with twinkling lights. It looked almost romantic, the smoke from fires rising into the sky, people laughing and singing as they made their way to or from the only pub in the crater.

Anita found a well-hidden vantage point and settled down to wait. Alexander had never been a morning person, always preferring to meditate in the evening, and she hoped against hope that he'd stuck to this routine. She also hoped he would meditate by the Relic, as opposed to in some hidden room, far from prying eyes.

She waited for hours, eavesdropping on the conversations of anyone who came close enough, watching as their normal lives played out before her. It was after midnight, the town quietening down, when a movement at the top of the cliff caught her attention. A procession of four or five people descended the winding path, darkness shielding their identities, Anita having to move closer to the cliff's base to see who they were. She got as close as she dared, then waited for them to come into view, recognising them all as the torches beside the path illuminated their faces.

Timi and Amber came first, followed by Anderson, the Relic expert, and his wife, Bella. As the fifth figure came into view, Anita had to fight to keep her energy steady: Edmund, the traitor.

'He seemed troubled tonight,' said Edmund.

'He's fine,' said Amber, as though she knew the inner thoughts of whoever they were talking about. 'We're so close, that's all.'

'I'm not sure,' said Timi. 'I agree with Edmund; something seemed different tonight, not that I can put my finger on what exactly.'

'It's not our problem,' said Bella, taking hold of Anderson's hand. 'We've all played our parts. Now it's down to him.'

They walked away, moving out of earshot. Anita was sure it was Alexander they discussed, and if they'd left him alone up there, then now was her chance.

She circled to the back of the cliff, finding the route she had scaled earlier in the day. She climbed deftly, the lack of light making it trickier than before, but Anita's hands and feet instinctively knew where to go.

She pulled herself over the lip and walked to the crystal curtain, unafraid in the dark of being spotted from below. She peeked through the crystals, then pushed them aside and stepped into the temple, walking silently to where Alexander sat cross-legged before the Relic.

Without hesitation, Anita sat, mirroring Alexander's position, although she sat back-to-back with him, just in case she needed to make a hasty retreat. She lowered herself into meditation, pushing her mind into his, finding her way to his familiar centre.

It was more difficult than usual, almost like she was swimming through thick, gloopy treacle, but she eventually opened her eyes to find herself next to the pool underneath the temples in Empire; Alexander's centre.

She looked around and found, to her surprise, his familiar form lying on the ground, on the other side of the pool. It was odd; she was so used to him striding towards her, arms thrown wide as he welcomed her presence in his mind. Now he hid, as though scared someone might see him.

She went to where he lay, huddled into the side of the pool, eyes closed, forehead a tight knot of worry. She crouched beside him and placed a hand on his brow, trying to iron out the unfamiliar crinkles. His eyes flicked open immediately, and relief flooded his features as he recognised her, his hands finding her torso, pulling her roughly down on top of him, into a desperate, fearful embrace. He held her to him, lips kissing her hair. She clutched him, fighting back tears, her energy on a rollercoaster of relief and joy. It was really him. He was okay.

She felt the frantic beating of his heart, and the desperation in his arms. But, to her alarm, his energy remained static, as though he hadn't even noticed she was there. She pulled back from him and forced his head up to meet her eyes. He was reluctant, looking away, and anger filled her.

'Why won't you look at me?' she said.

He finally flicked his eyes up to meet hers. Solace crashed through her at what she saw.

He pulled her back to him, holding her as though his life depended on it. She pressed herself into him, calm washing over her as his hands slid up and down her back, pulling her close, showing her he hadn't left without good reason.

Anita forced him up, sitting astride him, wrapping her arms and legs around him, clinging to him as though she would never let him go.

'Are you okay?' she asked, finally breaking the silence.

He choked out a half-laugh. 'I've been better… but you're alive… I thought…'

'Me too,' she said. She buried her face in his neck, breathing him in.

He kissed her, long and deep, one hand in her hair, the other stroking her back. Weight fell from her shoulders with every brush of his lips. He hadn't abandoned her. He still wanted her.

He broke the kiss, pulling her cheek to his. 'I missed you so much,' he breathed.

'I missed you too,' she said, running a hand through his hair, pulling him closer. 'What happened? How did you end up here?'

'The temples came crashing down around me. I was thrown back into one of them—I think the Mind, but I don't know for sure. I got to my feet and was helping a couple who'd landed near me. I must have been hit by falling debris, because the next thing I remember is waking up here, monks fussing over me, Anderson and Timi hovering around wringing their hands.

'They told me the rest of the world had become uninhabitable. They spoke of death and destruction of colossal proportions. They said whole areas had imploded, that boulders rained down from the sky, that water supplies had turned sour. They told me the Cloud Mountain was the only safe place left, that we were the only survivors.'

'And you believed them?' said Anita, an edge of scorn in her voice.

'I didn't know what to believe,' he said, energy too low for a fight. 'It wouldn't have mattered anyway. As soon as I recovered, the Mind God occupied me. My centre is the only private place I have left, and he could force his way in here, if he so wished. I suppose at least some of the world must have survived, or you wouldn't be here.' He stroked her arm down to her hand, where he caressed her fingers.

Anita yanked her hand away in frustration. 'Everything they told you was a lie,' she said. 'The world is much as it was before, but the Descendants have been overthrown, and a democratic election took place.'

'Good,' said Alexander, determinedly taking her hand back in his.

Anita's energy lept at his touch. 'Why's your energy so static?' she asked.

'I have to keep it flat, otherwise the Mind God will know something's going on.'

Anita gave him a long look, weighing up whether to believe him.

'I couldn't look at you at first because I was fighting to control my energy. If only you knew how high it wants to soar at the sight and feel and sound and smell of you,' he said, a storm of desire brewing behind his eyes. He ran his thumb across her cheek. She leaned into it.

'Really?' said Anita, running a slow, seductive breath down his neck.

His energy pulsed in response, and he pushed her away, his features serious. 'Anita, don't. If he finds you in here, he'll kill you.'

A wave of rejection rolled over her. 'Fine,' she said, moving to get off him.

'Stay,' he said, pulling her back to him. 'I can't bear not to touch you.'

She sat back down, appeased, and rubbed her hands soothingly across his shoulders. 'What's he planning?' asked Anita. 'What's the ceremony for?'

Alexander's eyes went dark. 'He's planning to lure the other Gods here, so he can kill them.'

'How?' asked Anita, shocked.

'He knows they'll come eventually, to try and stop him.'

'And he's confident that he can take on both of the other Gods and win?'

'He seems to be, but I don't know why.'

'Because he's been using the Relic to syphon energy out of the world for decades,' said Anita, her tone grim.

'What?'

'That was why he put the Relic in the world in the first place,' she said, remembering that Alexander knew nothing of what Bakko and Cordelia had told them. She shared everything she knew, and he listened intently. 'But the other Gods won't interfere in the goings on of this world,' she finished, 'so I don't know how he plans to lure them here.'

'It sounds like they're going to come of their own accord,' he said. 'If they come as far as Joslyn's cave, it's simply a case of getting them into the mountain.'

'Then I'll have to keep them out.'

'Do you think the Mind challenge will really result in knowledge of how to send the Relic back?'

'I don't know,' said Anita, 'but that was the best idea we could come up with, so I hope so. In the meantime, we need to figure out a way to get you out of here.'

'Impossible,' he said, too quickly.

'Why?' Anita's face betrayed her suspicion.

'Because the only way to get me out, is to get the Mind God out of me first. Short of killing me, I don't know how we'd do that.'

'I don't know yet,' said Anita, 'but there must be a way.'

'You should go. The Mind God will end his meditation soon, and you can't be here when he wakes.'

'Why did he let me go before?' asked Anita.

'Because I attacked him, to stop him from chasing you. I don't have the energy to do that again right now. He's using a lot of my energy just being in here; it'll take time for me to recuperate.'

'I'll go,' she said, 'but I'll come back when I have a plan. Does he meditate every night, alone like this?'

Alexander nodded. 'Most nights,' he said, holding her to him like he might not release her. He kissed her hungrily, his energy flicking up once more.

Anita pulled away, feeling Alexander's energy turn reckless. 'I'll come back soon,' she said, pressing her forehead to his before lifting herself out of the meditation. It was a tricky thing to do, getting out of Alexander's mind without his help, and without disturbing the Mind God, but she managed it. It took all her willpower. Alexander's energy tried to suck her back in, and, of course, she didn't really want to go.

She emerged back into the world, opened her eyes, and sprang into action. She flew down the cliff, through the store, and back into the tunnel, barely conscious of her movements.

When she was back in the safety of Joslyn's cave, she slumped to the floor. Tears she'd locked away since Alexander's disappearance finally found their escape.

*　*　*　*　*

179

Anita told Marcus, Joslyn, and Draeus what had happened, and the mood in the cave turned sour. Marcus withdrew into himself, pointedly avoiding Anita. Joslyn and Draeus left them to it, spending every hour they could out of the cave. They said they were searching for some rare flower, although Anita suspected they wanted an excuse to spend time alone together.

A week after Anita's encounter with Alexander, she'd finally had enough of Marcus giving her the cold shoulder. 'I know this isn't how you wanted things to pan out,' said Anita, having found Marcus sitting on the edge of the cliff, feet dangling, 'but you can't refuse to speak to me forever.'

Marcus gave a shrug, tensing as Anita sat next to him. 'What are Draeus and Joslyn looking for today?'

'Lotus Cacti or something,' said Anita, looking out across the barren landscape. 'They never seem to find what they go looking for,' she added, with a wry smile.

'No.'

'Where do we go from here?' she said, turning her head to face him.

'*We* don't go anywhere,' he said, irritation creeping into his tone.

Anita sighed. Why did he always have to make things so difficult?

'I've requested my army join us,' he said. 'Seems pointless for them to be in Empire now the election's over, and we may need them here.'

'Where will they stay?'

'With my bodyguards. Sol's adamant they can find sufficient supplies to sustain everyone; the land where they are is bountiful, not to mention the army will bring a great deal with them.'

'When do you think they'll arrive?'

'Any day now.'

'Won't Amber's scouts see them?'

'What if they do?'

'They might attack,' said Anita, her tone testy.

'They might, but at least that would move us forward, one way or another.'

'Gods! Marcus, snap out of it,' said Anita, days' worth of anger boiling over. 'Why don't you just say it? Tell me how you hate that we've found Alexander. Shout at me. Just... stop avoiding it.'

Marcus turned slowly and looked her up and down. 'I feel as though the ghost of Alexander has reached into my chest and ripped me apart,' he breathed. 'I feel sick and weary and dead inside. Every time I look at you, my heart leaps with excitement, and then breaks when it remembers he's alive, that you are his, not mine. I can't stand being close to you, but not being able to touch you, kiss you, hold you. But when I'm not near you, I itch to move closer. Is that what you wanted me to say?'

Anita looked down at her hands as Marcus turned back to the horizon. 'No,' she whispered, her energy still. 'I'm sorry. I never meant...' But before she could continue, two figures appeared at the base of the cliff.

'Anita?' shouted Cleo, her voice eager. 'Is that you?'

Anita looked down at her best friend. Terrible timing, as always. 'Yes, of course it's me,' she said. 'Get your arse up here.'

Bakko and Cleo made short work of the climb. Cleo embraced first Anita and then Marcus, giving Anita a questioning look, given the tension in the air.

'Come inside,' said Anita, before Cleo could make a scene. 'I'll put the kettle on.'

* * * * *

181

They sat around Joslyn's table, drinking tea, and eating apple and cinnamon flapjack that Cordelia had insisted Cleo bring for Anita. The mood was strange; Bakko and Cleo fawning over one another on one side of the table, Marcus and Anita careful not to touch on the other.

'The election was a great success,' said Cleo, 'although Joshua pipped Gwyn to the post.'

'Who?'

'You know, the overconfident one who's always at Matthew's side.'

'Ah, yes.'

'The energy is still much as it was,' Cleo continued. 'Although, you could make a case that there's a very slight upward trend overall. And, of course, the Mind challenge bore fruit.'

Cleo turned to see if Bakko wanted to take over. She ignored Anita's surprised smile and resumed the story when Bakko showed no interest in picking up the reins. She relayed the ins and outs of the challenge, missing no detail.

'So, the symbols around the Relic depict that the three people in the drawings need to join their energy?' said Anita.

Cleo nodded.

'Then they need to half wake from the meditation and somehow use their combined energy to return the Relic.'

'Possibly, but, as I mentioned, the second way of interpreting the symbols is that they indicate a dual.'

'Maybe the people meditating have to duel with the Mind God?' said Anita. 'Or the Relic?' she added, as an afterthought, wondering if it were feasible to dual with an inanimate object.

'Maybe,' said Cleo, nodding and shrugging at the same time.

'Who do you think the three people are?' said Marcus, voice quiet but menacing.

Cleo flashed Anita a questioning look, but continued anyway. 'I think the most likely candidates are you two and Alexander, but that's only a guess, and assumes he's even still alive.' Cleo flicked a look at Anita.

'Because Anita allegedly felt energy tingles with both Alexander and me?' Marcus asked, unconcerned by the awkward tension ratcheting up a notch.

'Yes,' said Cleo, her voice small, reaching for Bakko's hand under the table.

'We found Alexander,' said Anita, sending Marcus a stern look.

'You what?' sang Cleo. 'Why didn't you tell me that straight away?'

Anita looked at her as though she were an idiot.

'Oh,' said Cleo, dropping her eyes.

'The Mind God has taken him hostage, and is possessing him.'

'But you're working on a plan to get him out?' said Cleo, as though this went without saying.

'Yes.'

'No,' said Bakko, firmly, surprising them all. 'You can't force a God out of a person; it's too dangerous. He could easily kill Alexander out of spite when he realizes what you're trying to do.'

'We can't just leave him there,' said Anita, hotly. 'And if we need him for the plan to send the Relic back, then we need to get him out.'

'As I said,' said Bakko, testily, 'you can't force the Mind God to leave Alexander, but there are other ways.'

'Jealousy,' said Anita, almost as a reflex.

'Sorry?' said Marcus.

'You said the cylinder in my Mind opened because it was jealous,' said Anita, looking Bakko squarely in the

183

eye. 'So maybe the Mind God is naturally jealous too. Maybe we need to find someone he wants to possess more, and coax him into swapping,' she said, her eyes darting between Bakko and Cleo.

'No,' said Bakko, standing up and planting both hands on the table as he leaned towards Anita. Rage hit her from both his voice and his energy. 'You will not put Cleo in harm's way.'

Bakko sent a force of energy so strong it knocked Anita backwards, onto the solid stone floor. Her head hit the ground with a sickening thud.

A blur of motion followed, everyone moving at once, Bakko somehow standing over Anita before she had time to blink, Marcus lashing out at Bakko, pulling him away, and Cleo moving to crouch over her best friend, protecting her from further assault.

'Leave her alone,' said Cleo, rounding on Bakko, her voice heavy with quiet anger.

He heeded her words immediately, moving back to his seat, silent and brooding. Marcus went to Anita's side, helping Cleo sit her up. They leant her against the jagged stone wall before Marcus fetched a fur to place between Anita and the cold, hard rock.

'What was that?' said Anita, no anger in her energy, only curiosity.

'I'm sorry,' said Bakko. 'That's never happened before.'

'Cleo has a strange effect on people,' said Anita, dryly.

Cleo rolled her eyes. 'Obviously no real damage done,' she said, giving Anita a light shove before returning to her seat. Marcus sat protectively next to Anita, his back against the wall, supporting her weight as she leaned against his arm. He glowered at Bakko.

'Seriously, what was that?' Anita repeated. 'How did you force me backwards without so much as a touch?'

Bakko looked perplexed. 'Energy, of course.'

'Like when Patsy duelled with Cleo in the Mind Challenge?'

'Yes.'

'You need to teach us,' said Anita. 'If we're to jointly meditate, and use our combined energy to send the Relic and the Mind God back, then we need to know how to use our energy like that.'

'We do not interfere,' said Bakko, his features set.

'The Mind God won't hesitate to use his energy against us,' said Anita. 'All you'd be doing is levelling the playing field.'

'We do not interfere,' Bakko repeated.

'Is that why you were leading the rebels before Matthew stepped up?' said Draeus from the entrance.

'Dad!' squealed Cleo, jumping up and giving him a hug.

'How do you always do that?' said Anita, marvelling at his ability to sneak into a room without giving himself away.

'Top secret tricks of the trade I'm afraid,' said Draeus, with a smile, before turning his attention back to Bakko. 'Or maybe we should talk about how Cordelia has been leading the Institution all this time? Which of those two activities constitutes *not interfering*?'

'And then there's how you inhabit people,' said Joslyn, her tone hostile as she appeared behind Draeus, a bunch of buff-coloured flowers in her hand.

'Joslyn,' said Bakko, flicking a look towards Cleo.

'She doesn't know?' said Joslyn.

'No,' said Bakko, 'but now is as good a time as any.'

'What don't I know?' said Cleo, looking from Bakko to Joslyn with a curious mix of emotions.

'I inhabited your mother for a brief time, while she was living with the rest of the Magnei, in The Jungle.'

'You are one of the Magnei?' said Cleo.

Joslyn didn't take her eyes off Bakko for a second. 'Yes,' she said, 'and he found his way into my mind.'

'For only a few moments before...'

'... before you realized my mind was too dark a place for even a God to thrive.' She laughed, the sound light, but her eyes were made of steel.

'As I told you all those years ago, that is not the case. But now, as then, I cannot make you believe me.'

Cleo looked between Bakko and her mother, her energy turning harsh.

'Will you teach us, or not?' said Anita, refusing to allow their conversation to be derailed, not when so much was at stake. 'Seeing as you've interfered before.'

'Please,' said Cleo, shaking off her rising anger, placing a hand on Bakko's arm, begging with her eyes.

He breathed heavily. 'Fine, I will teach you, but Cordelia isn't to hear a single word about it.'

'Not a single word. We promise,' said Cleo, giving him a victory kiss on the cheek.

* * * * *

After more tense discussion, they agreed on three key areas of focus. Firstly, how to get Alexander away from the Mind God and back to the cave, so they could prepare him for his role in the plan. Secondly, Anita and Marcus would practice joint meditation, with the added difficulty of half waking. Thirdly, they would learn how to energy duel. Opinions differed about whether the duelling would really help, but, seeing as they had nothing else to do, they set about their tasks with vigour.

The next few days were difficult in the crowded cave. Cleo and Joslyn spent hours together, catching up on everything they'd missed in each other's lives.

Draeus avoided the others, going back to Marcus' bodyguard at least once a day, to gather supplies and check for news. Bakko, Marcus, and Anita practised joint meditation, to varying degrees of success. And in the evenings, they all partook in post-dinner energy duelling.

The joint meditations were successful or otherwise depending on Anita and Marcus' moods. The tingles between them were acute, and to start, they could concentrate on little else. Anita found it frustrating not being able to control her energy, and Marcus was simply embarrassed. Bakko's remedy was for them to spend all their time together, touching if possible.

After a couple of uncomfortable days, they slipped back into old habits, small touches between them becoming natural. Their knees and arms brushed when they sat, and they always stood close together. Bakko was pleased with their progress.

They could now half-wake from their meditations in two out of every three attempts, and it was getting easier with each successful effort. But the more comfortable they became, the more thoughts of intimate activities came unbidden to Anita's mind.

Marcus and Anita sat facing each other next to Joslyn's bed, legs crossed, fingers entwined, as they meditated into Bakko's mind. They found it easier to learn new skills when Bakko hosted their meditations, as it was one less thing for either of them to worry about.

They walked through Bakko's ever-morphing landscape, holding hands, Marcus idly running his thumb down the inside of Anita's palm. This level of intimacy was now so normal, Anita barely even realized he was doing it.

They stopped beside a pool of bubbling water, and before she could stop him, Marcus jumped in, pulling

Anita with him. They broke the surface and Marcus swam away, laughing as Anita splashed and chased him. She caught him and jumped onto his back, about to dunk him, when Bakko appeared.

'I thought you were practising half-waking, or am I mistaken?' said Bakko, amused.

'Don't look at me,' said Anita, slipping off Marcus' back, pulling him towards the shore.

'Thought I would lighten the mood, that's all,' said Marcus, slipping his arm around Anita, tickling a spot between her ribs. She squirmed away from his fingers.

'Don't let me keep you if you have more important things to do,' said Bakko.

'Come on,' said Anita, breaking contact as she climbed out of the water, feeling a gaping loss at the absence of Marcus' touch.

Marcus climbed out after her and took her hand, harmony settling once more. 'Okay,' said Marcus. He turned to face Anita and took her other hand. 'Ready?'

'Of course,' she replied, closing her eyes, concentrating on coming half-way out of the meditation.

It was a tricky thing to do, as they had to move at exactly the same speed. If they went too quickly, they were liable to miss the half-way point and catapult to full consciousness, and if they went too slowly, one would invariably reach a half-conscious state before the other, which would pull them out of the meditation too.

When she was confident she'd reached the required state, Anita opened her eyes to see Marcus blinking his, adjusting to the light in the room. She felt the same relief she always did when they achieved a half-wake and looked around to see the others waiting for them.

She felt the familiar strangeness, with its almost dream-like quality. The edges of her vision were a little blurred, reactions a half beat slower than usual. Bakko assured her this was not really the case; she simply felt like that, her mind having to work much harder than usual, balancing between two states. She found it off-putting nonetheless.

'Right,' said Bakko, 'let's get to work. Cleo, you attack Anita, and Joslyn, you have a go at Marcus.'

They set to their tasks, Cleo sending a volley of energy at Anita. Her energy was strong, but there wasn't much of it, and Anita managed to absorb it, having to take only a small step back. She sent the energy back towards Cleo, who easily sidestepped the attack, but Anita had anticipated that, and sent a follow up straight away. This hit Cleo squarely in the chest and knocked her off her feet, Bakko responding instinctively, sending an energy wave towards Anita's feet. She saw it just in time, and jumped over it, but it took out Marcus, who was facing the other direction, having just sent a wave at Joslyn.

Marcus thumped to the floor, and Anita had to cover the next assault from Joslyn, which she deflected towards the ceiling. Most of it was absorbed into the stone, a small wave bouncing back, ruffling her hair as she looked around to see what would come next.

'Enough for today,' said Bakko, looking a little sheepish under Cleo's stern scrutiny. 'You two meditate into one of your own minds and wake up from there; it'll be good practice.'

Anita waited for him to elaborate about which skill they should practice, but Bakko turned and stalked after Cleo, leaving them to it. They shrugged and lowered themselves back to the floor, pushing into Anita's mind, to the Great Hall of the Magnei.

'This is where the cylinder was hiding?' asked Marcus, wandering around the space.

'Yes. According to Cordelia, this is the only non-natural structure the Gods built when they created the world.'

'And somehow it ended up in your head?'

'Yep, and even Cordelia doesn't know why.'

'The Gods are a little different to how I imagined,' said Marcus, running his hand across a tapestry. 'More like us than I would have expected.'

'I know what you mean,' said Anita, watching Marcus' progress around the room from her seated position on the floor. 'Bakko's relationship with Cleo is a good example.'

'Hmmm. I suppose they must have created our world using their own as inspiration.'

'You think there are other Gods, living lives similar to ours, wherever it is the Gods came from?' said Anita.

'It would be sad if only the three we know about existed…'

'Would it?' she said, humour in her tone.

Marcus finished his circuit and sat next to Anita on the floor.

'Maybe,' he said, taking hold of her hand, raising it to his lips.

The movement caught her off guard. She had become so used to being close to Marcus, to their physical contact, but she wasn't sure if his kissing her hand crossed a line. She looked him in the eye, questioning his intentions, and saw amusement.

'Confusing, isn't it,' he said, looking down, playing with her fingers. 'Holding hands, touching arms, hugging: all fine. But what about a kiss on the back of your hand?' he said, slowly, kissing her there. 'Or on your palm?' He kissed her palm, looking into her eyes.

A shiver spread across her skin as he ran his hand up her bare arm. 'What about my fingers on your neck, or tangled in your hair?' Anita's head dropped back at the tug of his fingers.

'A kiss on the cheek?' he whispered, his breath caressing her ear. 'Or on the lips?' he breathed, grazing his lips across hers, his eyes looking deep into her soul.

She closed her eyes and inhaled deeply, emotions warring: desire, restraint, longing, guilt. She tipped her head forward, her face rubbing against his, her fingers reaching for his cheek.

Gods, she wanted him, needed him, the comfort of his touch, the way he would cherish her with every press and nip and suck. It was so different to how it had been before between them. She wanted to lose herself in the cocoon of him, to explore. She wanted him to chase everything but this moment from her mind. But she couldn't. She loved Alexander, and he was inside the mountain, suffering every moment of every day. She pulled away.

Marcus exhaled, then dropped an arm around her shoulder, keeping her close.

'It is an interesting philosophical point,' said Anita, staring across the room.

'Where the line is?'

'I think Bakko's screwing with us, trying to challenge our preconceptions.'

'About energy?'

'About everything.'

'So our minds will be more open to new possibilities?'

'I suppose so,' she said, moving to face him, picking up one of his hands in both of hers. 'Marcus.' Her tone was serious.

Tension crept into his frame. 'I know,' he said, resignation thick in his voice. 'Alexander...' His voice trailed off.

'I'm sorry,' she said.

'I know.'

* * * * *

'You and Marcus seem more comfortable together,' said Cleo, several days later, as she and Anita enjoyed some rare time alone in the cave.

'I think we know where we stand now,' said Anita, sipping her tea. 'What about you and Bakko? He seems very... into you.' She sent Cleo a meaningful look.

'He's a little intense,' she laughed, 'but I knew that from the day we first met. He loves me, and strange as it may seem, he's never been in love before. He created energy tingles, and yet, this is the first time he's ever felt them. Can you imagine?!'

'Not really,' said Anita.

Silence settled over them.

'What'll happen when we send the Relic back, and the Gods no longer have a reason to be here?' asked Anita, looking intently at her best friend.

'We haven't spoken about it, so I don't know for sure, but I can guess,' she said. 'He has to go back to his world, where I don't belong, and I have to continue in this one, where he shouldn't be.'

'But he could choose to stay here?'

'I'm not sure it's that straightforward. Cordelia will need his help to keep Theseus from our world, so I don't think he can stay without putting us all at risk.'

'Unless they find a way to put an end to the Mind God for good,' said Anita.

Cleo shook her head. 'From what I understand, that's not what they want. They used to be the closest of friends. They want to go back where they came from and leave the world in harmony.'

'Bakko has to go.'

192

Cleo shrugged. 'All I can do is enjoy the time we have together, and deal with the rest when the time comes.'

CHAPTER 11

Cordelia sat in the office she had commandeered on the ground floor of the archives in Empire. She'd put in place an operation to find research relating to the Relic, and she ran it with military precision. Members of the Magnei—who had returned to Empire shortly after Cordelia—were helping to sift through the areas previously off limits to the public.

They'd been searching for weeks, all items methodically removed, catalogued by the archives' staff, looked over by a member of the Magnei, and put back, if they were of no use. Aside from several centuries' worth of scandal, mostly relating to the Descendants and other prominent families, they'd discovered very little.

They'd found research into energy transfer, which would probably have prevented the temple collapse, some stuff about the Relic's composition, which they kept, just in case it proved useful, and an original copy of some famous fairy tales, which made Cordelia nostalgic. Other than that, nothing.

The spring sun was low in the sky, shafts of light illuminating Cordelia's desk as she leafed through the fairy tales for the hundredth time. She smiled at the familiar illustrations; princesses and princes, witches and knights, spirits and demons, running her hands over the pages, when someone knocked on her door.

She closed the book. 'Come in,' she said, looking expectantly at the entryway. Patsy, the Mind challenge victor, appeared, carrying not one, but two books, a broad smile adorning her lined face.

'Good news?' asked Cordelia, a flutter of excitement flying around her stomach.

'I think we've finally hit the jackpot,' said Patsy, reverently placing the two items in front of Cordelia.

'Oh?' said Cordelia, raising a happy eyebrow. 'Enlighten me.'

'We know there was a time when a significant amount of Relic research took place, primarily right back at the beginning, when the Relic was first discovered.'

'Yes,' nodded Cordelia. 'Until the Descendants stamped it out.'

'Indeed,' said Patsy. 'Then, every so often, one of them would allow it again, just for another to come along a while later and put a stop to it once more.'

'Endless games of power and politics,' said Cordelia.

'Over the years, they were thorough in the destruction of related work.'

'Yes,' said Cordelia.

'But we've found two works in the Body vault, hidden in a secret compartment in the wall. The first speaks of the nature of the Relic itself, and the second makes a study of how energy is drawn to it.'

'Impressive,' said Cordelia.

'I don't think the author realized quite what they'd discovered, but… I think we know how to return the Relic.'

* * * * *

Cordelia and Patsy left for the Cloud Mountain at once. They gave strict instructions to those still searching the archives to send word immediately, should they discover anything further.

They made good time on the journey, and arrived at Joslyn's cave to a happy reception.

'Thank the Gods,' said Anita, as she saw Cordelia and Patsy crawl awkwardly over the lip of the cliff, gather themselves to their feet, and enter the cave.

Cordelia gave her a strange look as they embraced.

'Sorry,' said Anita, realising she'd just, in fact, thanked Cordelia and Bakko… 'Hard to break the habit of a lifetime.'

Cordelia smiled. 'It's good to see you.'

'You too, and about time,' she said, although she was a little wary of Cordelia now. 'We've been going stir-crazy up here; please tell me you have a way to return the Relic?'

'Maybe,' said Cordelia. 'Patsy's found several books that might prove useful.'

'That *might* prove useful?' Anita repeated. 'Cordelia, the time for staying aloof has passed, don't you think?' Her tone was harsh, weeks of pent-up irritation at being stuck in an overfull cave, with no end in sight, spilling over. 'If you would just tell us all you know, we might have a chance.'

'No,' said Cordelia, firmly, stepping past Anita and greeting the others.

Anita rolled her eyes and muttered under her breath, taking a seat on the floor of Joslyn's crowded kitchen, waiting for Patsy to share her news. Marcus sat beside her, taking her hand, entwining their fingers. There were minutes of agonising greetings, tea-making, small-talk swapping, and seat re-arranging before everyone was settled and ready to listen to what Patsy had to say.

'So, as you know,' she began, looking around at her audience, 'we have been conducting a thorough and methodical search of the archives, focusing on the areas previously off limits to the public. Austin, Marcus' father, put an end to Relic research recently, which indicated the Mind God was concerned someone was getting too close. But it's taken us weeks of searching to come across what we think he was worried about.' She paused and took a sip of tea before continuing.

'We searched the Mind Descendants' family vault first, thinking the Mind God may have kept whatever was troubling him, but we weren't to be so lucky. It was in the Body vault we finally struck gold, stumbling upon a hidden compartment with these two books inside.' She held up two small, worn books, one with a green leather cover, the other having lost its cover along the way. They were nothing more than notebooks, untidy handwriting scribbled across the pages, crossings out scattered here and there, additions crammed in the margins.

'This one,' said Patsy, showing the more dogged of the two, 'goes into detail about the nature of the Relic; its composition, character and preferences.'

'Its what?' said Anita, not sure if she'd misunderstood. 'Composition I get, but character and preferences? It has a personality?!'

'Yes. Apparently,' said Patsy.

'It's a lump of stone,' said Anita.

'Is it?' said Patsy, bringing Anita up short.

'Well, I thought so,' she said, now a little embarrassed by her outburst.

'Always challenge preconceptions,' teased Marcus, quietly, so only Anita could hear. She flushed, glad the room's attention had shifted back to Patsy.

'The text implies the Relic is more than a *lump of stone*—to use Anita's inelegant description. It suggests the Relic should be thought of… more as an animate object, albeit a stationary one.' Patsy looked around at the sea of confused faces. 'This means the possibilities for interaction are significantly increased. Indeed, it should be possible to meditate with the Relic itself.'

Anita felt opposition bubble inside her, but made herself consider the outlandish theory objectively before disregarding it. 'You're suggesting we attempt to mediate with the Relic?' she said. 'Does the notebook tell us how to do that?'

'Unfortunately, it does not,' said Patsy, 'but this is where the second book comes in. It tells us how energy is drawn into the Relic itself.'

'Someone realized the Relic was sucking energy out of the world? Who?' asked Anita, annoyed that someone else had worked out what neither she, nor Bass or Elistair, had managed to.

'It's not clear who the book belonged to, but obviously someone both very intelligent and with an open mind,' said Patsy, pointedly.

Anita gave her a dirty look, but kept her mouth shut.

'So how is energy drawn to the Relic?' asked Marcus, eagerly.

'It's complicated,' said Patsy, 'but it appears the Relic absorbs energy waves, just like any other object. However, the Relic has a way of storing this energy, and becomes more and more powerful over time, using energy gained to attract increasing amounts of energy to it. The more energy it takes in, the more it attracts, or so the author hypothesises, which might explain why the energy crisis has gathered pace in recent times.'

'So you don't think the energy has anything to do with sentiment?' asked Cleo.

'I don't know,' said Patsy, 'and energy balance is a complex beast. They probably both play a part, but now there's less energy to go around, maybe any changes due to sentiment have a more profound effect.'

'So, we should try to stop it from absorbing energy?' asked Anita. 'By meditating into it, and destroy it from the inside?'

'Or maybe we could trick the Relic into absorbing our energy, by appearing to be just like any other energy source,' said Marcus, 'and get inside that way.'

'Or a combination of both meditation and absorption?' said Cleo.

'Remember the illustrations and words the Mind God gave us,' said Joslyn. 'There needs to be a coming together of a compatible Mind, Body, and Spirit— assuming that interpretation of the symbols is correct— and they need to *look to the light* when sending the Relic skyward.'

'But, assuming we somehow rescue Alexander, and jointly meditate into and destroy the Relic, without being stopped by everyone in the Cloud Mountain,' said Anita, counting out the steps on her fingers, 'how will we then eject the Mind God from this world?' She looked to Bakko and Cordelia for an answer.

Cordelia sized her up before shrugging. 'Bakko and I will take care of that bit,' she said.

'How?'

'Once the Relic is destroyed, the Mind God will lose his additional energy. It will be re-distributed back into the world,' said Cordelia. 'With his advantage gone, Bakko and I will, together, have greater power than Theseus. Between us, we'll remove him from this world.'

'Removing yourselves at the same time,' said Cleo, looking surprised at her own words, like she hadn't meant to speak.

'Yes,' said Cordelia, firmly.

'We need to come up with a way to get Alexander out then,' said Anita, 'while keeping the two of you out of the way,' she said, to Cordelia and Bakko.

'And why is that?' asked Cordelia.

'Because, according to Alexander, Theseus is planning a ceremony where he intends to put an end to your opposition once and for all.'

* * * * *

They filled the next few days with tense strategizing. They all agreed their best chance was to get Alexander out, and for Anita, Marcus, and Alexander to practice joint meditation as much as possible before attempting to meditate into the Relic itself. But, the only way they could think to get him out, was to use someone else as bait.

That Theseus was jealous and selfish, and therefore, that it was a plan that would work, was not in dispute, but the only ones who made good bait were Cleo and Cordelia, or at least, the part of Cordelia that wasn't the Body God. They were the only ones who meant something to the other Gods.

Cordelia and Bakko flat out refused to go along with it, even though Cleo was keen to help. Knowing this, Bakko spent his time following Cleo everywhere she went, not trusting Anita and Cleo not to do something radical behind his back.

Given their stalemate, they settled on Plan B: for Anita to sneak back into the mountain, meditate with Alexander, bring him up to speed, and see if he had any escape ideas of his own. Draeus would go with her into the mountain.

They went at dusk, as the sun dipped under the horizon, making their hasty way up through the tunnel and into the storeroom above. They headed out into the night air and reached the base of the cliff without incident, Draeus marvelling at the settlement that nobody in the outside world had a clue existed.

Draeus stayed at the bottom, as lookout, and Anita scaled the familiar route to the top. She paused, listening, feeling for the presence of others, and was about to hoist herself over, when faint energy waves and then voices floated to where she hung against the cliff face.

'You're sure she'll come back?' asked a hushed male voice.

'Of course she'll come back, eventually, and everything is in place for when she does,' said Amber, her voice a low snarl.

Anita froze. Who were they talking about? Did they mean her? Their energy disappeared, presumably back through the curtain of crystals, and Anita snuck a look over the lip to see what was going on. She couldn't see clearly through the curtain, but she could make out more than one figure moving around beyond.

Warnings flashed in Anita's mind; she had to abandon the attempt to contact Alexander. Something strange was going on, and she couldn't risk running headlong into a trap. She climbed down, and Draeus appeared from a crease in the wall, concern written all over his face.

'What happened?' he asked. 'Did someone see you?'

Anita shook her head. 'I heard two voices: Amber's and a man's. I think they know I was here before, and I think they've laid a trap.'

'Are you sure?'

'They didn't use my name, but they talked about someone, a woman, coming back, and said everything was in place for when she did… and it sounded like they were trying to keep their conversation secret from whoever else was up there.'

Draeus furrowed his brow, taking in her words. 'What are our options?'

'Wait until the others leave the temple and hope the Mind God stays up there. Maybe, if he meditates alone, I could get to him. Or return to the cave.'

'Or we could stay up here and observe for a day or two,' said Draeus.

'We could do that, but… if they were talking about me, does that mean Alexander is in on their plan? I didn't think the Mind God could access Alexander's centre without him knowing…'

'I'm not sure it's that straightforward,' said Draeus. 'You know how complex and uncertain things can get when you're dealing with a person's mind. Maybe the Mind God found a way to go undetected.'

'Maybe,' said Anita.

'What's it to be?' said Draeus. 'Retreat, or stay?'

'We have to move forward,' said Anita, 'and we won't achieve that by going back to the cave.'

'We stay.'

'Yes. Hopefully I can get to him tonight. We'll watch the front of the cliff to see if they come down. If that doesn't work, we'll have to stay up here and wait for another opportunity,' she said, her mind made up.

'Okay,' agreed Draeus, with a firm nod of his head.

They traced their steps back the way they'd come, until they reached a hiding place with a good view of the front of the cliff. They made sure they were out of sight, between a cluster of large boulders, and settled down to wait.

Several hours passed. They were stiff and cold, the night air full of bite, before torchlight appeared at the top of the path. They strained their eyes, trying to make out how many people were coming down, but it was impossible to tell. They waited for them to come closer, adrenaline pumping as they watched the shadowy figures make their painstaking approach. It seemed to take an eternity for the group to reach the bottom, but they finally made it, close enough for Anita and Draeus to see who they were.

They watched like hawks, careful not to let a single person slip past unseen, Anita focusing her energy and her eyes. She identified Amber, Anderson, and Bella, Anderson's wife. Amber and Anderson conversed loudly about how they were masters of the universe, while Bella followed in their wake, energy strangely low.

Draeus and Anita waited for them to pass before comparing notes. 'Three?' asked Anita.

'Yep,' said Draeus. 'Amber, Anderson and Bella.'

'Same,' said Anita.

'What now?'

'I climb back up to the top and hopefully find Alexander meditating alone.'

'Right you are,' said Draeus, his tone more appropriate for a Sunday picnic than their current circumstances. Anita smiled into the night.

They moved carefully back to Anita's climbing route, picking their way slowly, with only the distant light of the town to illuminate their path. They made it, and Anita wasted no time before scaling the cliff. She reached the top and listened. She held her breath, blood rushing in her ears as she concentrated on picking up any faint sound or trace of energy.

After a few minutes, satisfied there was no one outside the crystal curtain, she pulled herself up over the edge, crouching like a hunting cat as she took in her surroundings. The place was quiet and empty, no signs of life on either side of the curtain, although a dim glow snuck through the crystals, betraying some source of light beyond.

She stayed perfectly still for several minutes, watching for any movement, listening for any sound. There was nothing, not a single hint of another person. Crouching low to the ground, she approached the crystal barrier. She paused as she reached it, once more straining to discover any evidence of life on the other side, but, as before, was disappointed.

She took a deep breath and lay flat on the floor, her stomach pressed against the freezing stone, a shiver working its way down her spine. She reached her hands forward and parted the crystals a fraction, enough only to get a glimpse of what lay inside. She scanned the open space, careful to take in every detail.

To her surprise, and gut-wrenching disappointment, other than the Relic, and a handful of torches around it, the temple was empty. She lay still for a moment, considering her next move. Should she retreat to Draeus, or inspect the Relic?

She weighed it up for several frantic heartbeats before crawling slowly forwards. Once through the curtain, she was up on her feet, legs seeming to move of their own accord, mind trying to stay calm and focused, but distracted by her recklessness. She reached the Relic and lay a hand on it, the familiar jagged edges as cold and uninviting as ever.

She felt it all over, searching for anything they might have missed before, or any small clue that their plan might work. She found nothing. She focused on the space around her, trying to feel the energy of the Relic, but again, nothing. She took a deep breath and turned, heading back to Draeus, but as she did, a movement on the other side of the Relic, right by the crystal curtain, caught her eye.

Anita froze and retrained her eyes, fear and dread filling her as she searched for the cause. Once again, her eyes found nothing, but a trace of energy suddenly buzzed against her back, and she spun around to see who or what was behind her. A gasp escaped her as she picked out a figure in the shadows, every ounce of self-preservation screaming at her to run. But there was nowhere to run to, because the figure had blocked her only exit.

'What are you doing here?' asked Alexander's familiar, rich voice, his body still hidden from view. The voice chilled her; it was Alexander's, but not the Alexander she knew.

'I wanted to see what all the fuss was about,' said Anita, motioning back towards the Relic, 'but that piece of junk seems as benign as ever.'

Alexander stepped slowly into the light and raised his eyebrows, mocking her. 'Benign junk?' he asked, smiling a sinister smile. 'Curious, for a benign object to put the world in such a spin, don't you agree?'

'Hence my curiosity,' said Anita, edging towards the crystal curtain, her only chance of escape.

He spotted her movement and easily headed her off, toying with her like a cat with an injured bird. 'Going somewhere?'

'I've seen everything I came to see,' she said evenly. 'It would be rude to outstay my welcome.'

'Have you?' asked Alexander, pausing. 'Seen everything you came to see, that is?'

He suddenly dropped to his knees. Anita took an involuntary step towards him before forcing herself to stop. He looked up at her and his eyes were familiar once more, a look of horror contorting his features.

'Run,' choked the real Alexander, before his eyes went dark once more.

Anita froze. 'What have you done to him?' she said, as he got to his feet, shaking his head.

'It's a great honour to be possessed by a God,' he sneered. 'I have done as I please, as I am entitled.'

Rage chased away her caution. 'Your sense of entitlement has caused a great deal of suffering; inflicting that is not your right.'

'How unfortunate for you,' he said. 'Fortunately for me, I don't have to listen to people like you. I'm a God, and can do as I please. Timi, lock her up, I'm sure we can find some use for her.'

To her astonishment, two hands seized her from behind. She hadn't felt his energy until this moment, yet he'd been standing right behind her. She responded immediately, spinning Timi over onto the floor before he realized what was happening.

She wasted no time, pelting for the place in the crystals where she'd entered, but moments before she reached it, a splitting pain struck her mind, lightning flashes cascading across her vision. Then her body fell, mid-sprint, to the unforgiving floor, and everything went black.

* * * * *

Anita disappeared over the top of the cliff, and Draeus waited a few moments to make sure she didn't immediately reappear. When she didn't, he made his way back to the front of the cliff, from where he had visibility of anyone leaving or entering the temple. He settled down and waited, tension gripping him as the minutes ticked by, still with no sign of Anita. He told himself this was a good thing; she was probably meditating with Alexander, but he couldn't shake the feeling of foreboding that was creeping up inside.

Only a few minutes later, a flame torch appeared at the top of the cliff. It waved left and right in an obvious signal to someone watching below. Draeus waited, holding his breath, knowing in his gut that Anita had been discovered.

Five figures appeared out of the darkness and flew at the steps up the cliff face, their torches betraying their progress. They made it to the top with alarming speed. They disappeared behind the crystal curtain, reappearing moments later, several of them grouped together, moving more slowly than before. The torches made pitiful progress down the descent, but as they eventually passed nearby, he could make out a female figure slung between two men, Timi bringing up the rear, his smug smile menacing in the flickering orange light.

Draeus slunk back into the darkness, fighting to keep his energy under control so as not to betray his presence. They disappeared into a tunnel in the crater's side, and he waited ten full minutes before moving from his position, making sure they really were gone, watching for any further movement from the temple. None came, so he crept slowly back to Joslyn's cave, a knot in his stomach as he tried to work out how best to break the news.

CHAPTER 12

Anita's eyes flew open as she came around, memories of what had happened flooding back, setting her on guard. She bolted upright, blood rushing to her head, making her dizzy as she sat, disorientated, on the floor. The fuzz cleared, and she forced her eyes to focus, taking in her gloomy cell, enclosed on all four sides by jagged rock walls. The only interruptions were a solid metal door and a recess holding an energy lamp, which cast a sallow glow across the room.

'Finally awake,' crowed a voice from behind her, making her jump, and sending a cool shot of adrenaline through her blood. She spun around to find an unfamiliar man leaning against the cell's wall, but she knew immediately who it was.

He was tall, lithe, and attractive, with brown skin and spindly fingers. His features were fine, with light green eyes like pools of water, mocking her where she sat.

'You're finally showing your true self,' said Anita, after several moments of careful study.

'And?' he taunted, walking towards her, 'I'm just dying to hear what you think.' He walked closer, circling her. 'Who wins? Me or Alexander?'

Anita was taken off guard by his approach, feeling helpless, like she was the prey of a snake, slowly coiling around her. A cold lick of fear took hold. 'What do you want from me?' she said, trying to divert him from his current course.

'I plan to drain your energy, slowly, until I possess it all and you die,' he said.

Anita paled, shocked by both the content and nonchalance with which he delivered the news.

'Well, you did ask,' said the Mind God, shrugging and rolling his eyes as though her reaction were melodramatic. 'But don't worry,' he continued, 'first, I plan to possess you awhile; see what all the fuss is about.'

'Where's Alexander?' asked Anita, suppressing a wave of panic that threatened to engulf her.

'Boring sod, that one. He's around somewhere. I'll probably drain him too, just to keep things tidy. But you're the one I really want... after all, you're the one who killed my favorite.'

'That's what this is about?' said Anita, incredulous. 'You want to kill me because I killed Austin? It was self-defence.'

'He was my favorite.'

'Your favorite what?'

'Host, of course. But there's also all the stuff you've been doing with the Relic... which is... irritating.'

'But you're killing the world you helped create,' said Anita, eager to learn as much as she could.

'Of course I'm not,' he snapped, rounding on her. 'I'm making it better.'

'By killing off most of the people?'

Theseus disappeared into thin air, and a splitting pain filled Anita's head. The world faded in intensity, somehow now beyond her grasp, just a little too far away for her to impact.

'Now, where shall we start?' asked a sniggering voice from inside her head.

'Get out,' said Anita, out loud.

He laughed. 'Learn to talk to me without speaking, or everyone will think you're crazy.'

'Get out of my head,' Anita thought.

'Better.'

'You can listen to all my thoughts?' asked Anita.

'Most of them. Now, let's have a look around.'

Anita sat down and meditated, following Theseus as he tore through her private spaces.

'A horse in a stable? Seriously?' He laughed, mocking her.

'You and your fellow Gods designed how this works,' she said. 'You only have yourself to blame if you don't like the results.'

Pain seared through Anita's mind.

'I won't hesitate to punish you if you displease me. Ah, strange centre... tribal... earthy, typical of a Body, I suppose. But now, this boat is unexpected, lots of Mind here, and...'

A scream filled Anita's mind. She tried to close her ears to it, but didn't know if that was even possible, when the sound was coming from inside. She shook her head, until, moments later, a great weight lifted, and she felt suddenly free.

Anita pulled herself out of the meditation, blinking as her eyes took in Theseus, slumped on the floor. She stifled a smirk. 'What happened?' she said, as the Mind God got to his feet.

'What was that?' he said, Anita surprised to find a hint of worry in his, until now, entirely self-assured tone.

'What was what?' she said, trying to hide the confusion from her face.

'I tried to link from the boat to the next place in your mind, but it wouldn't let me in,' he said, fear creeping through him, before turning to anger. He rushed to where she sat and wrapped a hand around her throat. 'What have you got in there?' he demanded, face inches from hers, hand squeezing her windpipe.

'I don't know what you mean,' choked Anita, her hands scrabbling at his fingers.

'Or who then?' he said, tone borderline hysterical. 'Are you harbouring another in there? One of the other Gods?' He pushed Anita backwards, so she was lying on the ground, a knee on her chest as he continued to choke her.

'I have nothing and nobody in there,' she whispered, 'only another place… a hall. It was hard for me to find... took a long time.' Her head swam.

Theseus let her go and exploded to his feet. 'A hall? What hall?'

'I don't know,' she lied, her voice still small as her hands assessed the damage at her neck. She hoped he wouldn't be able to make out the lie amid the cacophony of emotions mixed up in her galloping energy. 'You couldn't get in?' she asked, sitting up, curiosity trumping self-preservation.

'No,' he said, pacing around the cell.

'Has that ever happened before?'

'Of course not,' he snapped. 'I'm the Mind God; all minds are open to me.' He paused, looking curiously at Anita. 'Except the minds of the other Gods.' He rounded on her once more, his hand returning to her neck. 'Which one is in there?'

'I honestly don't know what you mean,' she said, taking comfort that his hand was a little less tightly wrapped around her throat than before. 'I've never been possessed by anyone other than you, just now.' She willed him to read her energy, to see she was telling the truth.

He pushed her back to the ground, discarding her, and started pacing.

He paced faster and faster before letting out a roar of anger, thundering towards her. 'Mark my words,' he said, in a slow, menacing voice, 'I will drain you of your energy, and it will kill you.' He left the room, slamming the heavy metal door with terrifying force.

* * * * *

Draeus finally heard voices as the others returned to the cave. It was dark, but he'd lit only one solitary light. Cleo and Bakko entered the room, Bakko pushing her up against the wall, before realizing they were not alone. He spun around and met Draeus' eyes, feeling Cleo's embarrassment and Draeus' dismay at the same time.

'What happened?' Bakko asked, taking a step towards Draeus.

'Where's Anita?' said Cleo, looking around for her best friend.

'Get the others,' said Draeus, and Cleo jumped to it immediately. She was quick about it, fetching Joslyn and Marcus from the kitchen.

'What happened?' demanded Cleo, moving around the room and turning on the lights.

'Anita was captured,' said Draeus. The others stayed silent, knowing more would follow. Draeus recounted the entire story before anyone uttered a word.

'They knew she'd been up there,' said Marcus, 'and that she'd come back.'

'Assuming Anita was the woman Anderson and Amber were discussing, then yes,' said Draeus, 'but we don't know that for sure. And we don't know what else they have going on up there.'

'You said they took her into the mountain itself?' said Bakko. 'They didn't say where they were headed?'

'No,' said Draeus, shaking his head. 'The guards didn't say a thing, and nor did Timi, who was following them.'

'There was no sign of Alexander?' said Marcus.

'No,' said Draeus.

'We have to go up there and get her,' said Marcus, resolutely. 'We have to go tonight. Hopefully we'll get there before they hurt her.'

'Your plan is to waltz into the mountain, with no idea how many people are up there, or where they're holding her?' said Draeus. 'Not to mention, we have no idea what else they have up there; energy weapons and the like. And you think we should, what? Wander around for a bit, until we find Anita and Alexander, and then, what? Escape back the way we came?'

'Who said anything about rescuing Alexander?' said Marcus.

Cleo rolled her eyes. 'Much as I don't like the idea,' she said, 'we can't just leave her there. If Anita was who they were discussing, they said everything was ready for the ceremony. You've got to admit, that doesn't sound good.'

'I agree we have to do something,' said Draeus, 'but getting ourselves captured out of sheer stupidity isn't going to help anyone.'

'We could create a diversion,' said Joslyn, quietly. 'We,' she gestured at everyone in the room, 'will go into the mountain through the tunnel. We will find out where they're holding Anita and Alexander, and what they have planned. Then we'll find a way to rescue them. At the same time, Marcus' army will attack the front of the mountain. Cordelia should lead this attack. They'll think she's enraged because of Anita's capture, and hopefully that means they'll take the threat seriously.'

'At the very least, it should draw Amber's attention away from what's going on inside,' said Marcus. 'Hopefully it'll cause chaos; none of the monks will know what to do.'

'I wouldn't go that far,' said Joslyn, shooting him a warning look. 'They are clever, astute, and they're all readers; a dangerous combination.'

Marcus looked a little abashed as the others agreed to the plan.

'Where's Cordelia?' asked Cleo.

'I'm here,' said an unfamiliar voice from the entrance. It was light, like the wind, and twice as mesmerising. A tall, beautiful woman stepped into the dim light. She was athletic, with olive coloured skin. She looked to be in her late thirties, dark hair cascading down her back, green eyes taking them all in.

'Cordelia?' said Cleo, unsure.

Bakko smiled and strode to embrace the woman. 'Finally,' he said with a laugh, 'Tatianna walks in the world we created together. At last, we can have some fun.'

* * * * *

'I possessed her,' said Theseus, pacing at the top of the mountain, where Timi had previously held court, 'but there was a place in her mind I could not reach.' He paused, looking from Amber to Timi for answers, the dramatic sunrise casting him in a golden glow, making him look every bit the God he was.

'I thought that was impossible,' said Timi.

'I am the Mind God; it's supposed to be impossible.'

'So, it would stand to reason that the other Gods had something to do with it?' ventured Amber.

'Yes,' he said, 'but there was no trace of either of them in her, and they could not have hidden from me.'

'Maybe they left something in there?' said Timi. 'An object?'

'Unlikely. It was no object, but a place.'

'Did you try to force your way in?' asked Timi.

Theseus rounded on him. 'Do I look like an imbecile?' he snarled. 'I was expelled from her mind when I tried.'

Timi paled at the implications, at the thought he might have picked the wrong side.

Theseus felt it. 'Out,' he screamed, 'get out of here.'

They both made for the exit, Timi's relief palpable as he scuttled away. 'Not you,' he said, indicating that Amber should stay.

She obliged, moving back to stand by the Mind God, waiting for his next move.

'Sit,' he said, eventually.

She did as she was told, lowering herself to a pile of rugs on the floor, keeping her eyes trained on him. 'You would like to possess me?' she asked, arching an eyebrow.

He took a long while to respond. 'It would be… strange for me,' he said, watching her.

'Because of Austin?'

'In part.'

'I know how it relaxes you,' she said.

He watched as she leaned back and unbuttoned her blouse, revealing a lace bra beneath. His mouth twitched at the corners, amused by her actions. 'How did she get in?' he asked, prowling towards her, making her lift her head to keep her eyes on him.

'I don't know,' she said, 'not yet, anyway.' A steely edge crept into her tone, but her eyes were inviting.

He walked behind her, out of her view, and her skin prickled with concern. She was used to toying with others and didn't like it when the tables turned. She felt vulnerable, unable to see his movements, fighting the urge to turn around and face him. A blur of action exploded behind her, and she felt an impact on her back. Her energy spiked, no idea what was happening, but she forced herself to remain still. She took an involuntary breath as two hands pressed into her shoulders, pausing for a moment before kneading away the tension.

'I don't think I'm the one who needs to relax,' he whispered, nipping her ear with his teeth.

She leaned back into him, her back against his chest, her head under his chin, his warm, strong hands massaging their way down her arms, across the palms of her hands, to her fingers. 'I plan to possess you,' he said, his rich voice mesmerising, 'but it'll be no fun for me if you're wound so tight.'

Amber tipped her head back and closed her eyes as his fingers intertwined with hers, tugging them gently. He wrapped his legs around her and his body heat thawed the tension in her soul, months of strain and pressure melting under his touch.

'I plan to drain Alexander and Anita together. Tonight,' he breathed. 'I need you on top form for the ceremony. We must make sure nothing gets in the way.'

'Of course,' she murmured, 'whatever you need.'

'I need to rest, and so do you,' he said, wrapping his hands around her, still holding her fingers, so her arms went with his. He lay down, pulling her with him until they lay flat, Amber on top of him, her head resting back against his chest.

They lay for several moments, their energy mingling, when, unexpectedly, Amber thudded to the ground. She arched her back, a shiver of intense pleasure running down her spine as she felt him take control. She smiled; he was finally with her, his power pulsing through her mind.

* * * * *

Sol, Marcus' most trusted strategist, sat in the cave, anxiety rising as he listened to the plan. He looked around at the strange collection of people, and tried to calculate their chances of success. He had to consider, after all, how many of Marcus' army—*Sol''s* soldiers—could be killed or seriously injured in the fight.

Marcus finished speaking, and Sol arranged his thoughts, formulating a response. 'So,' he said, looking round at their expectant faces, 'if I've got this right, the plan is for me to lead the army up the front of the mountain, assuming we can get through the checkpoints.'

He paused, and Marcus nodded.

'We will then try to force our way in, by climbing both the path to the top, which usually takes the best part of a day, but also, by finding other potential routes up the sheer cliff face.' Scepticism laced his words. 'You, in the meantime, will slip in through the back entrance, find Anita and Alexander, and then slip out again, before anyone realizes what's going on.'

'You will provide a distraction, yes,' said Marcus, failing to cover his irritation.

'But what I don't understand,' said Sol, 'is why you want to get them out so quickly.'

'I'm sorry?' said Cleo.

'Don't get me wrong,' said Sol, holding his hands up to pacify them, 'I know why this seems like a good idea, and, of course, you want to get your friends back to safety, but this is a one-time plan. If we do this now, we lay all our cards on the table. You'll more than likely be chased out of there, assuming you get out at all, which means you'll lead them to the tunnel. Then, you'll have to block it off, or they'll follow you back down here. Not to mention, we will lose men in the assault on the front of the mountain. Morale is not exactly at an all-time high, and we'll have given Amber the opportunity to experience an attack, identify her weaknesses, and learn for next time.'

'What do you propose as an alternative?' said Marcus. 'Seeing as you're not in favour of our plan.'

'In fact, I am in favour of your plan,' said Sol, 'but with a few moderations. The army is restless out here, with nothing to do, on short rations, and with reports of the energy still dropping. Soon, there'll be defections, either to Amber's army in the Cloud Mountain, or back to the cities. We need to take action sooner rather than later. And I agree, the best way to distract Amber and her army is to attack.

'However, given this will be our one and only chance to get into the mountain, we need a bigger plan. One that does everything in one hit,' he said, looking around for confirmation of their understanding.

'You think we should try to send back the Relic at the same time?' asked Draeus.

Sol nodded.

'But they haven't practiced joint meditation, at least, not all three of them together,' said Cleo, wrapping her hair round her finger in distress.

'If we wait to be entirely ready, the war will be over, and we will have lost,' said Sol.

'You think we can find Anita and Alexander, get us all to the Relic, and then send it back, with all manner of chaos going on around us?' said Marcus.

'Yes. A small force should go with you into the mountain. Once people realize what's happening, you'll need help keeping yourselves alive.'

'What about Bakko and Cordelia... I mean, Tatiana?' asked Cleo.

'They come too,' said Marcus. 'Once we've returned the Relic, we'll need them to deal with the Mind God.'

Cleo paled. 'You're right,' she said, her voice small, as she got up and left the room.

* * * * *

The door rattled open, and Alexander looked up from his cot on the floor, his energy a mix of curiosity and fear. He didn't hide his obvious surprise when he recognised Timi's agitated form. 'What are you doing here?' Alexander asked, his voice even, having learned that fighting his captors wouldn't get him anywhere.

'Come with me,' said Timi, worry written across every fibre of his being. 'Now,' he snapped, when Alexander didn't move, poking his head back through the door. 'Quickly... and be quiet.'

Alexander jumped to his feet. He didn't ask where they were going, or why, staying silent as he followed, tiptoeing through the maze of tunnels inside the mountain. Alexander let himself hope... was Timi setting him free? Had Timi been a triple agent all along? His thoughts were interrupted by Timi's hand pushing him back out of view as two monks sauntered along the corridor, too consumed in their own conversation to pay a couple of calm energy signatures any attention.

'Good,' said Timi, 'you'll need to keep your energy under control for the next bit too.'

Alexander nodded.

'Stay here and keep out of sight,' said Timi, as he rounded the corner.

'We are changing protocol to maintain security,' said Timi, his sullen voice travelling to where Alexander stood. 'I am relieving you now, fifteen minutes early.'

'What?' said a surprised voice, presumably a guard. He was clearly torn between leaping to obey and following his existing orders.

'As I said,' said Timi, 'we are concerned about security. I will oversee the transition to the next guard, and you may not be here for the changeover.'

'But...' started the guard.

'... when the Mind God gives me an order, I tend to obey it,' said Timi. 'Immediately.'

Silence followed, the guard hesitating. Alexander could only imagine the look Timi was giving him.

'Should I report to anyone?' the guard asked.

Alexander heard the shuffle of feet and jangle of keys.

'No,' said Timi. 'Do whatever it is you would normally do at the end of your shift, and consider yourself lucky for the extra time off.'

The guard disappeared without further comment, but confusion racked his energy. Alexander watched him go, waiting until his footsteps had disappeared before approaching the door where Timi stood, the key now in the lock.

'You can thank me later,' said Timi. 'Whatever you do, make sure you're quiet. The next guard will have no reason to enter... unless you give him one. Around midday, they will open the door and slide some food in on a tray. The guards are not permitted to enter, so if you stand behind the door, out of view, you should be fine. When they discover you've escaped, this is the last place they'll look.'

'What do you mean? Who's in there? Why not just let me go?' said Alexander. 'You've already shown your true colours and gone against the Mind God, so why not set me free?'

'You may think that's what I've done, but as usual, you've missed the point; I want the ceremony to go ahead,' he said, a sick smile pulling at his thin lips. 'Now, you can waste time out here trying to persuade me to do something I will never do, all the time risking that the next guard appears for his shift early, or you can walk through that door.'

Alexander gave a slight shake of the head, not for a moment understanding the motives behind Timi's actions. He reached out and twisted the cool handle, pushed the door inwards, and stepped through into the dim light beyond.

The door swung closed behind him and the lock clicked back into place, but Alexander barely heard. His eyes were fixed on the woman lying on the floor on the other side of the cell.

* * * * *

Anita had been asleep until the rattle of the door brought her back to consciousness, fuzz still clouding her mind. She lay with her eyes closed, tempted to give into the powerful pull of darkness, urging her back into its clutches, but her senses told her there was someone else in the room. Soft footsteps approached, and she forced herself awake, opening her eyes to find a figure crouching before her, brushing hair off her face.

Anita's eyes went wide, and she sat bolt upright, confusion flooding her energy. 'Alexander?' she choked. He pulled her to him, engulfing her, and she revelled in the feel of her face against his chest, his scent, his hands on her back.

221

'Are you okay?' he whispered into her hair.

'I'm fine, but… how did you get in here?' A spike of wariness shot through her energy, and she pulled back to look at him.

'Timi,' he said, hands going to her shoulders. 'He seems to have had a change of heart, unless this is a trap.' He sat, pulling her into his lap. 'What did they do to you?'

'The Mind God possessed me. He tried to force his way into the hall in my head, but somehow he got kicked out.'

'You expelled the Mind God?'

'I don't think it was me, exactly, more the place in my mind didn't want to be discovered.'

'How is that possible? Our minds are a part of us; they don't have abilities independent of us…'

'I don't know, but it turns out the hall in my head really exists, and it's the only non-natural structure the Gods put in the world. So maybe it's an exception to the normal rules.'

'Does the Mind God know that?'

'No. I told him it was a hall, but said I didn't know where it was.'

'He might work it out.'

'He might, but, even if he does, that doesn't mean he'll be able to force his way in, and I have no intention of letting him possess me again.'

'How are you going to stop him?' said Alexander, lacing his fingers with hers. 'With the power of your Mind, or your superior Body skills?' He ran his nose down hers, then placed a light kiss on her mouth.

'Both, if I have anything to do with it,' she said. 'I do have superior Body skills.' She smiled, feeling light for the first time since her capture.

'Shhhhh,' he said, silencing her with his lips, 'we have to be quiet. The new guard will be in position any minute, and I'm not supposed to be here.'

Anita ran her hand through his unruly hair and pulled his mouth back to hers. 'Then stop talking,' she whispered.

Alexander obeyed, slowly caressing her lips. She savoured the contact they had so long been denied. He ran his fingers down her side, sending shivers through her, chasing away the tension, kisses deepening with every touch. He rolled them to the floor, and she arched her back into him, the warmth of his body radiating into her soul.

Her hands reached under his shirt, finding bone and sinew where there had once been muscle. 'Alexander…' she whispered, making him look at her.

He said nothing, but looked down into her eyes, then kissed her neck, chasing away all thoughts. Their hands explored each other, revelling in the unfamiliar feel; drawn, scared flesh that had once been soft and smooth, eaten away by struggle and worry and pain.

Their energy intertwined, making Anita feel whole for the first time since before the temples collapsed. She hummed as he nipped her neck, tipping her head back, fisting his hair. He pushed down her trousers, then his own, then covered her with his body, the shock of heat as their skin met making them both gasp.

Anita wrapped her legs around his him, tipping her hips up to meet him, and barely stifled a moan as he pushed into her, clutching his back, holding on as though he might not be real. They moved together, slowly, bodies working as one, tension building, until waves of pleasure hit them, rolling through them, their energy combined.

It eventually subsided, but they clung together, minutes ticking by, neither wanting to leave the warm cocoon of their embrace.

'I missed you,' murmured Anita, stroking his face.

'I missed you too.' He pressed his lips to her's, the kiss gentle but deep.

She kissed him back, then forced herself away. She sat up and began pulling on her clothes. 'We have stuff to do,' she said.

'Shhh.' He lifted himself onto one elbow and ran his thumb across her lips. 'The guard will be in position by now,' he said, his voice low, 'and who knows how much time we have...'

'... before I'm drained of my energy?'

'He told you?'

'Yes. We have a plan though,' she said, watching his pupils dilate as he studied her, 'to return the Relic.'

'Tell me,' he said, reaching for his clothes, then settling her back in his lap.

'You, me, and Marcus need to jointly meditate, half wake, then meditate into the Relic itself.'

Alexander looked sceptical.

'I know, it sounds crazy,' she said, 'but we think that's what the images around the Relic are about. It's a long story, but it's our best chance.'

'Well, we don't have many other options,' he said. 'Show me how.'

'Okay,' she said, kissing him again, just because she could, before moving to the floor, settling opposite him, with her legs crossed. Alexander sat the same way.

'We need mediate jointly, and then both push our energy back towards the outside world. We have to be careful not to push too far, otherwise, the meditation will break, and we'll fully wake up. But obviously we need to go far enough to half wake. It's a balance that's taken Marcus and I some practice. Once we've done that, one of us needs to take the lead, the other two following unconditionally, remaining mostly passive, but lending all their collective energy to the actions of the lead.'

'You'll be the lead?'

'We think it makes most sense. Marcus and you both get tingles with me, and I get tingles with both of you,' she said, pausing as his energy dipped, taking his hand. 'I'm sorry; you know you're the one I want.'

'I know,' he said. 'I feel bad for Marcus.'

'I feel terrible, but either way, someone was going to get hurt, and I love you. Anyway, it makes sense if I'm the lead, because of the words the Mind God put next to the Relic: *she who dares will surely triumph*.'

'Makes sense to me… so, we all meditate to your centre, then we pull ourselves halfway out of the meditation, careful to maintain our connection, and then we push all our energy into you, so you have enhanced power?' he said, with a questioning look.

'You don't push your energy into me,' she said. 'If you did that, your energy would keep travelling in the direction you sent it. It's more subtle than that… you need to give up control of your energy, but at the same time entertain the notion of my controlling it, and no one else.'

Alexander raised his eyebrows but gave a willing smile. 'I'll give it a go,' he said. 'Sounds like we need all the practise we can get.'

'We do,' she confirmed, before they each sent their energy into Anita's mind.

CHAPTER 13

The sun made its ponderous way towards the earth. Clouds glowed purple and orange as its rays sliced through them, the temple's crystals casting full spectrums of light both inside and out.

'It is time,' said Theseus, sending the thought through Amber's head. 'First Alexander, and then Anita. I want to see her face when she sets eyes on him, his life force draining into me.'

Amber signalled to two guards who stood nearby, and they sprang into action, rushing off to get Alexander, to bring him to his fate.

Amber and Theseus made their way up the cliff, him still inside her mind, sucking her energy into him, bolstering his force for the ceremony to come. It felt good to be inside a Mind once more; so much easier to possess one of his own than a Body or a Spirit.

They progressed to the summit, to the temple that belonged just to him, but as they reached the top, a shout from below made them turn back. A guard raced up the path to meet them. Something was clearly wrong. They started back towards the guard, moving as fast as they could without risking a fall, Amber's mood dark.

'What is it?' Amber snapped, making it clear the guard should not hesitate in getting to the point.

'We're under attack,' she spluttered, 'an army.' The guard tried desperately to catch her breath. 'Coming up from the base of the mountain.'

'Whose army?' said Amber, unable to hide the dread clutching at her insides.

'We don't know; they haven't identified themselves.'

'Go,' said Theseus' voice, before Amber felt a weight lift from her. She turned to see Theseus standing behind her, fury contorting his face. 'Go and put a stop to this. Use whatever force is necessary. I will continue as planned.'

'Of course,' said Amber, almost wishing the Mind God good luck, but thinking better of it. Instead, she turned back down the mountain, descending at speed, the guard trailing in her wake.

* * * * *

Theseus made his way back to the top, to his temple. He walked through the curtain and a wash of power flooded through him. He took a deep breath, revelling in the sensation. Edmund, Bella, and Anderson awaited him.

'Everything okay?' said Bella, nervously.

'Of course,' he said. He couldn't let them get distracted at this crucial stage. Bella shot Anderson a look, which Theseus did not miss. 'Where is Timi?' Theseus demanded, itching to possess someone for as long as he could.

'Um… we haven't seen him,' said Bella. 'He's been gone for a while.'

'Update,' Theseus barked, ignoring that issue for now.

Edmund leapt to respond. 'We have everything ready.'

'Stand up straight and try to have some strength of character,' said Theseus.

Edmund attempted to pull himself upright, but it did nothing to help. Theseus looked to Anderson to continue.

'The crystals around the Relic are in place,' said Anderson. 'We've tested them ourselves, and the energy drain works... most effectively.' He looked apologetically at his wife.

'Good,' said Theseus, 'now get out until Alexander arrives.'

Theseus felt a presence outside the temple's boundary. A terrified person hovered at the perimeter. 'Wait,' he said, and the three of them stopped in their tracks. 'Edmund, show in whoever's outside.'

Edmund said nothing, but snapped to his task, pulling back the crystal curtain and ushering the scared man inside. 'What is it?' Theseus demanded, rounding on the man.

'I'm sorry,' the man started, faltering under the weight of their collective appraisal, 'but... but... Alexander is... um... gone.'

With a blur of movement, Theseus was standing over him, holding him by the neck. 'What did you say?'

'He was gone when we opened the cell,' the man choked. 'Someone must have let him go.'

Theseus flung the man to the ground. 'Anderson, get Anita. Do not return here without her. Take a contingent of guards with you. Edmund, find Timi, and bring him here immediately. You,' he said to the man cowering on the floor, 'search for Alexander. Put the whole place on alert. And you,' he said, whirling to face Bella, who was edging towards the exit, 'stay with me until they return.'

* * * * *

Sol surveyed their motley crew as they emerged in the storeroom. Cleo and her parents, the two Gods, Marcus, and twenty of their best soldiers stood in the near dark. He was relieved they'd made it this far without detection, and tried not to worry about the long road ahead…

'Everyone clear on the plan?' asked Sol, giving them one last chance to ask questions before they entered the fray. They all nodded, nobody hesitating for a second, and Sol nodded too. 'Good. In which case, Draeus, lead the way.'

They followed Draeus to the door at the front of the storeroom, too thick to hear through, so they had no idea what they would find on the other side. 'Open the door,' said Sol, indicating for two of his men to pull the door open a fraction, positioning himself to be able to see through the crack once they had.

'It's stuck,' said one of the men, throwing all his weight behind the task.

'It must be locked,' said Marcus. 'When Anita opened it, it swung easily, with no effort.'

'As it did when I opened it yesterday,' Draeus confirmed.

'Shit,' said Sol. 'Spread out and search the room,' he said to his men. 'Floor grates, wall grates, ceiling grates, doors, cracks, holes, I want to know about them all. Go.'

The men fanned out and methodically searched the space, which they all knew would take an age, given the sheer size of the room.

'Likelihood is they won't find anything,' said Cleo, looking around at each of them. 'We're inside a mountain made of solid rock, and even if there is another way out, there's no guarantee we'll find it.

Nobody's discovered the tunnel we came through, and Joslyn's been using that for decades.'

'So, what do you suggest?' said Marcus.

'This room is full of supplies, some of which are military. We need to force the door.'

Sol let her words sink in, considering their options. 'If we do that,' he said, 'we'll announce our arrival to everyone within earshot; we'll lose the element of surprise, and our only means of escape.'

'There must be a way to do it quietly,' said Cleo, 'and anyway, most of the noise will be in here, muffled by the door.' Nobody spoke, so she continued. 'Marcus, Dad, you never saw guards around this area, or in the town, so unless that's changed, we won't be met by an immediate force. And the door's away from the town, right? So there's a good chance no one will hear us at all, meaning, if we do this, we'll still have a real shot at being able to slip into the mountain unnoticed.'

Sol found himself nodding.

'And anyway, we don't have a great deal of choice.'

They stood in silence, considering her words.

'She's right,' said Marcus, 'we don't have time to waste. Who knows what they're doing to Anita, right at this moment, as we stand here and delay.'

'Fine,' said Sol, knowing they'd made up their minds. 'I'll give the order.'

It took half an hour of searching before they discovered a box of suitable explosives, and energy devices capable of detonating them. Sol himself placed the weapon in the lock and armed the detonator. He walked around the group, giving final orders to his soldiers, ensuring everyone was well out of range of the expected blast. When at last he was satisfied, he crouched behind a rack of shelves, did a final visual sweep, then executed.

A muted bang filled the storeroom, bouncing a little around the stone walls before being absorbed by the liberal quantities of stuff everywhere. A soldier ran to inspect the results, ushering the others forward once she'd confirmed the job was done. They swung the door open, and the small force ventured through, the soldiers sweeping the way ahead before motioning for the others to follow.

Sol was pleased to see he'd done a good job on the explosives, the door still mostly intact, only a small section blown out where the lock had previously sat, and a small amount of blackening creeping up the door, both inside and out.

They moved quickly, seeming to have gained entry without discovery, keeping low, using boulders for cover, doing all they could to avoid the notice of the milling crowd in the town below. They hurried towards where Draeus had seen Anita disappear into the mountain the night before, searching the rock carefully when they got there, no door or opening apparent.

It took less than a minute for Tatiana to discover the entrance, concealed by a fold in the rock. It looked like a natural fissure in the stone, but a few paces in, opened up into a fully fledged tunnel, torches adorning the walls, lighting the way.

They followed the tunnel, careful not to make a sound, the floor inclining steeply upwards after a short time on the flat. There was nowhere to hide if someone came this way, so their best chance was to move swiftly.

The climb was long, and after several hundred metres of steep incline, sweat trickling down their backs, Sol wondered if it would ever end. The floor levelled abruptly, and the tunnel suddenly opened up.

'Back,' Sol hissed, 'to the floor.' He waved them down with his hand. He too crouched, observing the space above the lip, creeping forward slowly to assess their options. The tunnel opened out into a circular intersection, five tunnels crossing, an intricate compass mosaic on the floor, showing north, south, east, and west.

Sol could see no clue as to where each tunnel led, and they all looked identical. 'Come up,' he said, quietly, only just loud enough for the others to hear. Draeus and Marcus stepped forward and looked around, searching for anything Sol might have missed, trying to identify anything familiar from their previous visits.

'I'll go a little way down each tunnel,' said Draeus. 'Hopefully I'll recognise something.'

Sol nodded. 'Be quick, and be quiet,' he said, 'and if you run into anyone, act like you're supposed to be here.'

Draeus smiled. 'Will do,' he said, heading off down the first tunnel, just to the left of where they'd emerged.

Draeus found nothing in the first two, each appearing to go on for some distance without change. However, the third tunnel told him exactly where they were.

'We're up by the main entrance,' he said, when he returned to the others. 'That tunnel is one of the ones around the central courtyard. There are windows looking out over the fountain.'

'Did you see anyone?' asked Cleo.

'No,' said Draeus, looking worried, 'but every other time I've been here, it was busy.'

'It's close to the front entrance though,' said Marcus. 'Maybe they've all hidden inside because of the attack.'

'Maybe,' said Sol. 'Or maybe they know we're here and soldiers are heading in our direction as we speak.'

'In which case,' said Draeus, 'we should get a move on.'

'And do what?' asked Sol. 'Do you know where to go, now we're up here?'

This had been one of Sol's biggest concerns when they'd been planning the mission: that nobody had a clue where to look for Anita and Alexander once inside. They were hoping for a lucky break, which was never a course of action which sat comfortably with him.

'Yes,' said Draeus, 'we should start with Timi's quarters at the top of the mountain and work our way down from there. At least that way, we shouldn't miss anything.'

'And when we come across monks or soldiers?' asked Cleo.

'We capture them and put them in a holding cell,' said Sol, 'and hope there aren't so many of them that we get overrun.'

Marcus looked sceptical, and Sol rounded on him. 'I had reservations about this plan from the get-go, but now we're here, we have to see it through,' he said, firmly. 'If you want a sure-fire way for us to fail, then arguing between ourselves will do it.'

'I'm with you,' said Marcus, sending Sol an apologetic look. 'Let's move.'

* * * * *

They cleared the area, finding only two monks. They held them in a dark room off the courtyard, several soldiers keeping watch as Sol peppered them with questions.

The monks didn't hesitate to share everything they knew. They confirmed that some were hiding because of the attack, but, more importantly, people were scarce because the Mind God had announced a ceremony would take place at sunset, and all mountain residents were to attend. The monks had been checking on an experiment before heading to the temple. They were in the dark about the purpose of the ceremony, but were clearly eager to witness whatever it was.

Convinced no one else was hiding in the area, they finally reached the stairs to Timi's quarters. Four of the soldiers went ahead, to ensure no immediate threat waited at the top, but it was also abandoned.

'I'll check the sleeping quarters,' said Marcus, leading two of the soldiers through the tunnel which led to Timi's rooms. To his great surprise, he found Timi, sitting cross-legged on the floor. Timi looked up at Marcus, his expression open, curiosity and excitement lighting his eyes. His palms were out to the side and facing upwards, showing he carried no weapons.

'What are you still doing here?' asked Marcus, warily. 'Don't you have a ceremony to get to?'

Timi laughed. 'What could you possibly know about that? Obviously not enough to know that's where you should be, if you wish to save your girlfriend.'

Marcus' face creased into a snarl.

'Oops, I forgot,' said Timi, 'she's not your girlfriend any longer. Her actual boyfriend is by her side.'

Marcus took a few deep breaths, looking into Timi's reckless eyes. 'You didn't answer my question,' he said calmly. 'Don't tell me you've fallen out of favour?'

'As I said,' said Timi, 'if I were you, I'd head to the temple. The ceremony you speak of is already underway, which means Anita has limited time left in this world.'

Joslyn appeared at Marcus' elbow. 'And why, pray, would we believe any words uttered by your deceitful lips?' she asked, looking him over.

'Because I now realize I've backed the wrong horse,' he said, 'and I am a pragmatic sort of man. The

Mind God can be defeated, and I believe Anita is the woman for the job, but she won't be able to do it if he drains her of her energy.'

'He's doing what?' said Marcus, reeling.

'As I suspected...' said Timi. 'The purpose of the Mind God's ceremony is to link Anita and Alexander to the Relic, then use it to drain them dry. It will kill them, and he will be strengthened by their energy.'

'How do we stop him?' asked Marcus.

'I don't have all the answers,' said Timi, shrugging. 'All I can do is tell you what I know, point you in the right direction, and hope you succeed. Or indeed, if you fail, that the Mind God doesn't suspect my betrayal.'

'Won't he already be suspicious, given your absence?' said Joslyn.

'Yes,' said Timi. 'Now, the quickest way for you to get to the temple is to follow me. If I leave you to your own devices, who knows how long it'll take. You might even arrive too late, and that might not be good for me.'

'You want us to follow you?' said Marcus, full of disbelief. 'How do we know you're not leading us into a trap?'

'You don't, but Joslyn can read my energy; she's extremely adept and will tell you I'm not lying. If you don't believe me, feel free to try and find your own way there, but I pray to the Gods you're not too late.'

Marcus looked to Joslyn for confirmation, refraining from asking how they knew each other so well. She nodded, but Marcus wasn't convinced. 'We could just go back the way we came.'

'Does that tunnel take you right to the temple?' said Timi, voice slick and irritating.

'Fine,' snapped Marcus; they didn't have time to waste. 'I pray, for all our sakes, that you're telling the truth.'

They returned to the others to find Edmund on the floor, Cleo pinning him, a knee on his back, his arms locked behind him.

'Traitor,' he shouted, as Timi emerged.

'Bit rich coming from you, don't you think?' said Cleo, twisting his arm.

Edmund yelped in pain. 'Let me go,' he said, sounding like a petulant child. 'You can't win. All you can do is beg the Mind God for forgiveness.'

Sol rolled his eyes, took a baton out of his belt, and calmly hit Edmund over the head. He went limp, his head thudding to the floor. 'Tie him up,' Sol ordered. Two soldiers snapped to it. 'And for Gods' sake, make sure you gag him.'

* * * * *

Anderson returned at the head of a column of ten men, smiling like a Cheshire cat as he and his prize swept past the gathered crowd, into the temple. His mission had yielded results far better than he could have hoped for. He looked triumphant as he assessed the ranks of senior monks and soldiers now assembled inside the temple. But his smile vanished as he saw Bella fall to the floor, the Mind God appearing before him.

'Your wife was a most amenable host,' said Theseus, watching Anderson with obvious interest. 'I believe you have something for me?'

'Um, yes,' said Anderson, faltering, his emotions raging as he fought the urge to run to where Bella lay. 'Someone moved Alexander to Anita's cell.' His eyes kept flicking to his wife. 'Nobody knows who put them together, and, of course, they're refusing to tell us.'

236

'Is that so,' said Theseus, walking slowly towards Anita and Alexander, who had been forced to their knees between several guards. 'Who put you together?' he asked, lightly, his eyes meandering backwards and forwards between them.

They looked up at him with blank expressions. They were neither hostile nor accommodating, neither scared nor comfortable, giving nothing away. Theseus' temper flared.

'I asked you a question,' he said, voice menacing and low, but Anita and Alexander kept their expressions neutral and their lips shut. 'We can play that game if you want to,' snarled Theseus, suddenly rounding on Anita, backhanding her across the face.

Alexander flinched as Anita's head snapped round, but he didn't move, and she didn't cry out. She simply returned her head to its previous position and assumed the same blank expression as before.

'Interesting,' said Theseus. 'Let's try something else,' he said, as he turned to Alexander, slowly, making his intent clear, trying to provoke a reaction. He watched Anita as he kicked Alexander in the ribs.

Alexander doubled over, winded, gasping for air, a pained expression on his face. He turned his gaze to the floor, visibly pulling himself together, forcing air back into his lungs, then lifted his head, and straightened his back. His expression returned to a carefully crafted mask of calm.

* * * * *

'No matter,' said Theseus, circling behind Anita and Alexander, knowing a prolonged and brutal interrogation would be needed to get either of them to talk. Time he didn't want to waste. 'It will be of little consequence once I'm through with you.'

The Mind God whirled away, his cloak billowing around him as he approached the Relic. 'Bring them here,' he said.

The guards immediately complied.

'First her,' he said, pointing towards Anita, his energy a torrent of venom that surprised even him.

They brought her to the Relic, forcing her to sink to a cross-legged position, chaining her hands to the ground in front of her. No hope of escape. Once they were certain she couldn't move, they brought Alexander to his tether point and repeated the process.

'Good,' said Theseus, a cruel, triumphant smile adorning his lips. 'We will begin.'

He turned and walked towards the crystal curtain, which parted as he approached. It remained open as he stood on the threshold of the temple, addressing the mass before him. Every resident of the mountain had collected, either somewhere on the ascent, or around the cliff's base.

'My people,' he said, arms wide in welcome, voice carrying with clarity to every single soul, 'my loyal and accomplished subjects.' He paused, taking a moment to savour the adoration on the faces of his devoted followers.

'This is but the first of many similar occasions that will soon come to pass. I know some of you will be curious as to what you are,' Theseus broke off, smirking, 'and, I suppose, I, am doing here. But here, in this moment, in the dying light of day, inside *my* temple, I reveal to you our collective purpose.'

He stopped a moment to dwell on his accomplishment. 'Anita and Alexander are traitors to our world, plotting and scheming both energy and political ruin, and, in part, they have succeeded.

'There are others. They did not act alone. However, they were the catalyst to our world's recent demise.'

A collective intake of breath rippled across the cool evening air, but no one dared utter even the lowest whisper.

Theseus smiled a reassuring smile. 'Today, we take control of our future. We begin to clear from our path those who wish to stop us, who wish to destabilise the world.' He built his words in a crescendo. 'When we look back in years to come, when we are living a peaceful, plentiful life, we shall site this day as the beginning. The foundation. The opening ceremony of our fight; a fight we cannot fail to win.' The crowd cheered, despite themselves, baying for the blood of the two traitors in the temple.

The Mind God turned to Anderson. 'Begin,' he commanded, striding back to the Relic, disappearing from view for most of the crowd. A self-satisfied glow settled over him.

'You lose,' he said to Anita, crouching down to take hold of her chin. 'You have lost, and Austin is avenged.' He whispered the words, squeezing her face so hard that he knew pain radiated out from his touch. She said nothing, looking into his eyes with the same steady, blank expression as before.

He threw her face away and stood up, barely able to contain his fury. 'Get on with it,' he snapped at Anderson, who was hovering on Anita's other side.

'Of... of course,' said Anderson. He picked up a string of crystals from the floor and attached it around Anita's throat. One particularly big crystal sat snugly at the back of her neck, another hanging down to lie flat against her chest. Once Anita's crystal connector was in place, Anderson quickly saw to Alexander's. It pleased Theseus that the fit was tight and uncomfortable.

Anderson nodded to Theseus once his work was done, stepping back to where Bella lay on the floor. He crouched at his wife's side, feeling for a pulse, eyes closing with relief when he felt the blood pumping under his fingers.

Theseus stepped up to the Relic. He crouched, picked up the end of Anita's crystal chain, and wrapped it around the Relic, so the crystals lay flat across its surface. A convulsion racked her body, and Theseus smiled, victorious.

Alexander paled.

Theseus picked up Alexander's chain and wrapped this too around the Relic, careful the two strings didn't touch, and that each had good contact with its surface.

One look at Alexander showed he felt the pull of his energy being drained. Theseus stood back in triumph, raising his arms to demand applause from those who could see what he'd done.

His audience responded without hesitation, unable to tear their eyes from the spectacle. Their pattering claps spread, growing as they travelled out of the temple, down the path to the crowd below. The people knew not why they were clapping, but a wave of excited energy grew as the applause travelled, the crowd believing the lies that Theseus had told them.

CHAPTER 14

Timi led them through a maze of tunnels, which twisted and turned through the mountain. They had no idea where they were going, other than that they were losing height. Cleo was becoming increasingly suspicious that he was leading them into a trap, when they popped out into the crater, the dying light of day taking them by surprise.

They were on the other side of the cliff to the storeroom, but thankfully, close to the cliff's base, around which a mass of awed humanity had gathered.

They heard Theseus' voice from above, all eyes fixed on the top of the cliff, no one paying them the least bit of attention, which was lucky, seeing as Marcus and Timi were both highly recognisable.

'Come,' said Timi, 'we need to hurry, while their attention is elsewhere.'

From above, they could hear Theseus' speech coming to a close, so they followed without protest as Timi made for a gap at the back of the cliff. They had only twenty metres to cover, but breathed a collective sigh of relief as they ducked into the shadow of the cliff, confident that only a handful of the crowd had even looked in their direction; probably not enough to cause a scene.

'We don't have much time,' said Timi. 'Theseus is about to attach Anita and Alexander to the Relic, using a string of crystals. The crystals will drain their energy. It's a slow process, but they'll need every ounce of strength they can get, if they want to return the Relic.'

'We've got to get up there,' said Marcus, 'and looks like we're going to have to climb.'

None uttered a word against the plan.

'Draeus, Marcus,' said Timi, 'where did Anita climb before? At least we know her route is a viable way to the top.'

'Round here,' said Draeus, searching for the familiar spot.

'Look for other routes up,' Sol ordered his soldiers. 'The more of us climbing at once, the better.'

They nodded and obeyed, spreading out and scanning the rock for routes to the top.

Draeus found the place where Anita had scaled the cliff. He pointed out the route to Bakko and Tatiana, who silently assumed the roles of first climbers. With barely a hesitation, Tatiana stepped onto the climb, scaling the rock at speed, as though it were as easy as walking up a set of stairs.

'Bodies!' exclaimed Bakko, rolling his eyes before pecking Cleo on the lips. 'I might not climb as elegantly, but you watch, I'll be as quick.'Cloe couldn't help a smile as she watched him climb. He was right; he was as quick, and the Gods were halfway up by the time Cleo had even chosen her first foothold.

'Cleo,' said Draeus, 'what are you doing?' He urged his daughter to take her foot off the cliff. 'Stay down here, with me.'

She didn't even falter. 'Dad, now is not the time.'

By the time Cleo reached the top, Tatiana and Bakko were nearing the front of the temple, where the crystal curtain had been pulled apart. Cleo followed them, noting that the soldiers had found three other routes up, three soldiers making it to the top at roughly the same time as her. Good, she thought, as she trailed in the footsteps of the Gods.

* * * * *

Theseus revelled in the crowd's appreciation, sucking up the energy they were freely offering, when he sensed the presence of the other Gods. They were daggers against his energy field.

With a flick of his wrist, the crystal curtain fell closed. He pushed those inside the temple out of his way, so he could walk the perimeter, searching frantically.

He moved wildly around the edge, feeling for them, trying to track their movements, finally locating them as they neared the front of the cliff. Those inside the crystal cocoon shot each other worried looks at his erratic behaviour, but Theseus ignored them. Something far more important than disciplining errant subjects occupied his mind.

* * * * *

Tatiana and Bakko stopped when they reached the front of the cliff, finding their entrance barred. They knew better than to try and force their way through the crystals, which were—no doubt—a trap laid especially for the two of them.

'Come out, Theseus,' said Tatiana, her voice soft, caring, luring. 'We mean you no harm.'

Theseus laughed. 'You think I'm that gullible? Tell me why you're here.'

'We're here because you're destroying the world we created,' said Tatiana. 'You're killing innocent people, and causing suffering where it need not exist.'

'I'm making the world the place it should always have been,' said Theseus. 'The place we created was imperfect. It lacked obedience. They were forgetting all about us.'

'And rightly so,' said Bakko. 'Our vision was for a self-sustaining world. One that didn't need us. So what if they forget us? What's it to us?'

'An insult,' he hissed. 'A disgrace. A humiliation.'

'It's what we planned,' said Tatiana.

'It's what you two planned.'

'You shared our vision at the start,' said Bakko.

'Liar,' said Theseus, through gritted teeth.

'Come out and talk to us,' said Tatiana. 'Why involve the mortals in our fight?'

'Because they belong to me, and I say they stay.'

'They belong to no one,' said Bakko. 'They have free will, another point on which we all agreed.'

'Come out and face us. We were all so close, we shared so much, we can find a way back to what we had,' cooed Tatiana.

'Leave,' said Theseus, his tone cold, 'before I set this entire place the challenge of ending you.'

Bakko smirked and shook his head. 'As if you could,' he said. 'As if they could.'

His self-assurance riled Theseus.

Tatiana shot Bakko a stern look.

'Find a way back? With him?' said Theseus. 'I think not.'

Theseus turned his back and walked away, towards the Relic.

'Where are they?' demanded Cleo, her hostile tone startling all present, no one having noticed her approach.

'Cleo, no,' said Bakko, his voice commanding, his eyes pleading. He took a step towards her, but she was too close to the curtain for him to reach her. The lure of the crystals would be too strong for him to resist.

Theseus turned, and Bakko could feel his prickle of interest.

'To whom do you refer, young Mind?' said Theseus, his voice smooth.

'Unless you're entirely witless, you know very well *to whom I refer*. Where are they?'

'In here with me,' said Theseus. 'You're welcome to join us. Simply step through the curtain, and you'll see them for yourself.'

'Cleo... no... please,' said Bakko, shaking his head. Dread like he'd never felt gripped him.

Cleo took a step closer to the threshold, as did Theseus from the other side. Marcus arrived, along with Joslyn, Draeus, and Sol, but she ignored them.

'I want to see them,' said Cleo, edging even closer.

Bakko's energy went wild, his arm reaching toward her, beckoning to her. Cleo didn't look at him, and that fractured his heart.

She threw Marcus and Sol meaningful looks, inclining her head towards the curtain. 'Help me,' she mouthed silently, the crystals obstructing her face from Theseus' view. They nodded, catching her meaning, and crept to stand either side of her, closer to the curtain than Bakko could go.

'The curtain won't hurt me if I try to step through?' she asked, now so close to Theseus that they were almost touching.

'It's designed to lure Gods, not people. You're not at any risk,' he said.

She reached out her hand, hovering tantalisingly close to the barrier. Theseus' hand mirrored hers from the other side.

'Very well,' she said. 'I suppose I'll have to trust you.' Her fingers met the crystals and Theseus' hand shot out to grab her, taking hold around her wrist. As soon as he made contact, she threw her weight backwards, Sol and Marcus already in motion, surging forward to grab Theseus' arm. Using their combined weight, they pulled him free of his protection.

Theseus was half a beat too slow in mustering his defences. He hadn't expected a trap, and wasn't a natural warrior, nor in possession of much in the way of Body skills.

He'd been so caught up in Cleo's capture that he'd let down his guard. He gave a cry of fury as they pulled him free of the temple.

Bakko and Tatiana were on him at once, surging forward, grabbing him, then retreating to the cliff's edge, away from the safety of his temple.

* * * * *

Cleo, Marcus, Sol, and the soldiers stormed through the curtain, assessing the threat. They were met with little open opposition, most of those inside wearing traditional monk's robes, staring aghast at the events unfolding before their eyes.

There were, however, a handful of Amber's guards, who did what they could to repel the invading force. Marcus was glad to see that none of Amber's troops had weapons—presumably not permitted inside the temple—so they had no choice but to fight hand to hand.

Sol's force carried an array of tools: knives, batons, and energy stunners. They put them to good use, a neat row of Amber's guards convulsing on the floor in no time.

Cleo and Marcus dodged the fighting, making a beeline for the Relic, where Anita and Alexander sat on the floor.

Marcus crouched at Anita's side, relief written across her features. His hands moved to the crystals at her neck, working the clasp free.

Cleo made for the Relic itself, planning to tear the crystal ropes away from its surface.

'Wait,' shouted Anita.

Marcus and Cleo's movements ceased at once.

'The Mind God has made a connection between us and the heart of the Relic. We can just as easily use it for our own purposes. Undo these chains,' she said, rattling her hands to emphasise her point.

Marcus quickly searched the bodies of the convulsing guards, finding the keys on his third attempt. He undid the chains and Anita moved her hands to her throat, where her fingers worked the choker free. The pull of the Relic ceased as the crystals left skin around her neck. She kept hold of the rope, keeping the connection open, and instructed Alexander to do the same.

'Take my hands,' she said, holding out her hands to Marcus and Alexander. 'It's now or never.'

* * * * *

Marcus and Alexander nodded and reached for her, the familiar tingles spreading through each of them, their connection, at this moment, stronger than it had ever been.

'The inscriptions told us to *look to the light*,' said Anita, eyeing the sun, not far above the horizon. 'Face the light,' she said, and they stepped around the Relic, until they were facing the sun. 'Now, we meditate.' She pulled them down to sit on the ground. 'To my centre.'

Marcus and Alexander wasted no time before sending their energy into Anita, her mind lighting up at the influx of power. She'd never meditated with two others, and she felt lightheaded at the surge of strength that forced its way in. She opened her eyes to find Alexander and Marcus in her Mind's centre, their chests, as usual here, bare and distracting. They were both uncomfortable, staring at her with a look of concern.

'I'm fine. It's just… different having you both in here,' she said, relaxing enough to send them a reassuring smile. 'We've never done this all together, so how do we make sure we wake up at the same speed?'

'You two practiced?' asked Marcus, surprised.

'Yes,' said Anita. 'For some strange reason, Timi moved Alexander into my cell. We've had a few hours together.'

Marcus nodded. 'Timi helped us too,' he said. 'He told us where you were, what was going on, and then led us back here, to rescue you.'

'Someone's had a change of heart,' said Anita. 'Maybe the Mind God is too crazy, even for him.'

'How are we going to do this?' said Alexander, his urgency rallying them to their task.

'Let's just concentrate on getting back to our bodies,' said Anita. 'If we go slowly, it might just work.'

'Okay,' said Alexander. 'On three?'

Anita nodded. 'Ready?' she asked, not waiting for an answer. 'One, two, three.' They all forced their energy out of Anita, back towards the troubled world outside.

They went slowly, but rapidly picked up speed as they got closer to their goal. They missed the halfway state entirely and catapulted forcefully back into themselves.

'Shit,' said Marcus, 'that was way too fast. Maybe everything's amplified when there are three people?'

'Or maybe it's the crystals,' said Anita.

A raft of noise punctuated their concentration, and they looked around together. The curtain had been pulled aside, the defeated guards bound and lined up in a row. But Sol's force now faced Amber's reinforcements, who had just reached the summit, fighting their way over the top.

'We have to hurry,' said Anita. 'To my centre, now.' She closed her eyes and pushed her energy to her centre, finding Marcus and Alexander, once again, standing before her.

'Maybe there's another way,' she said, looking from one to the other. 'What if you give your energy to me now, and I try to control us waking up? Maybe if only one of us is willing our energy back to our bodies, it will slow things down?'

It was nothing more than a hopeful idea, but they had nothing to lose. 'Okay,' said Marcus. 'One at a time, or both together?'

'Um, I don't know… let's try both together? Just… do it slowly.'

'One, two, three,' said Alexander, the words slow and calm, so as not to rush them.

Alexander and Marcus relinquished control of their energy, giving it to Anita to utilise as she deemed fit.

Anita felt a shift. An even larger weight of energy landed inside her, but it was a lumbering, unstable force, tipping slowly to the point of unbalance, soon to fall off its axis. 'Stop,' she screamed, as the energy gained momentum. 'Take it back.' She coughed, strained, screwed up her face with concentration as she tried to control the immense crush of power.

Alexander responded first, his energy lifting from the rolling force about to snowball through her mind.

249

Marcus reacted a split second later, his body inside the meditation thrown to the ground by the force of his energy returning.

'Are you okay?' asked Anita, rushing to his side, crouching to make sure he was still conscious.

Marcus turned over, his eyes dazed. 'I think I'm fine,' he said, shaking his head to clear it. 'Just a headache.'

'Me too,' said Anita. 'I think we can chalk that one up as a fail.' She ran a frustrated hand through her hair. 'What next?'

'What about if we try to surface directly into the Relic?' suggested Alexander. 'That way, even if we end up going too far, it'll propel us in the direction we want to go.'

'Worth a try,' said Anita. 'Ready?' she said, looking at Marcus, who was struggling back to his feet.

He nodded.

'One, two, three,' she said, and they all pushed their energy towards the Relic. Anita felt the moment her consciousness emerged from inside her head. She felt a pull; her body trying to snatch her back, but the crystals were an anchor, a pathway to follow, helping her resist the homeward tug.

Her energy glided through the cold, stark crystals, shafts of rainbow light filling the air, the world a blur of technicolour. She picked up speed, hurtling towards the Relic.

'Give me your energy,' Anita somehow communicated to the others. She wasn't sure if she'd said the words out loud, but whatever she'd done, thankfully, they understood.

A flood of power bolstered her as the solid wall of the Relic approached. Her plan had been to ram their energy into the Relic, hoping the sheer force of their collective power would allow them entry, but two thoughts made her hesitate. The first was the scorn Bakko had shown her when she'd admitted trying to force her way into the cylinder in her head. The second was the phrase *look to the light*. She suddenly understood that she couldn't break into something as powerful as the Relic. She had to convince it to let her in.

She had only a split second before impact, but time seemed to slow. She had to get this right. The thought dawned on her that, at this speed, they could all die if she failed. She pushed the thought aside, seeking one of the light waves also travelling through the crystals towards the Relic. She found one, reached out with her energy, and anchored herself to it.

The wave continued, unchecked, towards the Relic, Anita jolting as the wave increased their speed. She scrunched her eyes closed, bracing for impact, feeling horror in Alexander and Marcus's energy as realisation dawned. The wave crashed into the stone, and, to her surprise, Anita felt nothing but a strange weightlessness come over her. She opened her eyes, momentarily blinded by light, briefly considering the possibility that she'd died on impact. But Marcus and Alexander's rough hands took hold of her arms, hauling her to her feet.

'You did it!' said Marcus excitedly, hugging her.

Alexander gave her a bemused smile as she looked up at him. 'It would appear we've safely made it into the Relic,' he said, gesturing around them.

'It must have absorbed us along with the light wave,' said Anita, looking around. The place was a blank, open space, enclosed on all sides as though they stood in the hollowed-out centre of the Relic. But instead of a pitch-black space, as would be expected at the centre of a rock, it was bathed in natural light, rays seeping in from outside.

The waves seemed to follow a curious path around the perimeter of the cavern before shooting upwards and punching out through the jagged roof above.

'Where do you think they go?' asked Anita, walking over to the place where the waves turned sharply upwards, playing her hands through the light.

'I don't know,' said Alexander, 'but the energy somehow becomes available to the Mind God, so there must be something that connects them.'

'Something up there?' said Marcus.

'Seems the most likely place,' said Anita. 'Alexander, let me stand on your shoulders, and see if I can get high enough to have a look.'

Between the three of them, they manoeuvred Anita onto Alexander's shoulders. Happily, once standing, she could reach the ceiling, so could stabilise herself and more closely inspect the surface.

The rock she placed her hands on was pleasantly warm. The whole ceiling radiated power, Anita a little wary as she explored. No sooner had that thought crossed her mind than the rock started to crumble under her fingers. First, grains as small as sand, then pebbles, then chunks the size of fists fell to the ground below.

One of the rocks hit Marcus on the shoulder. 'Ouch,' he said, stepping back from where Alexander and Anita stood. Anita ignored him, rubbing at the roof with her hands, slowly at first, and then frantically as the ceiling fell away, doing her best to avoid the debris.

'Do you think that's wise?' said Marcus. 'What if you make the place unstable, while we're still in here?'

Anita continued to ignore him as her hands worked at the ceiling. 'Take a step to your right,' she said to Alexander.

He did as he was told, asking no questions as he held her up.

Anita continued to scratch away, pulling larger and larger chunks free, until, at last, her hand met with no resistance. She looked up and held her breath as she tried to make sense of what she could see through the hole she'd made. A cascading ball of blue light swirled above them. She pulled another few slabs away, enlarging the hole, then jumped down from Alexander's shoulders.

'What is that?' said Marcus, joining the other two directly under the hole.

Alexander looked up and took in the sight. 'Do you feel that too?' he said, turning to Anita.

'The pull?'

'Yeah… it's like it's trying to suck us in,' he said, taking a half step back.

'It looks like a mass of energy,' said Marcus.

'That would make sense,' said Anita, her eyes full of wonder as she stared upward.

'How do we get rid of it?' said Marcus.

The words were barely out of his mouth when new chunks of rock started falling from above. They shifted their attention, and found, to their horror, holes appearing in new areas across the ceiling.

'The place is imploding,' said Anita, panic in her voice as she watched the ceiling disappear. The walls were disintegrating before their eyes, the pull from above becoming stronger and stronger. 'We have to get out of here.'

'How?' asked Alexander, his eyes tracking the progress of the Relic's destruction.

'The same way we came in,' she said, 'through the wall. Make your energy available to me. I'm going to throw our combined force towards the floor, there,' she said, pointing to a spot about to be destroyed, 'where the light is coming in. When that piece of Relic disintegrates, I'll propel us through, together, aiming to get back to my mind.'

She saw Marcus' sceptical look and rounded on him. 'Unless you have any better ideas?' She didn't give him time to respond; there wasn't any time to give. 'Ready?'

Alexander and Marcus nodded.

'Now,' she said, feeling their collective power rush to her control.

Anita waited for the moment the floor began to buckle, then pitched them forwards, visualising the hole they would travel through. She imagined their combined energy returning to her mind.

The world blurred, and time seemed to slow. She felt the weight of the outside settle on her, and belief took hold. They would make it; they were almost through.

Anita could see their bodies awaiting their return, the Gods fighting, Sol's soldiers holding back Amber's, when she felt something sucking at her, pulling her backwards. The Relic, now free of its stone shackle, slowed their progress until they halted entirely. Panic fluttering in Anita's stomach.

She threw everything she had at getting them away, but it wasn't enough. The Relic began to pull them backwards, towards the sea of angry energy at its newly visible centre.

'No!' Anita screamed, as they picked up speed, clawing forwards with every fibre of her being. Her mind rebelled against the pull of the Mind God's tool. 'No. This is not how it ends.' Although, the realisation began to dawn that there was nothing more she could do.

Anita turned to look behind her, the Relic coming ever closer, and she closed her eyes, furious at herself for bringing this upon them. She searched her brain for something that might help them get away, desperately trying to unearth any scrap of hope, when she felt the force pulling them backwards check, and then diminish. She didn't hesitate, propelling their combined force towards her lifeless body with renewed vigor. They inched forward, then picked up speed, seeming to fly across the space, until, finally, they were back in the safety of her mind.

* * * * *

Bakko and Tatiana pulled Theseus to the edge of the cliff before launching their combined assault. Tatiana held him in place while Bakko battered his energy, sending wave after wave of draining offensive at every part of his energy field.

Although he couldn't physically escape Tatiana's clutches, they all knew there was little Bakko and Tatiana could do to truly hurt him. Up here, Theseus had put in place layers of defences, and his power was even more formidable now than it had been back at the beginning, when he'd first beaten the two of them and escaped into the world.

Bakko's energy diminished, the assault taking its toll. Theseus' grin got bigger and bigger. He watched as wave after wave of his guards stormed up the path to the temple. He knew the small invading force couldn't hope to hold off the sustained defense of his considerable army. Then he laughed, because he saw through his crystal curtain, to where the Relic was falling apart.

Theseus could see the churning ball of energy—his energy—at the Relic's core, and took in the lifeless figures of Anita, Marcus, and Alexander on the ground. He knew this meant they'd found a way inside, and that they could never hope to escape. Another problem solved, he thought, as he let the onslaught from Bakko wash over him. This assault would only last a short time more.

* * * * *

Cleo heard the laugh escape Theseus' lips. She followed his eyes from the Relic to the crystal curtain, then back to the Gods who fought him. She saw Sol's soldiers slowing, their movements becoming laboured, the fighting taking its toll, and knew the tide was turning against them.

She frantically looked around, searching for something, anything she could do that might help. Draeus fussed over two of Sol's men, injured during the fighting. Joslyn stood over their prisoners, making sure they stayed put. As Cleo watched, one of their prisoners somehow got to his feet, his wrists and ankles still bound. It was a foolish move, and Joslyn leapt on him before he could take a single step. They were right next to the crystal curtain, and they fell through it, unbalanced by Joslyn's pounce. Strands of crystal caught between them, ripping from the ceiling as the two of them went down.

Cleo heard a sharp intake of breath from behind her. She spun and saw Theseus pale as he took in the sight. His eyes went skyward, and she followed his gaze as he checked the fixings holding the rest of the curtain in place, worry written plain across his face.

'The curtain,' Cleo whispered, realisation dawning. She snatched up the nearest strand of crystals, and swung from it, pulling down with all her weight. Nothing happened, so she redoubled her efforts, bouncing up and down with everything she had.

Eventually, she felt movement, and the strand gave way, unceremoniously dumping her onto the floor as it fell.

'Stop that at once,' said Theseus' strained voice from behind her, but Cleo didn't even look around; she was obviously onto something.

'Dad, Joslyn, help me take down this curtain,' she shouted, jumping onto the next strand. 'I think it's protecting Theseus.'

They looked up simultaneously and rushed to help. Draeus was considerably heavier than Cleo, and the strands he jumped on gave way almost immediately. Joslyn came to Cleo, so they could work together, their combined weight much more effective.

The Mind God was lashing out now, trying to free himself from Tatiana, who held him easily in place. The beginnings of a smile tugged at the corners of her lips.

* * * * *

Anderson saw what Cleo, Joslyn, and Draeus were doing, and looked from them to his wife, who still lay lifeless on the floor. He struggled to get up, his hands and feet bound, but Joslyn was no longer there to keep him in place. He grabbed the nearest strand of crystals, applying his full weight until it gave way, landing with a jarring thud on the floor.

The other bound guards saw what he was doing and hesitated for only a moment before getting to their feet to help. Most of them hadn't been aware of what Amber had signed them up for, at least, not until after they'd arrived at the Cloud Mountain. By that time, they'd had little choice but to comply with the Mind God's wishes. But they had seen what he was capable of, had caught glimpses of the world they could expect if he were victorious, and most of them didn't like it. So they got up and threw themselves into the effort.

Seeing this, the others in the temple—monks and senior laypeople—took up the cause, until all around the temple's edge, strands fell.

With each success, the Mind God became more hysterical, until, in one great rush of noise and movement, the whole structure suddenly came free, the crystals hurtling to the ground.

The noise was deafening, crystals smashing everywhere, those who realized in time crouching to the ground, covering their ears and faces against the onslaught.

The sound ricocheted around the crater, bouncing off the stone. Silence settled across the remains of the temple, cuts peppering all present, no one escaping the carnage. The silence was heavy as they took stock, even the Gods pausing to assess the damage.

Moments later, an almost visible release of energy leapt up from where the crystals lay on the floor. It radiated up and out with a whoosh, off to seep back into the world. The Mind God lost his lustre, the smug smile wiped from his face, leaving a look of panic as the playing field levelled a little, one of his defences gone.

* * * * *

Anita, Marcus and Alexander broke their meditation, launching to their feet as soon as they returned to their respective bodies, taking in the changed scene around them. The Relic was now a ball of swirling blue energy. The curtain was gone, people everywhere nursing cuts from the crystal shards, and the Gods were fighting at the edge of the cliff.

Sol's soldiers still had their hands full, some guards still coming up the mountain, but Sol's job was easier with the curtain down. Many of their opponents had fled, obviously afraid the temple's destruction meant defeat for their cause.

'Gods,' said Marcus, looking at a loss for anything better to say.

'We need to destroy the Relic,' said Anita, turning her attention back to the only thing that really mattered.

'And how do you suggest we do that?' said Marcus.

Joslyn came to stand with them. 'By following the instructions the Mind God gave,' she said. 'The three of you need to combine your energy and send the Relic back to the light, which is rapidly disappearing, so you had better do it quickly.'

Alexander took Anita's hand and stepped closer to the Relic. 'We might need a few tries at waking up together, given our last effort.'

'Okay,' said Marcus, taking Anita's other hand. 'Can we meditate standing up through? I just feel like it'll be easier.'

'We can give it a go,' said Anita. 'Ready?'

They nodded.

'See you in there.'

They closed their eyes and meditated to Anita's centre once more. Standing seemed to heighten the sensation in the meditation, and Anita felt light-headed. She had to grab onto Alexander to stop herself from falling over. Her energy raced at the contact and Alexander gave her a strange look.

'Are you okay?' he asked, looking into her eyes, which were fully dilated, even though it was light inside her mind.

'I'm fine,' she said, brushing off his concern, 'it just feels a bit weird, that's all.'

Marcus and Alexander exchanged looks, and Anita's temper flared. 'Let's get on with it, shall we?' she said, inadvertently running her fingers over Alexander's muscular back. He narrowed his eyes at her.

'Come on then,' he said, pushing her back a little, 'we don't have much time.'

'Hang on,' said Marcus, stepping towards the others. 'It's usually easier to be touching before trying to get back outside.'

Alexander and Anita nodded. Marcus put his arm around Anita and placed a hand on Alexander's arm. Alexander mirrored him.

Anita looked from Alexander to Marcus, a strange buzz running through her at their touch. Bloody energy tingles, she thought, shaking her fuzzy head to try and focus. She looked up to see the other two watching her with worry. She huffed. 'One, two, three, go,' she said, angrily, making them focus on the matter at hand.

Leaving Anita's mind was peculiar. Instead of the world going black, they seemed to levitate, then fly, somehow breaking through the roof of the hut in her centre and out into the sunny sky above. They turned slowly around, still touching, flying higher, and then, the sunlight blinded them.

They woke to find themselves back in their bodies, but their energy was shared perfectly between them. They looked each other, trying to make sense of the sensation, raw power coursing around the circle of their hands. It built with their excitement, as they realized they'd achieved step one.

'Don't let go,' said Anita, quickly. 'Come with me to the Relic.'

They followed her lead, still holding hands as they moved towards the furious ball of energy.

'In the images that were found around the Relic, the three people held up their hands and sent it skyward,' said Anita, 'towards the light, I presume. Let me have your energy, and I'll try to send the Relic towards the sun.'

They both did as she asked, and Anita's eyes locked on the Relic, willing their combined energy to lift it up and out of the world. She tried and tried, but nothing happened. She closed her eyes and visualised the Relic moving skyward, but again, nothing.

'It's not working,' she said, giving them back their energy, 'but I think I know what might.' Her words were hesitant; she knew they wouldn't like it.

'What?' said Marcus, impatiently.

'I think I need to touch the Relic; to physically lift it.'

'You can't be serious,' said Alexander, 'you'll be killed.'

'You don't know that,' she said, eyeing the last rays of sunlight still visible over the horizon. 'The writing around the Relic said *she who dares will surely triumph*, but if I'm hurt, and I have your energy with me, I don't know what'll happen to you.'

'The writing also said *knowledge is power*,' countered Alexander, 'and we have no knowledge of how this works.'

'And maybe that was the Mind God's real meaning,' said Anita. 'We have to take a risk when we don't have all the knowledge we need. We're powerless, and at the Mind God's mercy. The only way we'll ever return the Relic is to take a leap of faith and try.'

'And maybe die,' said Marcus.

'Maybe,' said Anita, 'but it's now or never. It's up to you two; I won't do it without your permission.'

Alexander took a deep breath. 'This might be the only chance we ever get,' he said, resolutely. 'You have my energy.'

'And mine,' said Marcus.

Anita looked at each of them, smiling as she prepared herself for what she was about to do. 'If this goes wrong,' she said, moving Alexander's hand to one of her shoulders and Marcus' to the other. 'I'm sorry, and I want you both to know, I love you; I have from the very start.'

She stepped towards the Relic, reaching for it. If they said anything, she didn't hear it. Everything but the task before her fell away.

She gathered their combined energy, inching ever closer to the blue orb, then finally, with aching care, reached out and touched the cause of all their heartache.

Her hands wrapped around the mass of energy, and a lightness filled her, lifting her spirits, elating her. It promised more. All she had to do was dive into its deep blue depths and surrender her energy.

For the first time since she'd met the Descendants, she felt carefree, euphoric, filled with the excited jubilance of youth. She wanted the feeling to endure… it would be so easy to give herself over. Her mind raced, her heart thumped with longing, her fingers grasped at the energy, never wanting to let it go.

She smiled a strange smile, foreign to her lips, her head fuzzy, struggling to focus, giving into the immense power of this… thing. She was almost ready to leap, to give her energy freely, when two dark, almond-shaped eyes filled her vision. They stared into her soul, mouthing words she couldn't quite understand.

She frowned, her forehead creasing in frustration as she fought to hear the girl glaring so intently into her eyes. She shook her head, pulling herself back, fighting an internal battle, terrible turmoil swirling within her as she tried desperately to remember what was going on. What she was here to do.

A faint memory of a primitive drawing popped into her mind. With a jolt, she remembered everything, and felt sick at what she had almost done. Her mind rejected the lure of the Relic, and the full force of her burden came crashing back, hitting her with renewed force.

Gone was the feeling of weightless joy. Her limbs were heavy, shaking with the effort of holding her upright. Her mind strained to the point of breaking, the pressure of duty weighing her down. The energy of the two men who had put their life force in her hands only added to her load.

Anita took a long, deep breath, knowing what she must do. She raised her head to where the sun's final rays were glowing orange across the mountain's crater. She focused on the path that connected them back to their source, to the greatest ball of energy there was.

Anita gathered every grain of her resolve, pulling to her command all that Marcus and Alexander could give. She combined their energy with her own diminished reserves, lifted her hands, then compelled the Relic's mass upwards.

The first movement was the hardest to achieve. The Relic held onto her, resisting her efforts to send it back. She dug deeper, knowing she could defeat this enemy, believing it, telling herself all she had to do was to persist. To endure.

She had been here so many times before, when competing. Although people attributed her success to her natural Body skills, Anita knew this to be a lie. She would succeed now the same way she had so many times before: because she made it happen, refusing to give in, digging deeper than anyone else was willing. She would combine the power of her mind, body, and spirit, sustain her fight, ignore the pain, and do what it took to win. Like she always did.

This battle was the same as any other. She would give everything she had: demand that the Relic move, command it to bend to her will, believe that it would. Believing was the first step in making anything true. To Anita, it was inevitable that her adversary would eventually relent, and relent it did, beginning its unwilling journey, rising inch by inch into the sky.

* * * * *

The Mind God saw Anita's actions unfold in slow motion. He tracked her movements towards the source of his advantage, gasped as he felt her reach out and grasp it, smiled when he felt its power seduce her, and cried out when she finally rejected it. Then he felt her assault it with a tirade of power and resolve.

He felt the strength of that resolve and knew he had to stop her, to end her once and for all. He should have done, the moment she'd come into his possession. But even as he thought it, a sliver of doubt cut through him. He had, after all, been unable to force his way into a place in her mind.

Panic flooded through Theseus. He had to stop her, and he had to do it now. He fought Tatiana, trying to get to his feet, but his focus on Anita left him vulnerable. The other Gods attacked him with their energy, which sent him reeling backwards, further into Tatiana's grip.

Theseus played dead, going limp. Tatiana loosened her grip, shifting her weight so she could see what had happened to him. He seized the only opportunity he knew he would get, and used his legs to whip Bakko's feet out from under him.

Bakko went down hard onto his back, distracting Tatiana further. Then, continuing the same motion,

Theseus rolled away from her, kicking her in the face as his legs swung around, knocking her off balance.

Theseus sprang to his feet and rushed towards Anita. The Relic was now halfway to its destruction, almost out of the crater and into the sun's rays. He leapt from several feet away, disappearing from the world as he crashed into Anita's mind with shuddering force.

He clawed his way into her centre, surprised to find it undefended and at his mercy. He laughed. 'Stupid child,' he roared, to ensure his words would find her.

He was about to destroy her centre, to rip apart the fabric of her being, when he remembered the place he couldn't access. He didn't hesitate to push his energy there. With Anita's attention focused elsewhere, he could force his way in.

* * * * *

Anita felt a hostile force enter her mind and knew it could only be Theseus. She felt him enter her centre and heard his words, *stupid child,* echoing, ringing in her ears. She knew he meant to throw her off, so she let the words wash gradually away, ignoring them as she focused with iron determination on returning the Relic. It was at the edge of the crater, so close to the rays of light. They were so close to freedom.

She felt the Mind God's change of intent and part of her breathed a sigh of relief; at least she had a little more time before he destroyed her from the inside out. She felt him reach the Great Hall and her curiosity piqued; was this place still closed to him? The answer was not welcome. Theseus flung open the doors and strode inside.

A roar of anger erupted as he took in his surroundings. 'Here?' he raged. 'How can this place be here?' His voice demanded an answer, but Anita couldn't have given him one, even if she'd wanted to. Again, she ignored him, her entire being engrossed in the task of inching the Relic ever closer to its destruction.

The Mind God left the Great Hall. He careered back to her centre in a fit of fury, ripping up everything he could find. He started with the smaller items: racks of drying herbs, the bed, utensils, sending them flying.

Anita felt the damage as a searing pain through her skull. She blinked back tears, but forced herself to keep going; just a few more seconds.

Theseus moved to the fire in her centre, smothering the flames with a nearby fur.

It felt as though Anita's mind were splitting in two, the light of hope inside her burning a little less brightly.

He targeted the walls next, finding a knife and cutting holes in the canvas.

Shooting, stabbing pain forked through Anita's body and mind. She cried out, but would let nothing pull her back from her task. She might die at the hands of the Mind God, but she would free the world first.

Theseus became frantic. He rushed back to the fire and grabbed a burning ember, throwing it onto a pile of dried twigs on the floor. It smouldered, and he flapped the canvas from the wall, fostering a fledgling fire. It caught hold with little encouragement, and a burning pain gripping Anita, her energy rapidly depleting. But even as the flames licked across her dying mind, a note of joy radiated through her. She pushed the Relic the last inch into the light. She'd done it. They had won.

* * * * *

All eyes in the temple tracked the Relic's laborious journey to the light. The fighting stopped. Marcus, Alexander, and Cleo pulled their eyes away from Anita, to follow the Relic's slow progress through the sky.

Every one of them willed it on. Even those who had recently been loyal to the Mind God wanted nothing more than to be free. For the world to find a tranquil equilibrium.

Anita cried out in pain and dropped to her knees. Marcus and Alexander caught her, dampening the impact. They willed every last ounce of their energy into her, bolstering her.

Cleo held Anita's head, helping keep her eyes on the Relic. She pushed her hair back from her face and offered words of encouragement, not caring that she probably couldn't hear them.

Anita started shaking, her whole body straining, face sheet white, eyes dull, lips blue, skin feverish.

'Just a little further,' said Cleo. 'Just a tiny bit more.' She willed her best friend on as tears rolled down her cheeks. The Relic edged ever closer to its destruction, only moments left to go. 'Come on Anita; I know you can do this.'

A mighty crack exploded across the crater from above. Cleo tilted her face up, blinded by a flash of light that consumed everything around them.

'She's done it,' whispered Cleo. Relief rushed through her as she watched the spectacle unfold above.

The Relic was being pulled apart by the light, holes peppering its surface until they reached all the way through, fireworks shooting out in every direction. The cracking sound came again, then again, and again, and then silence.

An eerie quiet spread across the mass of bodies watching from below. Fear raced wildly through them as they waited to see what would happen next, what would happen to the swirling ball still visible in the sky.

Mothers pulled their children close. Friends held hands, silently praying to the useless Gods for mercy. Not one of them so much as blinked.

Another blinding light exploded from the Relic, a shock wave following. It somehow radiated through the bodies it hit, as opposed to knocking them over. The only ones physically affected were Tatiana, Bakko, and Anita, who were flung, with considerable force, to the ground.

Marcus and Alexander had tight hold of Anita, which softened the impact a little, but they were pulled to the ground with her. Her eyes were glazed over, staring into space.

'Anita,' said Alexander urgently, turning her head to get a better look. She stared straight through him, eyes vacant, as though no person lived inside.

Alexander felt his depleted energy return to him. Then Anita's eyes rolled back in her head, her body starting to convulse. Alexander and Marcus held her as best they could.

Bakko and Tatiana appeared at their side. Tatiana placed a piece of leather in Anita's mouth, then cradled her head. 'We have to go in,' said Tatiana. 'This is where it ends.'

'You'll kill her if you go in there,' said Cleo.

'She'll die without question if we don't,' said Bakko, turning to Cleo, soothing her. 'Trust me,' he said, his eyes locked with hers, so much he wanted to tell her; no time to find the words. Instead, he pulled her to him, and whispered, 'I love you, Cleopatra.' He kissed her deeply before turning back to Anita.

Tatiana nodded to Bakko.

'Wait,' said Alexander. 'I want to find her, wherever she is, inside her mind, and help her endure this.' He looked desperately from one God to the other.

'I don't see why not,' said Bakko, 'but...'

'But what?' said Marcus.

'If she dies when you're in there, as a result of what we have to do...'

'... then I'll die too,' said Alexander.

'We'll die too,' said Marcus.

Alexander looked at Marcus and nodded; Anita needed all the help she could get. 'Every second we waste, she gets weaker. Cleo, can you hold her down?'

'I'll try,' said Cleo.

'Sol, help Cleo,' Marcus shouted across the temple, not waiting for a reply as he and Alexander pushed their exhausted energy into Anita's mind.

* * * * *

Anita cowered in the flaming remains of her centre, crouched, knees to her chest, pain pinning her. Her body refused to respond to her commands. She sobbed silently as wave after wave of torment hit her, as Theseus worked his brutal way through every piece of her mind.

She closed her eyes and rocked backwards and forwards, barely moving an inch. She focused on that, not the torture. Her mind faltered, blackness claiming the edges of her vision, agony muddling her thoughts. She squeezed her eyelids tightly shut and threw everything she had into rocking: backwards, forwards, backwards, forwards.

Theseus reached the Great Hall once more, and the onslaught paused. Anita's pain eased a little as he walked around, taking in the space. 'Everything's here,' he said, voice laced with astonishment. 'Just as it was at creation.' He strode to a tapestry and ran his fingers across it. 'Remarkable. But too dangerous to be left.' He raised the knife he'd used to slash through Anita's mind and hacked at the tapestry.

Anita braced herself, tensing. But to her surprise, the pain never came. Or at least, it didn't get any worse.

'We can't destroy the one true temple; you know that well enough,' said Bakko's voice, from inside her mind.

A great reservoir of energy suddenly filled her, the weight almost too much to bear. So much power flowed through her that she worried she might not be able to hold it, to stop it from ripping her apart.

'Anita,' said Alexander's warm voice, as he pushed his way through the burning walls of her centre and rushed to her side. He wrapped his arms around her, pulling her to him. 'What has he done to you?' he said, stroking her hair.

'Destroyed me,' she whispered. 'My mind.'

'No,' said Alexander. 'You're going to be okay.'

'We have to put out these flames,' said Marcus. 'We need to contain the damage.'

'Yes,' whispered Anita, 'help him. I can't... I've tried... the well, outside...'

Alexander kissed her hair. 'We'll put out the flames; just hold on.'

Anita bowed her head as Alexander and Marcus rushed to the well, filling buckets, beginning their futile attempt to staunch the blaze.

* * * * *

'This isn't the temple we built,' snarled Theseus, whirling around to face his fellow Gods. 'She won't survive with all of us in here.' He laughed, then said to Tatiana, 'Your precious Anita, killed by your energy.'

'Anita's stronger than you could imagine,' said Tatiana, stepping carefully towards him. She held her hands up, as though he were a frightened puppy. 'It's over. The Relic's gone, and the people know the truth about you; they'll never follow you now.'

'They're loyal to me,' he said vehemently, swinging the knife around, bearing it at Tatiana. 'Stop. You're close enough.'

'Come back with us,' she said softly, coaxingly.

Theseus smirked. 'To what? To solitude?'

'To where we belong,' she said.

'To where we were banished.'

'That won't last forever,' she said. 'It will end soon enough.'

'No,' he snapped. 'Not soon enough.'

Bakko took a deep breath. 'What we did was wrong; we had to be punished. We knew there would be consequences if they found out what we did. It won't be more than another couple of hundred years, and then we'll be back, like nothing ever happened.'

'I will not endure it for so much as another second,' Theseus shouted, 'so you'll have to either kill me, or leave me here.'

'Or do neither of those things,' said Tatianna, surging towards him. She easily disarmed him, then pulled his arms behind his back, pinning him on his knees in front of her. 'I can't tell you how glad I am that we're back on a level playing field,' she said, throwing Bakko a victorious smile.

'Look, Theseus,' Bakko said, crouching down in front of him. 'I know it's difficult for you. It was your plan that failed, not Tatty's Body skills, or my Spirit skills. But you were unlucky, that's all.'

'Someone tipped them off,' said Theseus. 'I didn't fail.'

'Regardless, whatever way you look at it, the plan failed, and that was down to all of us. Had we been more considered about the whole thing, maybe we would have decided not to do it at all. But we didn't. We were young and foolish, and now we're paying for our actions. When our punishment is over, we'll put all of this behind us, and never try to do anything so stupid again... or, I won't at least.'

'Now,' said Tatiana, forcing Theseus to his feet, 'let's see if the door works the same way in here as it does in the hall in the real world.'

Bakko led them to the tapestry Theseus had been trying to destroy, and pulled it aside. 'Ah yes,' he said, with glee, 'the door's just where it's supposed to be.'

'Such a foolish addition,' said Tatiana. 'If anyone had found it, and worked out how to get through it… we would have been banished for eternity.'

'Or they would have killed us,' said Bakko.

'True,' she said, as she forced Theseus to stand in front of the three slabs of stone stacked horizontally in front of them. Each was a different colour.

In front of the door, the enormity of what they were about to do became real, and Tatiana looked at Bakko. 'We could put this off until we've had a chance to say goodbye,' she said, thinking of Cordelia, her host for so many years, and Cleo.

Bakko shook his head, a shadow passing behind his eyes. 'They've done their bit. It's time to do ours.'

Tatiana nodded, and Bakko placed his right hand firmly on the top slab of stone, the lightest and porous in texture. Tatiana placed her right hand on the next, grey stone, then forced Theseus's right hand into the centre of the hard black slab at the bottom. He resisted, but she pinned him to the floor with her knees and used her free hand to hold his in place. They pushed their hands into the stone, and it turned to dust under their fingers, a deep blue void opening up beyond.

'No,' said Theseus, staring into the abyss. 'I can't go back. Don't make me go back.'

'You know we have to,' said Bakko, grabbing Theseus on one side as Tatiana firmly grasped the other. They hauled him to his feet, Bakko and Tatiana looking at each other, so many unspoken words passing between them.

'Ready?' she asked.

Bakko nodded, and they stepped through the opening, forever leaving the world they'd created, returning to the exile that waited beyond.

* * * * *

Anita watched as Marcus and Alexander doused the flames burning through her centre. They weren't raging through the place as they might have in the outside world. Instead, they hopped laboriously from one area to another. Each jump chipped away a little more of Anita's resolve. She began rocking once more, barely even realising she was doing it.

Marcus rushed back and forth to get pales of water, while Alexander smothered patches of flame with an animal hide. They made slow progress, but a small kernel of hope grew as Anita watched. This, in turn, helped stem the spread of the flames.

Once she realized she had an element of control, her resolve strengthened, and she forced what paltry energy she had left into helping extinguish the fires. Within moments, the fires went out, but Anita collapsed backwards, the effort leaving her unable to even sit by herself.

Alexander and Marcus rushed to her side. Alexander scooped her up and carried her to the charred bed. Marcus hastily gathered as much padding as he could find to put beneath her.

They settled her down and Marcus took her hand, Alexander's hands on her face, stroking her hair, telling her it would all be okay.

'What's happening?' she asked, looking up into Alexander's concerned eyes. 'There's more energy in here than just ours.'

'The Gods came in with us,' said Alexander, stroking her forehead. 'They're fighting Theseus, presumably in the Great Hall.'

Anita's eyes flew wide. 'You two can't be in here,' she said, trying to sit up, to force them out.

'We'll be the judge of that,' said Marcus, squeezing her hand, 'and you're too weak to expel us. If I were you, I'd focus on staying conscious until Bakko and Tatiana have dealt with the Mind God.'

At any other time, Anita would have thrown them out without hesitation, but he was right, she was probably too weak. More than that, she wanted the comfort of their presence, and their energy. She wasn't sure she could stay conscious without their strength.

She lay back, collecting herself after the exertion of trying to sit. 'I don't want you to get hurt,' she said, her eyes fluttering closed.

Marcus pulled on her hand. Alexander tapped her face. 'No, Anita,' said Alexander, 'you can't go to sleep.'

'I wasn't,' she protested, although it was a lie; sleep pulled hard at her mind. The effort of staying awake was inordinate, and lying down wasn't helping. 'I need to sit up,' she said, giving Alexander a look that told him not to disagree.

'Okay,' he said, pulling her upright, her legs folding under her, so she sat cross-legged on the bed.

He made to sit behind her, to support her weight, but she stopped him. 'No,' she said, placing a hand on his arm. 'I need to keep myself awake. If you want to help me, think of a way to do that.'

Marcus began pacing, prowling up and down like a lion. 'How about I go to the Great Hall and find out what's going on?' he suggested, without looking at Anita. 'Maybe the Gods need help.'

At that moment, the ground beneath them began to shake, tattered canvas walls flapping wildly. 'This is it,' said Anita, her very foundation fracturing. 'You have to go.'

'No,' they said together.

'Yes,' she whispered, gathering up every remaining iota of her energy, using it to expel them from her mind. It worked, and they disappeared from her centre. Anita felt lighter without them there, but heavier without their support.

Pressure closed in around her, like solid walls, squashing her consciousness into the smallest of spaces. She felt no pain, only compression, as the force of whatever the Gods were doing filled every crack and crevice of her being.

She leaned forward, grabbing her head in her hands, scared that her mind would implode. She rocked, holding her head, shaking her head, doing anything she could to try and ease the burden. It got worse, and she screamed. She rocked back so hard she fell, and everything went black.

CHAPTER 15

Marcus sat at Anita's bedside, holding her hand to his lips, taking in every line and detail of her face. A light spring breeze floated in through the open window, curtains moving gently as it flitted past.

The scent of viburnum filled the room. A simple flower decoration sat on a round table to one side of the bed. The rest of the ample space was filled with cream furniture and understated artwork.

The room was bright and airy, one of Alexander's guest bedrooms in his cottage outside Empire. It was tranquil and restorative, uncluttered and homely. But Anita lay unconscious on the bed, as she had for the last ten weeks.

Alexander and Marcus had been kicked out of Anita's mind just as the Gods' energy disappeared from the world. No one knew what had happened inside Anita's head, but the world's energy had instantly rebounded to levels as high as anyone could remember. According to reports from the Magnei, the Great Hall in the Wild Lands had crumbled to dust and disappeared. No one had any explanation as to why.

Amber, and those loyal to her, had melted away when they'd realized they were beaten. Most of those left behind surrendered, pledging their allegiance to the new democratic system of rule.

Their elected leader, Matthew, had made an announcement shortly after word of the Relic's return reached Empire. He told the world that the prophecy had been fulfilled—genuinely this time—and offered energy readings from the observatory as proof.

The power of the Descendants was already as good as forgotten, and those who had been councillors found their reputations in the gutter. Even the idea of the Gods held little sway now. Only the truly devout turned up to worship, and that tradition would surely only last as long as they did.

The temples themselves were still a focal point, used to host weddings, funerals and other ceremonies. But the pull was tradition and a love for the beautiful old buildings, rather than fear of the Gods and a belief in their supremacy. The change had been so swift as to be almost indecent. Memories were short, and the elation of their newfound freedom had made the people bold.

Not that everyone had forgotten how things had been. It would take longer for scheming, social climbing mothers to entirely disregard the old bloodlines. But they were as keen, if not more so, on the new political class, for they now held the reins of power.

For everyone else, life went on much as it had before: fishermen fished, farmers farmed, academics studied and taught, the young flirted, the old complained, and all the best gossip was found at The Island.

Cleo popped her head around the door. 'Any change today?' she asked, setting a new vase of blossoms on the table.

'No,' said Marcus, placing Anita's hand back at her side. 'Nothing. I'll leave you to it.' He watched the rise and fall of Anita's chest one more time before standing to leave.

'She'll be okay. You know that, don't you?' said Cleo, placing a reassuring hand on Marcus' arm.

'I don't know anything,' he said, wearily, 'but I always hope.'

Cleo sat at Anita's side as the door clicked shut. 'Well,' she said, looking at her best friend's face, 'this is getting ridiculous. I never had you down as a lazy person, but you're pushing this beyond reasonable bounds. It's been ten weeks. *Ten weeks*! Are you hearing me?' She hovered over Anita's face.

'It's rude not to give any indication that you're paying attention, by the way. I know you've been through a tough time, but we're getting into territory where you could be accused of milking it. I'm just saying,' she said, throwing up her hands. 'Don't blame me; I only speak the truth. So, if I were you, I'd bloody well just wake up.' She looked again at Anita's face, scrutinising it for any slight twitch. Nothing.

'Fine, be like that. You're not the only person who's been through a rough patch.' Her voice was light, but the memory of Bakko summoned tears. She blinked them away. 'Bakko upped and left me, just like that; not even a proper goodbye. I know it wasn't his fault; he was doing his bit to save the world and all, but I hope you realize that you have not one, but two, gorgeous men fawning over you out here?

'If I were you, I'd hot-foot it out here and capitalise. I mean, just think how much running around they're going to do for you; too good an opportunity to pass up by anyone's standards. Not to mention, I'm dying to find out how you're going to navigate those two lovesick idiots. I won't lie, it's going to be awkward, and I'm looking forward to my front-row seat.

'So, you see, you owe it to me to wake up, to provide entertainment, to ease some of my suffering. I've never pretended to be selfless, and you've been away for ten weeks; you've got a lot of making up to do.'

Cleo took a deep breath and stood up, walking to the window to look out over the garden. 'The weather's been lovely,' she said. 'Perfect for outdoor yoga, or a run by the river. Perfect for sitting outside at The Island and talking about the ridiculous girls fawning over the politicians. It's just like it used to be, only with a whole new group of guys; it's really freshened things up, you know?' She was barely even aware of what she was saying any longer, thoughts drifting.

'Any change?' came a voice from behind her. She turned to see Alexander standing in the doorway; she hadn't even heard the click of the latch.

'No, but I'm sure she'll be back with us soon. She just needs a bit more time.' Cleo said the words as positively as she could, willing herself to believe them.

Whereas Marcus had thrown his energy into creating a new life for himself, utilising his army, turning them into farmers, labourers, and business people in his new empire, Alexander had done nothing but look after Anita, waiting for her to return.

He spent long hours at her bedside. He read to her, relayed the events of the world, talked about all the things they would do when she woke. But the strain was starting to show.

'You should come to The Island for a drink later,' said Cleo. 'I could use a drinking partner who's not my father, or Marcus. All they talk about is business, and it's getting old.'

'Maybe another time,' he said, sitting on the side of the bed, stroking Anita's hair.

'A few hours out will do you good.'

'I said no,' he snapped, not even looking at her.

'Okay, well, we'll all be there in case you change your mind,' she said. But he'd already stopped listening.

She left, and he breathed a sigh of relief when they were alone.

Alexander closed his eyes and pushed his energy towards Anita's mind, finding his way to her centre. It was no longer the yurt, but an open landscape of fields and woods atop a cliff, overlooking the sea.

He walked to the treeline and sat, as he had every day for the last nine weeks, observing the movement of clouds across the sky, waves coming into land, the rustling of leaves in the breeze. He sat, waiting.

When he'd first dared to explore her mind, a handful of days after they'd returned to Empire, he'd searched for other places; anywhere she could have been hiding. None existed. This was all that was left; one vast open expanse of countryside.

When he'd first entered, a storm had raged overhead. Waves crashed into the cliffs. Trees swaying dangerously in the wind, great cracks echoing out as branches broke, crashing to the ground. Since that day, every visit had seen slight improvements in her mood, and the place had come to life. Rabbits raced across the fields, birds appearing in the sky, wildflowers popping up and dancing in the wind.

Every time he came, Alexander made his energy available to her, willing her to feel it, and use it. At first there had been no response; all he could do was sit and observe Anita's torment. But slowly, she'd begun making use of him. She took only a little of his energy at first, a tentative draw, but over time, she'd taken greater amounts, and the landscape had calmed and bloomed more quickly.

Days ago, Alexander had noticed an eagle circling high overhead, its big brown wings spread wide as it coasted on the wind. He'd looked up and openly tracked the bird's progress. At his interest, it had fled, leaving Alexander frustrated with himself.

The following day, when the bird came, he tracked it only from the corner of his eye, resisting the temptation to shift his head when it flew out of view. It stayed much longer, circling, then swooping low before leaving him.

Over the days that followed, the bird had swooped right down in front of him, then landed in a nearby tree. Yesterday, it had landed just behind him, at the edge of the woods. Alexander hadn't been able to resist shifting a little to see her. It had made her fly away, but he was filled with excitement at the prospect of what she might do today.

He waited, caring little for how long it took, and was surprised when eventually he heard a rustling in the undergrowth behind him. He froze, forcing himself to stay where he was, looking forward, towards the sea.

The rustling came closer, followed by the snapping of a twig; it was no bird that moved behind him. He breathed out slowly, his heart thumping wildly in his chest. The movement stopped and his mind raced, trying to decide what to do.

'Will you run away if I turn around?' he eventually asked, his voice barely more than a whisper.

There was no reply for an eternity, then, 'I don't want you to see me.'

'Okay,' he said, fighting the urge to ask why. 'What do you want me to do?'

'Stay exactly where you are,' she said, creeping closer. 'Please don't turn around.'

'I promise I won't,' he said, high on the bliss of her company.

She stopped just behind him and sank to her knees, fingertips lightly brushing his shoulder. A ripple of energy passed between them, and Alexander shivered, closing his eyes to savour the sensation.

He sat still, battling the urge to wrap her in his arms. She placed a hand on his shoulder, then the other on the middle of his back. Alexander bowed his head, then tipped it to one side, his eyes still closed. He braced against the sensation of her energy running through him. He exhaled slowly, then breathed in deeply, using every ounce of self-control to keep himself still.

She traced the lines of his back, then inched her fingers under his shirt, across his rigid muscles. She moved one hand to his neck, running her fingers across his pulse, behind his ear, then into his hair. He leaned into her touch, dying to reach up and take her hand, forcing himself not to.

She shuffled forward, placing her legs either side of his body, pressing her torso to his back, wrapping her arms around him. He opened his eyes, and his blood turned to ice as he took in the cuts and bruises that littered her skin. It was a riot of colour; purple, green, yellow, red, and swollen. Her joints were barely recognisable, so much fluid lying beneath the surface.

Slowly, Alexander moved his fingertips to her hands, covering them. She flinched but didn't pull away. Instead, she leaned her cheek against his shoulder and closed her eyes, energy flowing back and forth between them.

They stayed there for hours, but eventually, Alexander broke the spell. 'I need to go,' he said, quietly. She held him more tightly. 'I'll come back later, I promise.'

'When will you come back?'

'I won't be more than a few hours.'

'What are you going to do?'

'Matthew's organising a party to celebrate the coming of summer,' he said, gently playing with her fingers. 'He's eager to make it a success, given the winter celebrations didn't happen. I said I'd help.'

'Now I'm intrigued,' she said. 'Tell me about it.'

'I don't need to tell you.'

'Oh?'

'Because you're going to be there, so you'll see it all for yourself.'

'Alexander... I...'

'... I'm not forcing you to do anything you don't want to do,' he said quickly, before she could pull away, 'but you're healing well; your strength is returning, and... you've got to come back to us sooner or later.'

'I was planning on later.'

'Why?'

'Because it's easier that way.'

'Since when have you ever chosen the easy option?'

'I was thinking I might give it a try.'

'Anita, you saved us all; not even a God could stand in your way.'

'And I'd like to lie low for a while.'

'You're putting off the inevitable. If anything, it'll make the attention worse.'

'Not if I go and live in the Wild Lands.'

Alexander spun around to look at her, furious. Her face was unrecognisable. Her eyes were swollen, her skin the same array of colours as the rest of her body. He ignored it. 'And what about us? Are you leaving me behind, or expecting me to slink off into the Wild with you?'

Anita was clearly shocked at his reaction. She stared at him for several long moments. 'Look at me,' she said, motioning to her face. 'I'm broken and defeated. I wasn't taking anything for granted.'

'You're not defeated,' he said fiercely. 'You're healing.' He moved a cautious hand to her face. 'And healing quickly. It wasn't long ago that a storm raged across your mind. Now look at it.' He waved an arm around. 'The sun is shining, the waves roll gently into shore. There are even bloody flowers.'

'But look at me,' she protested.

'I am looking at you. You look like someone who's been through a lot.'

'There are pieces of me missing; this is the only place left in my mind.'

'Your centre has come together early, that's all,' he said, with such conviction that it stopped her in her tracks.

'Really?' she said. 'You think that's what's happened?'

'Yes, of course,' he said, as though this were the most obvious thing going. 'The Gods caused chaos in here. Theseus ripped through your mind, and who knows what the other two got up to. It's the logical response, for your mind to shape itself into what it'll be forever. It would be pointless to heal into a new version of what existed before.'

'You honestly think that's the truth?'

He looked her squarely in her anxious green eyes. 'I've never believed anything so strongly,' he said, a smile tugging at his lips. 'Well, apart from the belief that you and I are meant to be together, and that I love you, more than anything.'

Anita arched an eyebrow. 'Really?' she said. 'More than anything?' She stroked a hand down his cheek.

He nodded, sincerely. 'More than anything.' He leaned forward and placed a featherlight kiss on her lips.

'Do I look this bad on the outside too?' she asked, looking down at her mutilated body.

'No. On the outside you look as though nothing ever happened.'

'Gods!' she exclaimed, then looked surprised at her outburst. She sat for several moments, quietly contemplating, something brewing behind her eyes. 'I look like normal on the outside?'

Alexander nodded, and Anita's brows knitted together.

'Then maybe... maybe I could come back with you?' she breathed. 'I thought I looked like a monster out there too.'

'Anita, there's no way you could ever look like a monster. In here, or outside. We've all missed you so much.'

'Enough of the soppy stuff,' she chided, giving him a mock stern look. She took a deep breath. 'Let's go then.'

'Now?' he said, taken by surprise.

'Want me to change my mind?'

He pulled them out of the meditation, and they woke up looking at each other, Anita blinking as her eyes adjusted to the light. 'Where am I?'

'At my cottage outside Empire,' he said, reaching for her hand.

'I thought we'd still be at the Cloud Mountain,' she said, looking around. 'How long have I been inside my head?'

'Ten weeks.'

'Ten weeks? I've got to get up.'

'Anita, slow down,' he said, placing a restraining hand on her shoulder. 'I'll help you up, but you've been lying down, not moving a muscle, for all that time. Go slowly.'

*　*　*　*　*

Anita took hold of Alexander's arm and pulled herself upright. The blood rushed to her head and made her dizzy. She clutched Alexander until the feeling cleared.

'I want to stand up,' she said, sliding her legs over the side of the bed.

Alexander helped her to her feet, but her legs buckled underneath her. He caught her before she fell, holding her until life came back into her limbs. She nodded, and he set her on her feet. He took some of her weight as she headed for the window, her progress slow.

'How do you feel?'

'Fine,' she said, but it was a half-lie. Her body was fine, but her head was killing her; jolts of pain shooting across her mind, flashes of light marring her vision. She looked out across the pretty walled garden and breathed deeply, closing her eyes, taking things one breath at a time. 'What happened after I blacked out?'

Alexander sat in an upholstered armchair. 'You kicked us out of your mind, and our connection with you severed. We tried to get back in, but seconds later, a huge pulse of energy sent every person in the temple sprawling to the floor. No one was hurt, but we were concerned about what might come next. We all just stayed there, on the floor, waiting.

'Marcus and I tried to wake you, to make sure you were still with us, but your pulse was weak. I could barely feel your energy, and we couldn't bring you round.

'When we'd waited long enough to feel foolish on the floor, we got up, called for help, got you out, and began the clean-up.'

'Are there still monks at the mountain?' she asked.

'No. Marcus' army cleared the place. They took the senior monks and army officers into custody for questioning, then forced their way into all the secret areas. Joslyn and Cleo led the search for anything interesting. The Magnei helped collect and transport everything back to Empire.

'What they found was made public. Anyone who wants access to the monks' research need only ask. Many of the monks have joined our ranks of academics. Most of them disagreed with Timi's policy of secrecy, or, at least, that's what they're saying now.

'The rest of the people living in the mountain were allowed to go free. Amber disappeared without a trace and is still on the run. Timi, on the other hand, was captured, put on trial, and is now serving a long sentence at the prison on Wild Island. Anderson, Bella, and Edmund are soon to join him.'

'What were the charges?'

'Various: aiding and abetting a plot to take over the world and all its resources, taking hostages, kidnap, attempted murder...'

'How long will their sentences be?'

'The rest of their lives, supposedly, but if anyone can talk their way out of a prison sentence, it would be Timi.'

'Hmm. So, what else?'

'The supplies they were hoarding have been brought back to Empire and redistributed. The Cloud Mountain has been shut down and cleared of any signs that the Mind God was ever there. There's a twenty-four-hour guard around the place for now.'

'What about the others? Joslyn, Draeus, Cleo, Marcus, Sol and his soldiers?' She paused. 'Cordelia?'

'Everyone got out alive. Joslyn came back to Empire with Draeus; they seem to have rekindled their relationship, much to Cleo's bemusement. Sol is head of our newly founded army, and Marcus is fast becoming a business mogul.'

'That was quick... Cleo?'

'Much the same as ever; managing The Island, collecting and trading in gossip… She's been taking energy readings from the observatory and relaying them back to Matthew and his parliament.'

'She knows how?'

'She has hidden talents…'

'What about Cordelia?

'She's gone back to her old life, the part of her that wasn't Tatiana, anyway. I've only spoken to her once.'

'Did she come and see me?'

'No,' he said. 'I think she's nervous.'

Anita tracked the progress of a bird as it hopped across the garden from the lawn, to a bench, to the wall. 'And what about you?' she asked, half turning to look at him. 'What have you been doing?'

He shrugged. 'I brought you back here as quickly as I could. Empire has the best doctors in the world, and I called on every single one of them to see if there was anything they could do. They've kept you fed and hydrated, but there was little they could do for your mind or your spirit, and the academics were no help either. I've been here, mostly, meditating with you, or talking to you, doing anything I could think of to bring you back.'

'What will you do now I'm back?'

Alexander laughed. 'I've been focusing on getting to this moment, and, I suppose, a lot depends on you… not that I'm expecting you to know what you want right away.'

'I know exactly what I want,' she said, walking over to him. She leaned down and kissed him, a smile dancing across her lips when she pulled away. 'A cup of tea.'

Alexander rolled his eyes and pulled her into his lap. 'That's all you want from me?'

'Well, that, and a couple of other things.'

'Such as?'

'I'd kill for a sandwich,' she said, her face serious. 'A crisp apple, and maybe some orange flavoured chocolate.'

'Anything else?'

'Hmmm, let me think. A long hot bath, a run by the river... and maybe one other thing.'

'Just one?'

'Just one,' she confirmed, searching his eyes. 'You.'

He lifted a hand to cup her cheek, then slid it into her hair, pulling her lips to his.

He pulled back and looked into her eyes. 'I'm glad you feel that way,' he said, 'because I have something for you.' He reached into his pocket and pulled out a ring made from two strands of gold twisted together, ends crossed artfully at the top. 'This was my mother's,' he said, sliding it onto Anita's index finger. 'It was her favorite, because my father made it for her with his own hands. Every time I look at it, I think of you.'

Anita smiled, holding up the ring for them both to admire. 'I love it,' she said, kissing him again. 'Thank you.'

'I was scared you would never come back…'

'When you went missing after the temples collapsed, I was scared too.'

'I can't live without you,' he said, pulling her to his chest.

She smiled into his shirt. 'Me too.'

CHAPTER 16

Matthew's party was at and around The Island. They had set up areas for games and food on each bank of the river, the main dance floor on the island itself. Boats filled with flowers and lanterns floated around, blossoms strewn liberally everywhere, the scent of lily of the valley in the air.

The sun shone, not a cloud in the sky as Anita and Alexander made their way across the bridge to the less crowded bank, where sheets of canvas hung between trees to provide shelter from the sun. They ignored the prying eyes of all who saw them, hushed voices murmuring as they passed.

They sat and watched awhile, as the gathering swelled in size. Anita smiled as she spotted Sol getting Cleo a drink, nervously handing it over. Apparently, this was their second date, and by the looks of things, it was going well. It was rare for Cleo to let things progress past one dinner, and she was still coming to terms with what had happened with Bakko.

Gwyn was fending off a drunk Joshua. She had become a diplomat, working for Matthew's government. Matthew's son, Henry, rescued her, swooping her onto the dance floor.

'It's nice to be around so many people,' said Anita, leaning into Alexander's arm.

'You mean this gossiping lot?'

'When the Gods, you, and Marcus were in my head, it was impossibly crowded. But when you all left, instead of feeling relieved, I felt empty. Being around so many other people, so much energy, it's driven the emptiness away. It's relaxing, oddly.'

Alexander shook his head, pulling her closer.

'Don't get me wrong, I don't want to be around people all the time. But when everyone's so happy and carefree, and playing and dancing, it's… nice.'

Marcus joined Sol and Cleo, and Anita froze. Since she'd woken up almost two weeks ago, he'd avoided her completely, having, according to Alexander, been at her bedside every day beforehand.

She'd sent him countless messages, but he'd ignored them. She'd tried to visit him at his castle, but each time, had been told he wasn't in.

'I'll be back in a minute,' said Anita, already on her feet, moving towards him.

Marcus looked up when she was close. Recognition dawned, and he looked like he might run. 'Don't you dare,' she said, placing a hand on his arm before he had time to get away. 'I need to speak to you.' She softened, releasing his arm. 'Just give me five minutes, then I'll leave you alone.'

Marcus nodded and let her lead him up the bank to the treeline, largely out of view from the revellers below.

'Marcus,' she said, looking him in the eye, 'I just… I… thank you.' He looked away, but she continued. 'At the Cloud Mountain, you gave me your energy. You came into my mind when you knew it was dangerous. You came to my bedside every day for ten weeks. I…'

'Are you trying to torment me?' he whispered.

'No. Of course not.'

'Then please just leave me alone. I've told you everything I need to.'

'But, Marcus, we're... friends.'

'Is that right?'

Anita had no words. She tried to put her hand on his arm, but he shrugged her away.

'I can't be your friend,' he said. 'Please, just let me be.' He turned and walked back to the party. Anita stared after him, then returned to Alexander.

'Are you okay?' Alexander asked as she sank down beside him.

'He won't even talk to me,' she said, tears in her eyes.

'I'm not sure I can blame him. If you'd chosen Marcus over me...'

'So, after everything we've been through, that's it? We never speak again?'

'Forever is a long time,' he said, gently. 'I'm sure he'll move on, eventually. Right now, it's raw. It'll be easier on him if he doesn't have to see you.'

She nodded, blinking away tears.

* * * * *

Rose and Melia watched from a distance as Anita and Alexander took to the dance floor. They danced close together, with none of Anita's unusual showiness.

'I can't believe anyone ever thought she was a Descendant,' said Rose, scrutinising Anita's every move.

'No, she looks too much like her mother for that,' said Melia, looking between her son, Marcus, and the girl who had repeatedly broken his heart.

'I suppose none of that matters any longer,' said Rose, taking a deep breath and tearing her eyes away. 'They found a way,' she said quietly, 'we're finally free.'

If you enjoyed Court of Crystal, I'd really appreciate it if you left a review on Amazon, Goodreads, Instagram, TikTok, or any other place you can think of... authors aren't fussy! Just a few words, or a line or two would be perfection. Thank you for your support.

*   *

*   *

Sign up here: https://www.subscribepage.com/r2a0n6

CONNECT WITH HR MOORE

Are you a Mind, Body, or Spirit? Sign up to HR Moore's newsletter to find out! You'll also get all the latest news about releases, book recommendations, and freebies too!

Sign up here: https://www.subscribepage.com/r2a0n6

Find HR Moore on Instagram and Twitter:
@HR_Moore

Follow HR Moore on TikTok: @authorhrmoore

See what the world of The Relic Trilogy looks like on Pinterest:
https://www.pinterest.com/authorhrmoore/

Like the HR Moore page on Facebook:
https://www.facebook.com/authorhrmoore

Follow HR Moore on Goodreads:
https://www.goodreads.com/author/show/7228761.H_R_Moore

Or check out HR Moore's website:
http://www.hrmoore.com/

ABOUT THE AUTHOR

Harriet's British, but lives in New Hampshire with her husband and two young daughters. When she isn't writing, editing, eating, running around after her kids, or imagining how much better life would be with the addition of a springer spaniel, she occasionally finds the time to make hats.

TITLES BY HR MOORE

The Relic Trilogy:

Queen of Empire
Temple of Sand
Court of Crystal

In the Gleaming Light

Nation of the Sun (coming June 20th 2021)

Printed in Great Britain
by Amazon